ALI AND ME

Muhammad Ali, My Joy and My Journey

Lawrence Seurynck

Kindle

Copyright©2019

DEDICATION

Dedicated with love, to my dear wife who made all the creative hours possible. Also, the wonderful team on the Ali Farm for all those years. The paint, crew Becky and Joe, for their great work and excellent humor. And to Lonnie, Muhammad's brilliant, loving wife.

INTRODUCTION

For a decade, I had the startling good fortune to work for Muhammad Ali. Volumes have been written documenting his boxing prowess, social activism, and public antics. This book traces remembrances of the times we spent together, his influence on my life, and the journey he set me upon. Here I want to share personal glimpses of the man and his reverence, mischief, magic, and compassion.

Globally, Muhammad was a warrior. He faced the most intimidating fighters of his day, often as the underdog. He absorbed thousands of blows, yet, he is most remembered for his gentle regard and his belief in humanity. Ali battled first as a sterling athletic specimen, then with the near expressionless mask of Parkinson's disease; Ali shook up the world, then he inspired it.

Understanding the historical arc of slavery in America brings into focus the implausibility of Muhammad Ali, aka Cassius Clay. Far more than a reaction to oppression, Ali was a force that illuminated the aching want of bigotry and the pettiness of tribalism. His compassion for people brought him joy, which was easy to see in his expression and how his eyes took people in. His grace uplifted everyone he met. He hugged them all. Most can tell you the day he reached out, and the power of his embrace felt deep in their heart.

As I contemplate "Ali and Me," there are stories to share, times on his farm in Berrien Springs, Michigan, the club we founded with his old boxing ring, and times he made people laugh. Ali was hilarious. These were good times; more significant was witnessing Ali's gentle capacity to inspire people to look inward to discover their own strength, to be stalwart, to be tolerant, to be Ali.

I had a friend who taught a class called "Autobiographical Fantasy." The point of the writing was not to adhere tightly to every irrefutable fact but to communicate a truth. I have written the remembrances of Ali in that spirit. I have trusted the details in my memory and given names when I cannot remember a minor actor. But the truth of the tale is exacting.

The parallel tale of our friend Zane is heavily researched, but his character is wholly fictitious. The account seeks truth in another way. Imagining a man like Ali a few generations earlier may give the reader an unvarnished moment to understand even a bit of the shameful blot of enslavement that continues to mark America today. Each of us embodies a response to the enslavement, be it denial, sadness, anger, humiliation, or pride for what was endured. Ali had his response; he showed us a way to heal. The world needed Muhammad during his lifetime, and that has not changed with his passing.

PROLOGUE

The space between the roof rafters and ceiling joists narrowed with the roof's pitch, inching to a thin black crease at the rear of the building. I laid on my stomach, guiding a four-inch hose that spewed cellulose insulation into the voids between the rough-sawn rafters. A switch in my right hand clicked the blower on and off. I steered the flow until the hose shuttered, then shut it off and waited for the air to clear so I could pull myself to the next position. When the bits of shredded newspaper flew, absolute darkness filled the narrow cavity; I could not see my hand even an inch from my face.

In the blackness with my goggled eyes closed, the sound of my breathing filled the space. I calmed my hurried breaths, then lay still, sensing the pulse of the old building, the subtle vibrations of cars passing by on the street below, and the grating rumble of semi-trucks thumping over tar strips mending the cracked pavement.

Lying tight alongside a wall, I pulled off a glove as I waited; I felt the bricks set laser straight, one upon the other. The wall rose thirty-five feet from the fieldstone foundation up through the old dry goods store and past the second-floor offices of an 1800s dentist. Mice stole teeth pulled from the mouths of townspeople and soldiers returning from the Civil War and left them in scattered piles beneath the gaped floorboards.

The wall continued up through the attic, then rose a few feet above the tarred roof as a last-ditch firestop to quell a fire ripping across the rooftops, one building to the next, a city block of buildings shared common walls.

I ran my fingers across the mortar between the finely laid bricks. I thought of the mason standing on a scaffold of tree limbs lashed with coarse hemp rope many decades ago. A simple pulley bound to the crude platform hauled buckets of mortar and stacks of bricks to build the wall a hundred feet long, three courses thick.

I thought of the hands that laid the bricks, bare and rough, the man too old to fight in the war. But the care. Even in that attic space, unseen and unused, the work was perfection. The sweep of my hand connected with the laborer those decades ago. Mine was probably the only hand to touch that wall since the mason in 1865.

The shredded newspapers settled between the rafters, the moment of reverie passed, I fired up the blower, and the space went dark once again.

Most of Dowagiac, Michigan's central business district, was built between 1840 and 1865. As we restored buildings, I learned to take note of the craftsmanship; the clever way rafters ran from a pocket notched in a brick wall across to a notch in the opposite wall.

Double rafters, called sleepers, frame openings for a stairway or roof hatch. The sleepers lock in place with square fingers chiseled right through the abutting beam, their seams so tight one must look closely to find all four sides of the end cuts.

Such joinery supports the first and second floors and the roof joists. All have held comfortably for 150 years without a single metal fastener, secured solely by the craft of a steady hand and a chisel.

History brought assurance to life in Dowagiac; we felt hidden away from the stresses of big city life. We gleaned comfort from the old buildings and the families that populated them.

The quiet of two-lane roads, apple orchards, and townsfolk. There were still grandparents who played together as children, raising families in the same houses, on the same streets, with a fresh generation of kids playing in the park.

When I spent time with Muhammad Ali, it was no great stretch to contemplate the generations that led us to those moments too. I often studied his hands, resting calmly as he spoke. Like a voyeur, I stole an intimate glimpse of the form, the white scars nicked into his knuckles and the breadth of his fists. Then there was the right hand, relaxed and casual, that at another time bore the power to knock George Foreman off his feet.

Most impressive in Ali's physique, even two decades after his last fight, were the thick muscles that rippled across his back. I thought he looked pretty much like a regular guy until I got a look at his back. His lats and shoulders made it clear he was at the pinnacle of the human physique.

Early on, I learned Muhammad had been named for Cassius Marcellus Clay, an abolitionist whose family also enslaved people. That tied the generations close together. I wondered if those enslaved workers were of Muhammad's stature. Were their backs, split by the whip, also thick with the same rippling muscles?

I dared to imagine Ali.

We typically distance ourselves from atrocities "all those years ago," "all those miles across oceans," ... "over there." But I wanted to sense the reality of it. I can't assess the validity of my contemplations, how enslavement strangles the mind, but my eyes took in the face of a man who 150 years earlier might well have borne the incomprehensible brutality.

Only with our eyes open to this juxtaposition can we begin to understand the audacity of Muhammad Ali. He fought, and he forgave. He was dazzling in the ring. He spoke poetic and loud. He made his stand on new ground that the rest of us might never even imagine.

PART ONE:

CHAPTER ONE

LEGEND OF THE FARM

At dawn, my hooded jacket dripped cold rain as I walked amongst the long rows of deeply settled tombstones, still reeling in my reverie. Memories nestled amongst the sweet rays of morning light. My mind drifted back, across time, to the old dairy farm in southwest Michigan. The manicured drive, the barns, the muddy water flowing lazily down the Saint Joseph River.

Legend has it the place was once owned by Louis Campagna, a Capone heavy operating out of Chicago, 90 miles to the west. That made sense of the escape tunnel that ran underground from the swimming pool one hundred yards to the river. And why the tunnel is lined with thin sheets of lead to slow a ricocheting bullet, like a baseball bouncing on wet clay.

Legend has it that in a tiny closet, hidden at the rear of a room above the garage, the floor is elevated a few inches, so a lookout, sitting tightly on an armless chair for long hours, peering out the window, would have a full view of the half-mile-long driveway leading in from the heavy iron gates.

A few years ago, a contractor remodeling the second-floor bath in the primary residence ran into a snag---twelve inches of reinforced concrete in the subfloor. The bath is directly above the formal entry. Legend has it the mobster "did not want to die on the crapper" if the feds blew the front door. It may seem paranoid, but Louis "Little New York" Campagna had reason to look over his shoulder; Campagna was a bookkeeper and bodyguard for Al Capone.

Initially founded in 1900, the peninsular property was a simple farm bound by the Saint Joseph river twelve miles upstream from Lake Michigan. In 1920 Campagna bought it and added barns and a training track to develop racehorses for the syndicate. After Campagna took possession, the main house mysteriously burned to the ground. Rather than rebuild, Campagna converted one of the barns into the main living quarters.

Capone and his men were a common sight in Southwest Michigan during Prohibition. For the wealthy and mobsters alike, Michigan brought relief from the stifling heat of summer in Chicago. The gentle flowing rivers, clusters of peach and apple orchards, and dozens of quiet inland lakes made for a little slice of paradise only a morning's drive from the Windy City.

In small towns, where everyone knew everybody, townspeople chit-chatted and smiled their hellos but kept to themselves--- as long as there was no trouble. Capone and his men kept quietly to themselves too. Publicly they came to relax. They kept their business out of sight. They enjoyed ice cream sundaes on Main Street with locals and resorters. They came and went freely without interference from city police.

The eighty-five-acre farm was their retreat, a lost parcel at the end of a quiet street. From outside the gates, thrill-seekers could glimpse a couple barns, but the mobsters, and the things they did, were hidden down the long winding driveway.

To me, the place was reminiscent of a scene in a bad gangster movie the mob boss says, "Take him to Michigan; the rat will talk in Michigan." More specifically, as legend would have it, the rat would "talk" in one of the two low-ceiling, block-walled rooms deep beneath the concrete-lined Olympic swimming pool next to the carriage house. The rooms were discovered when a contractor dug through six concrete liners to determine why the swimming pool floor had cracked yet again.

Still, for most visitors, the property was an oasis. A sweeping vista from the gentle tree-lined western boundary to the St Joseph flowing almost a mile along three sides of the farm. From the entry gates, the lane rolls into the heart of the property, then bends left along the crescent hill that rises up from the long flat flood plain of rich bluegrass blanketed out to the river.

The first impression is of a Kentucky horse farm, but there are no white fences. The eye follows the drive past several white barns to a towering stand of Michigan hardwoods: oak, maple, and elm trees. Along the way, acreage leased to a nursery is planted in long rows of Lambs Quarter, Sweet Woodruff, and Walker's Low.

In 1975, the idyllic farm became a retreat for a new owner, a self-described "bad man" who, late in life, came to pray five times a day and enjoy the closest thing to a family life his celebrity would allow.

Muhammad Ali found his oasis; he recuperated on the farm in the era of the "Thrilla in Manila" and "Rumble in the Jungle." In the midst of global bustle, Ali found peace on the farm in a quiet corner of Michigan.

CHAPTER TWO

BECKY

When we began our work for the Ali's, I was given a code for the main gate. Over the next ten years, we came and went; it felt like a warm, loving sitcom, I became the house painter who was always, inexplicably, there.

There was no end to the painting and restoration work, but there were also luncheons and encounters with visitors and with Ali. When there was a birthday celebration for one of the staff, we were there in our painter whites.

When Lonnie, Muhammad's wife, added a photo of another friend's newborn to her wall of baby pictures, she called me to her office to see the sweet new face. I was there to work, but in special times, I was there as a leisurely companion for Muhammad.

Everyone is blessed with talent; oddly, mine was the ability to cut a nice line with a paintbrush at Olympic speed. In college, I was the trim man on the paint crew. After college, I fell back on my skills to build a viable career in idyllic Southwest Michigan. Lake life and peace. A perfect place to raise our family.

Southwest Michigan is the state's counterpoint to Detroit and the sprawling suburbs covering the big mitten's southeastern heel. Along a thirty-mile swath from Lake Michigan inland, orchards dot the countryside.

In early Spring, the big lake moderates temperatures to prevent budding fruit trees from freezing, and in late Fall, its warm waters extend the growing season a few precious days. Amongst the orchards, there are dozens of small inland lakes surrounded by vacation homes.

Built as simple seasonal cottages, there are continuous projects to make the old cottages modern, year-round homes. Most of our work involved a lake home. In the days before cell phones, we spent entire days undisturbed in homes overlooking the water.

One afternoon in 1995, I got a call from a building contractor to help with a project at the Ali farm. I knew Ali had a place in the area; there were rumors of encounters with Ali. Stories of Ali spotted at the County Fair, the Dairy Queen, or the drive-thru at McDonald's. Even a story of Ali agreeing to follow a mom and her kids home from town so she could get her camera to take a picture of her children with the Champ.

I agreed to meet with the contractor the following day. My head swirled; I might actually meet Muhammad Ali. In the morning, soon after eight, the contractor picked me up in his white four-wheel-drive pick-up for the ride to the farm. The project was an office newly renovated for Muhammad. The carpentry work was near completion, and the contractor asked me to quote the paint finish work.

I was anxious as we approached the black iron gates. The truck slowed momentarily as gates swung open to the two-lane driveway, the center island dense with creeping shrubbery and flowering plants. The lanes converged where the drive bent left in front of a small, single-story barn, white with a dark shingled roof. A hundred yards further, a tall barn rested at the edge of the hill, gently gliding down to the floodplain.

Passed the barns down the sloping hill, the driveway ends in a cul-de-sac with a small central garden. To the right was a two-story garage four bays wide, and to the left was Ali's residence.

The contractor parked the truck, then fiddled with his clipboard and some papers before climbing out. I stood alongside the truck, surprised at Ali's simple home across the drive.

The walkout basement of the three-story house faced the driveway with its paved parking area. In the left corner, a single-aluminum storm door entrance abutted the drive. There was no canopy above the entry, only white-painted siding, lifeless up to the second-story overhang. There, a cape cod-style roof sloped upward to the third-story wall. Three dormers rose from the short wall that ran the length of the modest house, all of it itching to be painted.

The contractor finally jumped out of the truck as if he was in a hurry. We walked to a door around the side of the garages and climbed a stairway leading to the second floor. At the top of the stairs, to the right, we passed a small room (with the secret closet for a lookout in the back corner); further along, an office for Lonnie, and at the end of the hall, Muhammad's office.

My expectation for Ali's office was a grand structure with vaulted ceilings and wide-trimmed windows. But the office was a small room with a low ceiling tucked at the end of the narrow hallway above the garages.

Just inside the door, a dark wooden desk sat across from the entrance, tight to the outside wall. There were bookshelves alongside the desk with just enough room for a chair that faced a small sitting area.

A few upholstered chairs and a coffee table filled the sitting space. Framed photographs decorated the walls. The room felt like a cozy antique, but the low ceilings were claustrophobic; I could hardly imagine Ali comfortable in such tight quarters.

A door behind Muhammad's desk opened to a long-enclosed

porch that ran the entire length of the building. Above a knee wall, rows of wood-framed windows looked off to the river one hundred yards away.

The porch had become a storage room for Ali's fan mail. We often ate lunch there in the coming weeks while we thumbed through large grey mail trays, some opened some not.

There were letters from Presidents, athletes, and celebrities. There was a letter from Jimmy Stewart with a rabbit drawn in ink on the front. We staggered with reverence at a letter from the United States Supreme Court thanking Ali for having the courage to trust in the Court, the Laws, and Constitution; the letter, signed by all nine justices, laid open in plain view.

There were thousands and thousands of pieces of mail. Most were notes of thanks for the inspiration and peace Ali brought to regular people. One day I sat on the floor with a tray of letters. Ali leafed through them. He'd select a couple of notes, lean forward in his chair, and read. It seemed he read through each of them two or three times, then put them aside on his desk.

We began our work not long after my first visit. The carpenters still had some trim work to install, but we had plenty of prep work and ceilings to paint while they wrapped up.

On the second day at the farm, we saw Ali for the first time. We were at work in a front office above the garage. Several people had come out of the service door at the back of the house. The entourage stood talking alongside a black GMC Suburban. I watched from a second-story window and saw Ali come out of the door. I called my co-worker, Becky. We stood in the window, voyeurs. Ali walked, slightly hunched, from the house to the waiting car.

The scene seemed formal and foreboding. We were

mesmerized. Ali carried an aura, powerful; he appeared larger than life. If we ever met, what would I say to Muhammad Ali?

Becky was a great painter, friend, and confidant. We worked together for more than a decade. Her deep evangelical Christian beliefs guided her to be a caring human being. Still, for all her deeply held values, she was tolerant of the paint crew's smart-ass remarks and worldly attitudes. Her stern gaze at once seemed severe, but her strawberry blonde smile lighted the room.

Her burly, lumber-jack husband, George, thought Ali was easily the greatest boxer of all time. Becky appreciated Ali the boxer but felt far more for the man, handsome, charming, spiritual, the epitome of grace, masculinity, and courage.

On our first morning drive to the farm, we had talked about good manners; when Ali came around, should we disappear or say hello? We worried he might be grumpy. The farm was his private place away from the world where everyone wanted a piece of him. We decided to be professional and patient and wait for an introduction.

Several days after first seeing Muhammad, we still did not have a chance to meet him. Each morning we rode to the farm in my old burgundy Volvo station wagon that, for a time, ably served as our paint vehicle. I parked at the front of the garages. We unloaded our tools, climbed the stairs, and got to work finishing the second-floor rooms. We painted ceilings, walls, and newly installed trim in each office, hallway, and stairwell.

One morning, I worked in the upper hallway while Becky painted trim along the stairs. The hallway, and especially the stairwell, was narrow. It was a nuisance when anyone needed to pass by the wet paint. The walls were so close she had no option but to climb to the top of the stairs and wait for the intruder to pass.

On this day, Lonnie was busy in her office and in the house. She had come and gone to the point she apologized to Becky for the numerous interruptions. With foresight, Becky had come prepared for the opportunity. She pulled a brand-new Purdy paintbrush and a marker from her back pocket. She presented the brush to Lonnie and asked her to sign it.

Lonnie seemed surprised but casually offered, "Oh, I will sign it, but the one you really want is in the house having breakfast, just open the door; he is right there."

Becky paused. Could she burst in on Muhammad at breakfast? Lonnie sensed her hesitation. "Now, don't you be silly, go---he is just eating cereal!"

Becky descended the stairs, crossed the parking area then hesitated just outside the screened door. She knocked tentatively, waited, then opened the door just enough to see inside. Muhammad was there. He looked up from his bowl of cereal and motioned for her to come in. Becky opened the door and stammered something about Lonnie had told her to come over, that Muhammad should sign her paintbrush.

"Yes, yes, come here." Muhammad gestured with his hand and whispered in a soft, shaky voice.

Muhammad was unsteady, his hands shook, Parkinson's had descended over him. As Becky approached, Ali reached to take the brush in his left hand and the marker with his right. He had trouble coordinating the two. Becky stood alongside, compassionate. She sensed his frustration and leaned in to hold the brush steady. Muhammad still struggled. He tugged her right hand and gestured that he also needed help with the marker.

Becky moved behind Ali, still holding the brush with her left hand; she reached her right arm over his shoulders, stretching to steady the pen. Suddenly, she hung over Muhammad's back, straining to reach with both hands. Muhammad got right to signing the brush, but for Becky, her embrace seemed its own lifetime. With the brush signed, Becky quickly stood. Now, she shook more than Muhammad. Flushed and giddy, she thanked Ali and walked straight out into the sunshine.

I heard she was meeting Ali to sign the brush and hurried from the offices. I met Becky as she exited the house; her expression was utterly unfamiliar.

"Did he sign it?" I asked.

Becky, face flushed, stammered, "It was the most erotic thing that has ever happened to me!" Her eyes fell, and her head drifted faintly from side to side. Then, she looked up at me, very focused, "Don't tell George!"

CHAPTER THREE

ONE MOMENT

We labored for almost two weeks to complete the first phase of work in the offices; still, I had not met Ali. We moved on to the next project, the exterior of the main residence.

As usual, Becky and I met at the paint shop in Dowagiac, loaded supplies, and rode thirty minutes to the farm. We rolled slowly through the gates, windows down, the cool breeze crisp and invigorating. The air had that sweet, promising feel peculiar to summer mornings in Michigan. The optimism of a new day with the anticipation of something special happening---- probably before lunch.

While painting a house may be daunting for most people, we loved the challenge. We made painting an athletic event, crawling over the place like ants performing all the little tasks that added up to a structure reborn to look better than ever. We always finished by cleaning the windows so every surface gleamed.

The main house was originally constructed as a cow barn built into the side of a small hill. The first floor, with the kitchen and the family room, opened to the rear parking area. On the second floor, a large formal living room opened to gardens in the front. The third floor had four small bedrooms and a bath arranged in a circle around the stairway that rose in the center.

To the front of the house, gardens once bordered the original home that burned to the ground without so much as an alarm sounding in town. What remained of the building was pushed into the cellar and covered over with plantings. Beyond that low mound, a small two-car garage survives alone amongst the trees and flower beds.

Our first step in painting the house was to wash it. We needed to remove the screens from the windows on all three floors. We needed to go inside to release the latches that held the screens in place.

It was not yet eight o'clock that first morning, and we did not want to disturb Muhammad or anyone else who might be home. So, Becky and I did little jobs to eat some time. We staged the power washer and connected the water hoses. We pulled plastic sheets over the flower beds. We tied ropes around shrubs to hold them back from the siding so we could access every inch of the building.

"Do you think anyone is still inside?" Becky asked when we had run out of tasks. "Should we knock and just go in?"

It was about nine-thirty, and the house seemed empty.

"I'll double-check with Lonnie." I offered.

Lonnie had walked across the drive to her office above the garages shortly after we arrived. I headed to the office door when I heard the screen door to the kitchen slam. I looked back to see Michael, a house guest, leaving.

At the time, I was not sure who he was, but I called to him,

"Excuse me, we have to go through the house to release the screens. Is anyone home?" I asked.

"No everyone is gone. I was the last one up," he replied.

I said, "thanks" and turned back to the house.

Becky opened the entry door with some familiarity. She led me into the kitchen and pointed out the table where she had met Ali. Then Becky went to the first window to release the screen while I went to the second.

We hopscotched around the room, one window then the next. We finished the first-floor windows, moved through the second floor, and climbed the stairs to the third floor.

Becky took the first room; I went to the second. Hurrying right along, I swung the door open and took a few steps into the room. I froze.

Muhammad Ali, Olympic Gold Medalist, Athlete of the Century, and Three-Time Heavyweight Champion of the World, was asleep on the bed. Between the bed and wall, there was barely space to walk in the small room. I stood there, back to the wall, an inch from the bed, looking down at Muhammad Ali, buck naked, asleep.

My heart pounded in my ears. I was sure the thumping would wake him. There I would be, a "white boy" he had never met, standing over him.

No introduction needed; his first reflexive swing would smash me senseless against the wall. I could not move. My feet stuck to the carpet; they would sound like a stick on a washboard if I tried to move. Burning waves of panic swept up my legs and neck and scrambled my thoughts. I needed a plan. Fast.

Like a cartoon cat cheating death, I slowly took one silent high step, then another. Three stomach-churning steps into the hall, I carefully eased the door closed.

I took a breath and gasped with relief. Becky came out of the first room, "Oh my gosh, are you ok?" she asked, startled by my expression. I silently pulled her by the arm to the next room, closed the door, and whispered,

"He is in there! He is asleep. He's naked!"

If we had already met, if he was not Muhammad Ali, if he was not naked, I might not have been dizzied. As it was, I felt reckless and embarrassed to be "that guy."

"Oh my God, I would have passed out!" Becky gasped.

We hurried quietly downstairs and outside to breathe fresh air. There was no way I was going back into the house until we were sure Muhammad was up and gone for the day. We walked to the car and left the farm for an early lunch in town.

CHAPTER FOUR

DON'T SHOUT

The next day we were back at Ali's, preparing to paint the house. The power washer idled. Its burpy growl interrupted the tranquility of the dewy morning, but we had work to do. The house was a challenge. Built into the hill, it was difficult to move equipment and set ladders, and the grounds were thick with mature shrubbery in the gardens along the front and down one side of the house.

By itself, power washing is strenuous. Pulling the machine and hoses around a structure and then climbing up and down ladders to reach the peaks and overhangs, the activity is an excellent full-body exercise. It's constant work just controlling the powerful spray and ducking the blowback laden with dirt and debris that invariably swirls until it finds a path into your collar and down to the small of your back.

Happily, the power washer made paint scrapers all but obsolete and saved hours of preparation time. It quickly blew away dirt and chewed away worn-out paint; the fresh coat would bond perfectly. While I ran the gun, Becky set up the hoses and held back shrubbery, anything to help keep the washer washing.

By late afternoon, we had finished three sides of the house and the lower two floors on the back. Only the half wall and three gabled windows that rose from the second-floor roof above the parking area remained.

It was late afternoon when Becky headed home, and I stayed to finish. I never wanted to power wash two days in a row, so I was motivated to finish the upper level.

Lonnie came out of the house and said, "See you in the morning," as she walked to her car. She drove up the lane and met the office staff as they departed for the evening. The small caravan rolled to the gates and disappeared. Quiet settled over the farm; just me and Muhammad, who I had seen but still not met, remained.

I was worn out from running the power washer all day and chilled from the swirling spray that engulfed me all afternoon. I hustled to finish. I lifted an extension ladder against the rounded metal gutter that ran along the overhang. I arranged the power washer, spray gun, and fifty-foot hose on the pavement next to the ladder.

Once on the roof, I would clean the entire wall without climbing down to move equipment. I pulled the cord to fire up the machine and got set to haul the gun and long hose up the ladder as I climbed. I stood on the first rung and bounced the ladder a bit to see if it sat true. I didn't like resting a ladder against a metal gutter, both surfaces were slippery, and I worried the whole thing might slide sideways, but there was work to do. I climbed with the hose over my shoulder and the gun slung down my back.

Twelve steps up, I reached to take hold of the gutter. I took special care not to jerk the ladder to the side. Then, I pulled the hose up with my free hand and laid the coiled excess on the shingled roof. Once set, I climbed two rungs higher and swung my body onto the roof.

I sat at the roof's edge and took a deep breath to relax. I looked out past the garages to the river. The deep green lawn lay in shadows, the expanse almost as broad as my view. The floodplain was one-third of the entire property.

Then, comfortable with the roof's pitch, I stood and walked to the near end of the upper wall. I pulled the trigger and leaned into the powerful jet of water. The washer did its work cleaning the siding, then I swung around to rinse the debris from the shingles and edged along to the next section of the wall.

The sun was almost set, so I moved quickly, fortunate there were only minutes of work yet to complete. When I reached the far end of the wall, I looked back to the ladder with alarm. As I had worked across the roof, the coil of excess hose kinked, the knot pulled tight against the ladder, sliding it sideways along the metal gutter. The ladder leaned precariously about to tip down the side of the house. I took a breath and walked back across the roof, careful not to pull against the hose.

Bad enough, the ladder might slide completely down at any second, maybe break a window on the way and give Muhammad a heart attack, but I was deeply anxious just being on the short roof. A few years earlier, while working at my own home, I slid off a roof very similar to this one at Ali's. I fell fifteen feet to the ground.

It was mid-November, and the sun had just set. I was shingling a new room added to our second floor. While I stopped for a cup of coffee with my wife, who stood in the window I had just climbed out, the temperature fell to freezing as long shadows covered the tar-papered roof.

I knelt against the window chatting, then stood to move down the roof to a bundle of shingles. As soon as I let go of the window frame, the new frost on the roof whisked my feet from under me. I began my slide.

My wife was six months pregnant and terrified. She screamed. I told her, "I'll be fine." As I dropped over the edge.

I knew I would shatter my ankles if I tried to land on my feet. So, I rolled back, hoping to extend my body to distribute the impact. I slammed down almost flat and bounced on a smoothed-out pile of sand left from the masons' brickwork.

Our contractor was meticulous in keeping a clean worksite; there were no debris for me to hit. I survived with a cracked hip and shattered wrist. I mended with no lingering effects, ever grateful I did not land on a pile of broken bricks or a cement block.

Now I sat with my back to the third-story wall at Ali's, looking at the wet roof and only a hand's length of ladder still poking above the gutter. I reached down to the protruding leg with the washer's wand to ease the ladder back from its extreme lean. It straightened, but I could not tell if it was fully upright. With the roof's pitch, I dared not get close enough to look down the ladder as it reached up from the asphalt below. My heart raced.

I considered my options. I tried each of the windows that led into the third-floor bedrooms. Even if I "broke in," I could explain the situation to Muhammad, startled as he would be to see me coming down the stairs. But the windows were locked. I thought I could shout to get help, but Ali was the only person on the farm. I would NOT scream in fear to ask Muhammad Ali to hold my ladder!

I realized I had no good option. I had to trust the ladder was straight enough not to slide out under my weight. I edged down the roof. The shingles were worn and wet. I kept low and pressed my open palms against the cold roof, maintaining three points of contact to keep from slipping. I positioned myself above the ladder and paused to slow my breathing.

Still, my heart thumped when I swung my leg up and over the top of the ladder, and my toe reached for a rung. I found a step, then still lying on the roof, I shifted some weight to the ladder. It slid a few inches to the left but held. I quickly gripped the gutter with my left hand. If the ladder skipped out, I could at least hang drop to the ground. I stepped fully onto the third rung down, quickly taking hold of the gutter with my right hand so the ladder could not slide in either direction.

I saw the ladder was still a few inches off plumb. I slid it straight and relaxed for a minute. I let the hose slip through my hand, lowering the gun to the pavement, then I climbed quickly down.

There were parts of this job I did not like; climbing on and off roofs was the worst. Still, the next day I would climb back onto the same roof to prime the wall and window frames. It was comforting that Becky would be there so I would not have to contemplate screaming for Ali to hold my ladder.

CHAPTER FIVE

MEETING ALI

The following day, I finally met Ali. We arrived with anticipation and excitement, like every day that summer. The morning sun was sweet; the first bright rays warmed the chilly air.

Once parked, we collected our tools and quietly set about organizing the day. It was just past seven-thirty. With the house washed, we walked around to evaluate areas that might need hand-scraping or a coat of primer. When we completed our circle, Lonnie opened the screen door and called me into the kitchen to discuss the exterior wall color and an accent color for the entry doors.

Inside, out of the morning sun, the room was darkly shadowed. Only the sunlight beaming through the window in the door tempered the darkness. To the left was a small, heavily curtained window above an old porcelain sink. To the right, Muhammad was at the breakfast table with a glass of orange juice and a bowl of cereal. The ceiling was low. I wondered if he would have to duck under the light fixture mounted in the center when he passed.

He glanced up when he heard Lonnie speak.

She asked me: "Do you think we should paint the walls a standard white, or should we use a bit of color?"

Muhammad looked at me and seemed to nod. "Hello."

Then, spoon in hand, he looked back to his cereal. Gingerly, I said, "Good Morning, Muhammad."

He grunted something that must have meant "Hello" and continued chewing a mouthful of raisin bran. That was ingloriously it. I had met Muhammad Ali. Rather than thrilled, I felt like an intruder.

A strange intimacy comes with painting; we traverse the private spaces that spouses generally share only with each other. It can be awkward. We joked on the paint crew that we not only saw the inside of people's homes; we saw their sock drawers and the back of their closets.

Suddenly, there is a stranger in the bedroom pulling linens from the bed, handling the sundry boxes stowed underneath and in the closets. Every intimate item is potentially disrupted. This morning, talking with Lonnie, I tried to be respectful of Muhammad, peaceful in his own space, thinking of his day, enjoying a little cereal and sliced banana when suddenly a stranger is there smiling awkwardly, saying "hello."

It did not help my comfort level that I had secretly seen him just the day before. Sensing my unease, Lonnie said, "Oh, you two had not met." And she made a sound like, "Hmmmp," meaning, "what exactly is the big deal? I was asking you a question."

"Oh," I replied, continuing my clever repartee. I looked back to Lonnie and answered.

"Well, if you have a color in mind, the house does not have to be white. Something soft will look clean and give character."

Lonnie knew precisely what she wanted. She showed me a paint color card with a creamy pale southwest tone circled-- muted with notes of yellow and orange.

"Really nice," I said. "The color is warm; it will add strength."

We choose a deep tint of the wall color for the door accent, a rich rust. I was very ready to get back outside and breathe.

Underwhelming as the first meeting may have been, the encounter augured the Ali I would get to know. A regular guy at home enjoying small moments in life. I thought of him shuffling to dress in the cramped bedroom and then negotiating two sets of stairs to get to the breakfast table. It was remarkable that Ali lived with the inconvenience. Life in a single-story home would have been so much easier.

As it was, the kitchen and family room filled the lower floor. The kitchen cabinets were old, and the refrigerator was of an era gone by. Behind the kitchen, there were storage closets and a pantry. Adjacent to the open kitchen, the family room where the stairway rose behind a false wall anchoring a wide-screen television at the far end of the room.

The second floor was open with large windows along three walls with a grand piano and a fascinating array of mementos marking celebrity life. There were few trophies but many gifts of honor from kings and countries.

Still, the first level lacked sweet morning light, and the four bedrooms on the third floor were small. The barn-shaped roof cut into the bedroom ceilings, including Muhammad's, forcing him to crouch when walking along the far side of the bed. The house had charm but did not reflect its owner. At the time, it felt dull and worn. The remodeling work, yet to come, would be a transformation.

Ali cherished his time at home on the farm. He did not seem to care about the state of the house or the two levels of stairs he had to climb between the kitchen and bedroom. He just needed a place to call home; Ali's happiness welled from within.

"At home, I am a nice guy: but I don't want the world to know.

Humble people, I've found, don't get very far." Muhammad Ali.

PART TWO:

CHAPTER SIX

ZANE

Some Time Ago

The new dawn sun rose hot in the red morning sky; broad pools of water lay still in the fields after a month of late spring showers. The sun sweltered just above the eastern horizon. Without even a day for the land to dry, the thick air smelled of warm earth.

"Papi, can we swim before lessons? Papi, please?" Mira pleaded. Her bright eyes interrupted Papi's resolve to administer lessons as the morning's first task.

"Go just to the bend, and hurry; lessons in twenty minutes. Zane, you go, watch your sister." He relented.

Papi never said "No." to Mira. From the moment she was born, Mira was Papi's princess. When Zane made mischief, he was in trouble twice if Mira was with him. Papi said Zane would be her ruin, so he swatted his bottom once for the misconduct and once for involving Mira.

The first morning light warmed the hard clay walls of the Rondeval. Inside, cool night air lingered, smelling of boiled oats and Papi's tea. Zane sipped the last milk from his cup and wiped it dry with a corner of his sweet bread. He ran through the yard gobbling the bread and calling for Mira to catch up.

They leaped across the red dirt of the hard-packed earth, swept clean; they skipped past the old gate and ran the short stretch of road toward the river. At the bend, Mira sprang down the path weaving its way along the hill to the water below. Zane followed her, running, leaping into the swollen river. The red clay bank slipped under the flow of cool silty water cascading down the valley to the ocean, just over the horizon, where a sliver of the sun already blazed hot.

Mira and Zane soaked their heads in the cool water. They splashed in the deep swirling current mid-stream, then swam to shore, digging fingers into the slippery bank, pulling themselves up to the path back home.

Zane hurried up the hill, Mira at his side; she stopped where the brush rose head tall at the foot of the steep incline. She pulled at a protea bloom, pink, intricate, laced in green, still closed tight in the shadows ahead of the morning sun, its stalk held tight.

"Mira, let's go." Zane called, "Papi will whip me if we are late."

Zane hurried up the hard clay path while Mira lingered. Without slowing his pace, he turned again to Mira. He saw an odd question in her gaze. His mouth opened to again call to her when a man stepped from the brush.

"Hurrying to Papi?" he asked. Zane stumbled to the side of the intruder.

Zane did not recognize the smiling man, though he seemed familiar, hot fear spiked his legs. "Mira, run!" he shouted.

The man pounded his fist into Zane's stomach. He stumbled and fell to the ground. The man pushed Zane hard as he tumbled, then rammed his knee into his back. Zane's face pressed into the wet dirt that rose at the edge of the rugged clay trail.

Zane heard Mira shriek, but the sound quickly muffled; she moaned. A heavy hand crushed against the back of Zane's neck, and his mouth smashed into the dirt. The man again bounced his knee hard on his back. Zane gasped. The wet earth pushed into his mouth. Zane was choking.

With his knee rough against Zane's shoulders, the man pulled Zane's arms tight behind his back; he quickly looped a thin rope around his wrists and tugged till the twine cut hard. The man pulled Zane's face from the dirt, his thick hand clenched over his mouth. Zane spit mud against the hand.

He yanked Zane to his feet. Zane whipped his head to see the tall man carry Mira, his arm just under her shoulders, his hand over her mouth. Her legs kicked; her arms swung frantically. Still flailing, they disappeared amongst the bushy trees lining the path along the river.

Zane never saw Mira again. He never again saw Papi or heard Mumma hum the lullabies that sent him and Mira off to sleep as she finished a long day's chores.

"Run!" the man commanded. He picked up a long stick, thin and polished, then slapped Zane on the top of the head. "Turn," he whispered hard. "Run!"

Confused, Zane struggled upward a few paces. He hesitated where the path met the road just out of sight of the house. The man slapped Zane with the stick again, "Run!" he commanded. The man pushed Zane across the road to a trail that coursed behind the farmed fields, then up and out of the valley.

Tears filled Zane's eyes as he ran. In his head, he screamed, "Papi." He thought of Papi calling for him. He turned to look for him standing in the doorway, shouting, but they were already too far from the farm.

The thin stick struck his face, hard this time. Zane's cheek split. He yelped. The slice burned. He ran; his steps were confused, his eyes blind with tears.

The man whispered hard, "Run!"

The stick whipped viscously across his buttocks. The sting spiked through his legs, and he stumbled forward. Then he ran. Urine wetted his thin damp shorts.

Zane ran with the man close behind until the sun was high and they were far up the valley. Now trees were thick along the path. The man poked Zane's shoulder with the stick.

"Turn." He commanded.

A steep, narrow path led up the hill. The stick pressed into Zane's back. Zane ran up the hill, breathless. He ran until his head pulsed hot in the blazing sun. His stomach knotted. Zane vomited. He staggered from the path, hands swollen and numb.

"Quiet." The man whispered.

He grabbed Zane by the neck.

"Stop." He growled in an angry whisper.

The man gripped Zane's shoulders and pulled him into the brush. Zane squatted on the ground. He closed his eyes to stop the swirling. The forest fell silent around them. Nothing moved in the sweltering heat.

A dove cooed from the trees above them. The man cooed back. Then Zane heard mumbling. The low brush rustled. Three boys appeared further up the hill. A tall, thin man with long wiry legs poked at them with a small bundle of long sticks.

The thin man jabbed at the boys as they walked, then motioned for them to sit. Together the men spoke whispers. The boys trembled, fearful. They seemed older than Zane but were still boys. One boy, his nose split, one eye swollen shut, looked only to the ground. The mark of a stick ran across his face.

The men jerked Zane to his feet and laced a long stick against his back and between his elbows. The thin man yanked Zane's face to the sky, then poured water over his parched lips.

The men lashed the long sticks to the other boys; constrained, they could only walk the open path.

Zane's captor disappeared into the forest. The thin man faced the boys and smiled his command. "Run!" They marched on while the noon-day sun fell slowly to the horizon. Night came.

They climbed high along the last hill, looking far across the valley toward the farm where Papi and Mumma cried for Zane. Tears filled his eyes. The path rose upward one final time; they climbed over the crest, then walked downhill toward the sea.

Rising up the hills from the ocean, the night wind grew cold. Zane shivered in his worn cotton shorts and sandals. Stars lit the brilliant night sky. The slice in Zane's cheek pulsed as he hurried down the winding hill.

Zane thought about Papi running through the night, working his way up the path to find him. Zane thought about how Papi would beat the thin man and leave him tied in the bush. Or maybe Papi searched along the river to find Mira. Papi would save Mira and then come for him, he thought.

The trail left the forest, settling onto the flat plain. It smelled of fresh dirt and citrus trees that swelled with new buds and showed bright green leaves in the rising sun that lingered briefly just below the horizon. The strange reds of the brief morning twilight reflected down from low clouds ominous in the eastern sky.

They crossed a planted field and saw the outline of a village beyond the citrus trees. The man whispered his commands. "Quiet, run to the grove."

The sun peaked on the horizon, and dew glistened on the grass and the citrus trees. A short, squat building blocked their way at the end of the aisle.

"Stop," the man commanded. "Lay down."

The man went to a half-door cut low in the side of the rough wall. He knocked. Two men crawled out. They worked quickly, cutting the ropes from the boys' arms, pulling away the sticks, and dragging them, hands still tied, through the half door into the cramped space.

Zane inched into the room, hands bound, unable to crawl. He saw a guard sitting crossed-legged against the wall near the door. He saw an arm reach to close the door, and the room went black. Zane heard the sounds of many mouths breathing, the gentle, rhythmic snores of deep sleep. He felt the arms and legs of people lying all around him on the dirt floor.

His cheek throbbed, his legs ached, his hands burned at the wrists, and his fingers were numb. Zane closed his eyes and saw Mira frantic, kicking, and alone. He saw Papi running along the path, tears in his eyes. He saw Mumma on her knees calling for him. Silently he wept, then, mercifully, he slept.

CHAPTER SEVEN

THE CROSSING

Zane's shared nightmare spanned centuries, though it was only days since he ran to the river with Mira. Now shackled, he huddled in darkness on the dirt floor of a cramped holding pen. He lay exhausted with grief and exertion. He slept deeply but awoke to a surreal nightmare, only to sleep again.

Finally awake, he did not know how much time had passed. He lay on his side for long hours listening. He heard men speak in tongues he did not understand, then only troubled silence but for the breathing of bodies all around him. Once, in his confusion, he tried to stand, but the ceiling was too low even to sit fully upright.

Finally, the lone door cracked open. A prisoner was led out from the low cavern. Outside, in darkness, several men hurried past. Then there was the sharp clank of a hammer striking metal.

A guard swung the door wide, sending a whoosh of fresh air into the damp, acrid fume of the pen jammed for days with men bound and starving. Zane leaned his elbows into the noxious dirt; he crawled painfully toward the door, excited to breathe sweet air. Suddenly men crushed hard against him, each of them straining to escape. He felt panic when a man crawled over his legs; Zane could not move. His shoulders ached, and his chest burned with fear. The door guard led a second captive out into the night.

Zane pushed his way the last few feet to the open door. The cool air eased his panic, but his heart still raced. A hand reached out to pull him through the opening. The sweet night air smelled of a citrus grove. Zane breathed deeply. He saw stars in the sky and thought the worst of his journey had passed.

Zane was pushed into a fetid corral where fifty men sat huddled upon the uprooted grass and animal dung. Zane leaned into a rough post, his head on his knees, his arms wrapped lightly over his shins. He heard the intermittent clanking of a heavy hammer. A burly man came to Zane. "Stand," he ordered, pulling at his arm. Zane stumbled up. How long had it been since he stood alone? One day? Two? Zane realized he had no idea.

The escort bore scars, markings of a tribe Zane did not know. He led Zane, with some compassion, to a blacksmith, his face dripping sweat. The brute grumbled an unintelligible command Zane could not comprehend, but Zane had watched him work. He saw men dragging a broken foot from the stone now at his feet.

Frantic, Zane froze; his world spiraled away. Then he felt his foot jammed onto the heavy stone already laced with drying blood. Zane fell forward against his knee, gasping; his head bobbed numbly.

Time slowed. From a strange distance, Zane re-assembled the moment. He studied his own blurry shin; he followed sweat trails in the loathsome dirt. He felt the blacksmith yank him upright with an arm around his neck. His open hand slapped Zane hard across his swollen cheek. Zane choked, struggling for a breath.

A second guard wrapped a heavy iron ring around Zane's ankle in one swift motion. The blacksmith slapped a strap over the ends of the ring and drew it tight against Zane's leg. With two brutal clanks, the ends of the ring flattened over the backside of the heavy shackle; blood swelled where the crude metal tore Zane's skin. He lifted his foot from the stone and felt new terror; he was hobbled.

Again, Zane was led shivering into a corral; he could not look away from the shackle. His thoughts retreated to embrace the gentle touch of a dampened cloth cleaning his wound, his mother's tender words to soothe him. He was not so far from her, just over the mountain, across the valley. He thought he could return to her in only a day, "Just stand and walk." Then he heard the hammer thump without the clank of metal and the unworldly howl of bones crushed.

Men shouted in the commotion. His focus returned; Zane saw the shackle and felt his shoulders worn raw, his thin shorts encrusted with filth and days of dried urine. His senses roused; the stench was intense, even in the open air. He was not supposed to be here, he thought.

He was a boy; there were men all around him. He was taller than most, with broad shoulders and thick biceps from work in the fields with Papi. But he was a boy. Zane looked into the night sky and again thought of the farm just over the ridge across the green valley.

While the hammer worked, men already shackled were loaded onto wagons. One by one, horses drew the wagons across the yard to the lane next to the crude building. Two men bounced the prisoners onto the rough planks, then pulled a tarp over them and ordered them to be silent with the crack of a whip. Zane put his hand under his head to keep off the man beneath him. He smelled rot and excrement.

"I was in that hole for most of a week." The man beneath him whispered. "I am sorry, my legs are covered in shit."

"I am not supposed to be here," Zane whispered.

A sharp whip stung the tarp, "Silence." A voice commanded.

The horses tugged the wagon forward. Zane felt the wheels dig into the soft dirt in the yard and then onto the hard-packed road. Minutes later, he heard the wheels roll onto wooden planks. He listened to distant shouts and smelled the salty air that rolled in from the sea and crept into the blanketed wagon. Then the wheels stopped. When the tarp pulled away, heavy hands drug the men over the back of the wagon. Zane struggled up.

"Get out. Walk." A bearded man commanded as he yanked Zane to his feet and pushed him toward a ship tied alongside the wharf. As dockhands approached, Zane saw them pull short leather whips, Sjambols, from their waistbands. He hurried toward the ship. They were led up a broad plank onto the boat.

Zane stood at the rail and looked into the black water in the shadows between the wooden planks and pier. The ship rolled lightly under his feet while a sailor dressed in strange clothing barked commands Zane did not understand. Next to him, a man repeated in Zane's tongue, "Strip. Everything! Now!"

The prisoners muttered, confused, hesitant. The sharp crack of a horsewhip focused the men. Slowly they pulled off their garments. A guard walked amongst the prisoners, slapping one then another with his sjambok.

Zane stood naked in the cool air. Two captives carried piles of clothing onshore to toss them onto a fire burning alongside the wharf. Zane covered himself, but guards forced the men into a line along the ship's rail. A group of women huddled over children at the bow, desperate to keep them from the whips and chilling breeze.

Sailors climbed the rigging and rolled barrels across the decks. The landing planks were pulled from the wharf while three men inspected each prisoner. Zane was pushed forward to a ladder reaching down into darkness. He saw men sickly or with broken bones led to the ship's rear.

Zane felt numb dread as he descended. "Against the wall.

Get forward." A sailor barked, pushing the men forward with angry hands. A second guard came from the front of the ship with a chain that he laced through each man's leg shackle. Zane was mute with terror. He heard the words but understood nothing as he crawled forward.

The ceiling was too low to sit up except between heavy beams beneath the main deck. A wide hatch crisscrossed with heavy metal bars opened to the deck above in the middle of the ship. Light came from a few narrow seams in the hull and cracks between the decking planks above them.

Zane laid down on the rough wood deck; he brought his hands to his face to mask the awful stench permeating the hold. Sailors hustled across the top deck, loading crates and cargo. Captives by the dozen descended the ladder into the lower deck. Almost five hundred men would be crammed into the fore and aft holds when the ship set sail. Zane sat amongst them, hunched beneath the low timbers.

A tall, lanky man settled alongside Zane. "My name is Saye; I am my father's firstborn." He said to Zane.

"I am Zane; I am also my father's firstborn." He replied.

Zane told Saye about Mira and Papi, and Mumma. He told him about the crops they had planted between Spring rains and his swim with Mira just before his capture.

Saye told Zane how he lived in the valley far from a village. He had four sisters and lived with his mother, father, and grandparents, who depended on Saye to plant crops and hunt. He was to be given a wife when the Proteus fully bloomed.

When night fell, the hold was packed with men sitting shoulder to shoulder. The cook sent buckets of porridge ladled into crude wooden bowls. Zane's empty stomach knotted with the sudden lump of food. His body ached terribly as he and Saye struggled to find a way to lay on the hard-wooden planks. They ended up back to back on their sides; their ankles twisted painfully against the crude rings. Zane wondered how many nights they would sail.

Before dawn, Zane felt the ship gently roll and the wharf's sounds fade. He lay on the wooden floor, looking up at the deck and listening to the thumping of bare feet. Then he heard the sails snap and felt the ship lean with the wind.

Zane's heart ached far more than his split cheek, torn wrists, and bloody ankle. He thought about Mumma and Papi searching for him. "What has happened to Mira?" he thought. He cradled his head in his hands, and sometime before the sun rose, he slept.

Zane woke to the sound of the bow plowing into waves. He felt the heavy ship push deep into a wave, then rise up to drop into the next roller. Zane closed his eyes to steady his focus. He felt queasy. A man near him grunted aloud as his stomach spasmed and he vomited. The ooze flowed across the floor. The stench brought bile into Zane's throat. Then with a violent burst, Saye heaved. The hold became a wrenching mass of sick men bursting.

Through the grated hatch, barrels of seawater poured into rinse the hold and spill out the scuppers. Men beneath the hatch gasped, choking in the flow. Zane heard the shouts but did not understand; he lay wet and shivering. His gut ached with spasms. His shoulders howled against the wooden floor. Saye lay against his back, and a man Zane did not know lay against his chest. Zane closed his eyes; alone and silently, he wept.

PART THREE:

CHAPTER EIGHT

SOME BACKGROUND

One hundred and sixty years after Zane's journey and twenty-six years after Ali was born, I graduated from a Catholic high school in Waterford, Michigan. Our parish was a homogeneous suburbia forty miles north of Detroit. While in school, I cannot remember sharing more than a casual greeting with a minority of any nationality. My adventure in diversity began with my Latino buddy from the public school late in my senior year; we were friends and then housemates in college.

From our middle-class suburb, we watched the Vietnam war on the nightly news, then the riots of 1968 in Detroit. Throughout my high school years, there were racial confrontations across the South and protests in the North. The Black Panthers in Oakland, CA, and the Weather Underground in Ann Arbor, MI, challenged the war and police violence. Both ended in bloody confrontations.

My social group protested our grievances, too: new ordinances closed city parks at dusk and restricted hours at the county beach. Protest was the thing to do, so we protested.

Evenings in the summer of 1968, we drove twenty minutes to Birmingham, an upper-middle-class suburb of Detroit; there, we threw rocks at the police. Somehow, we rationalized an equivalency between restricted park hours, the Vietnam War, and racial oppression.

From this isolation, my eyes opened, if just a bit.

Mid-summer, I took a friend to the Cincinnati pop festival at the soon-to-be-demolished Crosley Field. It was a raucous event in an atmosphere of confrontation and a constant threat of violence. While rock bands played, fans taunted police officers bound arm in arm, lining the infield to keep fans off the grass. When about eighty percent of the audience had left the stadium at the concert's end, the police rushed the stands with their Billy clubs swinging.

My friend and I ran hard just ahead of a phalanx of police bent on cracking heads. We slipped into the parking lot and ducked behind the first line of cars; the police continued chasing kids that kept to the roadway. My red MGA coupe was only a few rows in; we stayed low and made our way into the car. We slunk low in the seats watching the frantic crowd running in terror with the police at their heels.

A van full of kids backed out of a parking space just across the aisle from us. Before they could move forward, a cop smashed his club through a rear door window. Then he slammed his club flat against the sides of the van as he ran to the front. There he pounded his club through the windshield and, with a second blow, hit the driver squarely in the face.

Another of the cops broke out a side window with the heel of his baton and then tossed a tear gas canister inside. Police surrounded the van and smashed out the remaining windows, then reached inside, swinging their clubs wildly as tear gas billowed from the broken-out windows.

Kids began falling out the doors, rolling on the asphalt, and covering their heads with their hands; Billy clubs pounded. Boys and girls alike took a brutal beating. I thought the driver was dead, lying motionless half under the van. We scrunched low in our seats, just feet from the melee.

That day I learned what it looked like for the Freedom

Riders attacked while rolling into Anniston and Birmingham, Alabama. I saw the kind of hatred that fueled murder.

I could not imagine being so severely beaten; I struggled to comprehend the courage to face such an assault willingly. Civil rights leaders routinely stood up to baseball bats and ax handles and suffered the daily humiliations of Jim Crow.

Born into this era, Ali bore the weight and rose to exemplify peace, understanding, and forgiveness.

Being white and raised in America meant confronting my inherent prejudice. Knowing Ali forced me to contemplate deeply the prejudice in our society. I began to see how racial bias, subtle and overt, is ingrained in American culture and its institutions.

I had some things to reconcile. One day I was a house painter in southwest Michigan; the next, I was hanging with Ali. One day I was comfortable with my unexamined sense of racial equality; the next, my world stood on its head.

I have some thoughts to share. I will not get it all right, so here, early on, I ask for your understanding. And I invite you to possibly imagine Ali born in a different era, born into the time of his great-great-grandfather.

CHAPTER NINE

AUNT JEAN

My first professional house painting was for my Aunt Jean and Uncle Howard--- "Uncle How- Weird." He was a walking string bean of dry, sarcastic humor. At family gatherings, he would chide the host for only cooking one ham or scold the grill master for pressing "cheap little burger patties," not because there was not enough ham or the burgers were not delicious but because that was Howard. He loved to needle people. Still, when the kidding stopped, Howard was a perfectionist. He kept his car waxed, and the windows washed. Yard clippings were neatly bundled, and the driveway was swept. Howard was a stickler.

Howard was married to Sarge, my Aunt Jean, my mother's second oldest sister. Jean was a stern woman but friendly and happy to comment on all aspects of my life---my choice of girlfriends included.

Howard and Jean lived life clearly in love. He adored her, and in his way, he let it show. He put on that she was the drill sergeant that kept him in line.

One year at Easter dinner with our family, Howard complained that their house needed to be painted, but his knees hurt too badly to climb ladders.

"I might put painting it off till Fall, but Sarge says it has to be done." He declared.

"I know you are too cheap to hire a professional, but Larry can paint the house for you---and do a better job!" my mother bragged. "He painted our trim outside and helped me with the girls' bedroom."

Howard looked me up and down, then took the challenge,

"Well, if he is that damned good, I'll even pay him five dollars per week! What do you say, Larry, want to make some money?"

I was fifteen years old. I was nervous about taking the job, but it would be hard to say no. Besides, I wanted to prove my skills, and if I could please Howard, I could work for anyone.

Their home was a simple brick ranch set in the rolling hills of an old apple orchard. The property was meticulously kept. Even though the orchard had long since ceased commercial production, Howard kept the trees neatly trimmed, the rows raked and mowed. Even the garage floor was not just swept, but it was painted deep forest green to match the exterior house trim, and Howard rinsed it off most every Saturday morning. Howard spent hours tinkering in the yard, the garage, and everywhere else around the house.

The current paint project was strictly for cosmetics, the paint had faded a bit, but the finish was not chipping or peeling. The overhangs and windows just needed a fresh coat to brighten them up.

It took Howard a few weeks to prepare for the paintwork. He trimmed the shrubs and washed out the gutters.

Then on a Monday in early June, my mother drove me to Jean and Howard's in our black Ford Galaxy station wagon. I was queasy with anxiety. I did not want to be left with Howard, let alone have him oversee my work. I had always been just one of the kids; now, I was in the spotlight.

When we arrived, Howard stood in the driveway smiling broadly. "Good Morning, Chief; ready to work?" he asked.

"Sure," I replied, "I'll start washing the overhangs."

Howard was ready. He handed me a big scrub brush on a long stick. He had the garden hose pulled around one side of the house... I followed the hose and assessed the house as I walked.

"The step ladder is in the garage with the drop cloths." Howard offered, "And be sure to cover the bushes when you paint. There will be World War three if you get paint on Sarge's shrubs." he warned.

"OK, I can do that," I replied.

I quickly soaked the brush and got to scrubbing the overhangs. With water flying around, I figured Howard might leave me alone.

I pushed forward along the first overhang. There was dew on the grass, and the toes of my tennis shoes were soaked even before I began spraying. Water dripped off the overhangs onto my head as I worked and ran cold down my back. I wished I had worn a ball cap.

I thought Howard had gone, but he suddenly stepped up close to my side and commented, "You know if you backed up ahead of the hose, that water would drip on the shrubs, not on you?"

"Yeah, OK," I replied.

"How stupid," I thought, "walking forward into the dripping water." All I had to do was back along the house so the spray fell where I had already been.

I thought of Mom bragging I would do a better job than Howard. He was happy to needle me; I thought he was looking forward to needling her too.

I sprayed the overhangs and scrubbed and rinsed them and the brick walls. My arms burned from scrubbing above my head with the big brush and long stick, but I did not have to climb a ladder, and it did not take long to work around the house. The best thing was Howard left me alone.

Howard called me for lunch when the noon siren sounded at the town's fire department down the hill.

"Ham sandwiches," Howard announced, "the good cured stuff, not that cheap cut your mother buys."

Aunt Jean sat in her chair at the pale-yellow Formica-topped table speckled green with a wide metal band around the outer edge. The chairs had slick vinyl seats, deep red over round, polished metal legs. There were three plates with a ham sandwich on white bread cut diagonally, showing mayonnaise and yellow mustard. Each dish had a big spoonful of potato salad and a pickle.

I said hello to Aunt Jean and sat uncomfortably. Howard took his place at the head of the table.

Noticing I was soaked, Howard began with a grin, "Well, Sarge, I don't think we have had wet pants at the table since Jim was in diapers."

"Haha, I think you are right." Jean laughed condescendingly.

"Sorry, I got pretty wet washing the house," I said, filling the silence. My face felt flushed. I hoped they could not see my embarrassment.

But then Howard offered, "Sarge, he is doing a good job."

Howard took big bites of his sandwich and pontificated in his deep baritone. Then he and Aunt Jean spoke in shorthand about the morning and what was on the agenda for the afternoon.

"Mail is late," Howard announced.

"No bills, that's good." Jean cheered.

"Frank got back last night." Howard jumped in.

"Don't get in a fuss about him." Jean empathized.

"I've got rattlesnakes and alligators at work this week.
There is no rest; I hope we can hire good help. Nobody wants to work anymore." Howard complained.

So, you go in after lunch?" Jean surmised.

"Back to the salt mine," Howard replied.

I tried not to stare as Aunt Jean worked hard to pick up her sandwich and maneuver her hand to her mouth. Her hands and wrists were knotty and inflamed. I ate my lunch and quickly downed a small glass of milk. I excused myself and hurried outside.

With the overhangs scrubbed and rinsed, I washed the windows and wiped down the frames. Howard insisted the right time to clean the windows was before painting so the window cleaner would not mess up the fresh paint. I did not argue; he had a good idea.

Howard was inside for a long time. I worked along the side of the house, then the front. There was a large picture window in the living room with six framed sections that showed in across the speckled beige carpet to the kitchen. As I cleaned the windows, I saw Howard carry Aunt Jean from her chair at the table to the couch in the living room.

I focused on washing the windows, but I could see him arrange her on the cushions and tuck pillows against her sides. He pulled the button to turn on the television and left the room.

Aunt Jean was suffering more and more from rheumatoid arthritis. For as long as I could remember, she moved slowly and sometimes grimaced in pain; now, she could not even walk.

I worked painting the overhangs for a couple of days and

relaxed a bit with the routine of eating an uncomfortable lunch. Finally, Howard went to the office early in the morning and departed immediately after lunch. He left me happily alone to do my work.

When I arrived the following day, Jean and Howard had already eaten breakfast, and Howard had arranged Aunt Jean on the couch. She sat with her arms crossed in her lap, her hands turned under, and her fingers clenched. It seemed courteous, so I stepped in to say hello. Jean replied, "Good Morning," and asked about my mom or what was on the paint agenda that day. Her hands quivered when she talked; I wondered if she hurt that much

With the overhangs painted, I began trimming windows. This was the acid test. I carefully edged paint just up to but not touching the panes of glass. It took some time to cut in the first window, but the second went a bit faster. My confidence grew, and I was excited for Howard to see my exacting work. When he returned for lunch, he parked in the drive, got out, and walked straight across the lawn to the last window I painted.

I stood with my can of paint in one hand, and my trim brush in the other. Howard inspected the window. He looked severe, then turned to me with a smile.

"Well, Ace, that is pretty damn good. But, don't you think it would make a better seal if you carried the paint about a sixteenth inch onto the glass?"

"Well, ahhhh, yeah. That's a good idea." I replied.

I went back over the windows and pulled a thin bead of paint along the sash onto the glass. It filled the narrow glazing line and made the windows look tight by eliminating that thin, somewhat irregular line. It was a little bit of perfection. This is how I trimmed every window from then on throughout my career.

A bit after five o'clock, Howard returned from work. He again parked in the driveway and hurried across the lawn. I could see him eying the windows. He stepped up to the first window; his head almost touched the glass as he inspected the frames.

"I'll be damned." He said. "I have tried to do that for twenty years and only made a mess. Nice work, Ace."

In two weeks, I finished painting the house. Some months later, mom told me Aunt Jean had been traveling twice a month, almost seven hundred miles, to the Mayo Clinic in Rochester, Minnesota. Jean was an early candidate for experimental joint replacement. Soon she had her elbows replaced and was able to comfortably feed herself.

Over time, they replaced her knees, then her hips, and she learned to walk again. Eventually, they replaced her wrists. Though the mechanical joints were rudimentary by today's standards, her recovery was miraculous. Jean went from fully incapacitated to functional as a patient in this groundbreaking field.

One late Fall day at my parent's house, when Jean was using a walker near the end of her convalescence, I said that I remembered how difficult it was for her when I painted the house.

I remarked, "The Mayo Clinic must really be something!"

"Yes, and you know what I really like about Mayo?" she asked rhetorically. "All the time I have spent there, I have never seen a nigger."

I don't remember saying anything at that moment. I do remember feeling like I was somewhere to the side of the room looking on. I saw my Aunt. She looked so much like my mother. I saw her able to walk, to use her arms and hands. I saw her hair in its stylish perm. Her tight skin was flawless.

Her lips pursed.

Yet even in my white-bread adolescence, I sensed how damaged she was. It may be unfair, but those words define her in my mind. She died not many years later; I never spoke with her about race. Our family always accepted that she and Howard were overt racists; still, that sad statement never left me.

CHAPTER TEN

OUR VISIT

It was the morning of our young family's life; we were privileged by time and place. The sun shone brightly on those young upturned faces. Love and security lent a warm embrace. I knew the times at Ali's were special and would be finite. I wanted to be sure my wife and children shared the experience.

Soon after I met Muhammad, I went to Kim, Muhammad's executive assistant, to ask if I could bring the family out for a visit. Kim said she would check and let me know. Later that week, Kim said Muhammad would be happy to meet.

"I can tell you he is surprised that anyone wants to see him," Kim told me. "Because he is ill, he thinks no one is interested anymore."

Indeed, this was a few months before the Atlanta Olympics when Muhammad again shook the world with his appearance to light the torch. Muhammad was having progressively more difficulty speaking; his hands trembled, and he shuffled when he walked. His stardom was rooted in his athletic abilities; now, they were severely diminished. It was not yet apparent to Muhammad that the world adored him for his courage, wisdom, and humanity.

Kim was the cheerful face of the Ali farm. She was the first person a guest met in the office or spoke with on the phone. Kim made me feel like the entire farm was excited that I phoned or arrived to work. She knew precisely how Lonnie wanted Muhammad cared for, and she lived it. With no real sense of privilege, everything was done for Muhammad. His meals were prepared, his clothes arranged, and his schedule set.

Kim also helped keep him in line. Left to himself, Muhammad would have lived on hamburgers and milkshakes and mischief. Even when Lonnie hired a personal chef to balance Muhammad's diet, he found ways to feed his appetite for burgers.

To arrange a day to formally meet, Kim looked through his calendar for the middle day of a three-day block when he was scheduled to be at the farm. Even before his Olympic appearance, business obligations kept Muhammad in steady demand.

Kim wanted us to visit with a day available before and after to buffer our date if Muhammad had to stay an extra day when he traveled or leave early for a meeting if plans changed.

We settled on a Wednesday about a month out. When the day arrived, we dressed the kids in their best school clothes and sent them off on the morning bus. They were in fourth grade, second, and kindergarten. We thought it would be fun to surprise them, so we said nothing of the visit. During lunch, they were called to the office. We met them there and told them we were going to meet Ali.

Our second grader was not happy that we took her away from her class spelling bee. But this was an adventure. The kids were playing hooky, and we were going to meet the Greatest Of All Time.

We drove to Ali's with the windows down, feeling the glow of an early summer's day. I stopped at the iron gates and punched in my code and the gates swung open. My son was impressed with the big gates hinged on the fieldstone columns.

I drove slowly, pointing out the old milk barn where Ali trained and the barns packed with memorabilia. Kim met us in the cul-de-sac outside the second-floor offices. She led us up the narrow stairs and down the hallway to Muhammad's office. He sat in a chair behind his desk.

When we entered, Muhammad quickly stood and turned to my wife. He looked at me and asked, "Is she your wife?"

"Yes," I replied.

Muhammad, his arms extended, fingers fluttering, locked eyes with hers and chanted dreamily, "Leeeeeave him, leeeeeeeeave him."

Then he looked at me and said, "Man, she is too pretty for you." (This was not news to me.)

Awkwardly I introduced our children, more than a bit perplexed that their mom and I were so amped up over meeting this boxer. But Ali quickly won them over with magic tricks. He made a scarf disappear, a quarter reappear, and pieces of rope string back together. Minutes later, we were laughing amongst ourselves when we heard Muhammad gently snoring.

Kim explained that with his illness, Muhammad had begun falling asleep at odd moments throughout the day. She apologized.

Then with Ali peacefully snoring, we stood one by one and quietly turned to go. Ali cracked one eye open, smirked, then burst into laughter. He pointed at me with a huge grin, "The great white dope!"

Over time I learned whenever Muhammad was not the center of attention, he found a way to re-focus the room. Kim knew his snoring was her queue.

Feeling more comfortable, we looked around the office at

pictures of Ali hung on the walls, told the kids more about Ali's fights, and enjoyed a few more magic tricks. After an hour or so, we left together, walking with Ali through the hall and downstairs.

Ali walked silently, gently guiding our son, his fingertips brushing his shoulders. Outside, we strolled lazily across the lawn toward the river. Ali held our little one's hand. It felt wonderful to be there in the sun with Muhammad, who seemed to be soaking up every ounce of the affection we shared.

Ali posed for a picture with each of the kids. He took time to set up our son for a classic punch to the jaw. Our guy looked so tiny and fragile with the great Muhammad Ali hovering over him. And while our kindergartener was typically very hesitant to ham it up for adults, he took every queue from Muhammad. The picture is a classic. A two-ounce fist right to Ali's jaw.

When it was time to go, we shared hugs all around and climbed into the car. I drove slowly up the drive while the kids hollered goodbyes and waved out the windows. Ali stood alone in the driveway, his hand shoulder-high waving. I watched him in the mirror, standing there looking very forgotten, and thought we should have stayed another hour or two.

We went in awe of the celebrity and left humbled by the man. He made us feel like he wanted us around him forever...I would learn he had that effect on most everyone he met.

CHAPTER ELEVEN

OLYMPICS

It was a special thrill to visit the Olympic torches in Ali's office, one from Atlanta and the second from Sydney, Australia.

The Sydney torch is artistic, a showpiece of polished steel with layered covers of white and blue anodized steel. I skipped a breath the first time I saw it. Ali was just back from his trip, and the torch was not yet hung. It was in the just completed offices, lying on the freshly carpeted floor. It looked like a sheathed sword, but being from Australia, the shape suggested a boomerang. It felt good to hold it; a little bit dangerous. I imagined the pride Olympians must feel winning their way to the privilege.

The Atlanta torch is less showy than the Sydney; it looks like a telescope, cylindrical with aluminum reeds separated by a hand grip of Georgia hardwood, the same wood used to make Louisville Slugger baseball bats. A gold seal at the base is etched with the name of each city that has hosted the Olympics. Near the top, there is a gold band with the symbol of the Atlanta games.

It felt delicious to hold the torch, to feel the same weight Ali felt when he stood in Atlanta with the whole world watching. The moment symbolized his fight with Parkinson's. His hands shook, his body bent forward as the torch flame whipped up around his fingers, fiercely gripping the hardwood. It took several seconds for the rabbit to light, then drag its way up to the cauldron.

Ali worried the rabbit would not light at all. In the midnight practice run, the rabbit lit with a whoosh and zipped instantly up the cable to light the cauldron. In view of the entire world, nothing worked well.

The Atlanta Olympics in 1996 were a coming out for Ali. It had been fifteen years since his last fight and twelve since the formal diagnosis of Parkinson's. It was a struggle for Ali to even appear in public during those years.

In a 1991 interview with Bryant Gumbel, Ali trembled and slurred his speech. It was apparent the Champ was suffering mightily. He told Gumbel he feared appearing in public.

"I realize my pride would make me say no, but it scares me to think I'm too proud to come on this show because of my condition." he said. Too prideful, Ali would not find his place in Heaven.

For Ali to present himself to billions of fans around the world in full battle with Parkinson's measures his fortitude. There were times Ali said the disease was a blessing because it slowed him down and forced him to confront the most important aspects of life. He considered Parkinson's a divine test of his will.

His selection to light the torch was one of the greatest secrets ever kept. Ali was not told he would light the cauldron at the centennial Olympics until the week of the event. The short notice was probably good because it gave Muhammad less time to worry about his presentation. The world had not seen him deep in his battle with Parkinson's, and he worried. Others were concerned he would drop the torch or just not get the rabbit lit.

At the moment before Muhammad left the staging room to present the torch to the world, Lonnie assured him he would be fine; it was just another arena of people. A security officer at the door added, "Yes, the arena and three billion people on tv."

Ali swore he was not nervous until the rabbit did not light. Then the flames fluttered up the torch and appeared to burn his arm. Dave Kindred of the Atlanta Journal said, ..."he looked like a great man about to burn himself trying to light the family grill."

Muhammad was glorious that night. He moved slowly, he shook with Parkinson's, and he struggled. But when the cauldron lit, he held the torch high, and around the world, tears flowed. It was an iconic moment when people who once thought they hated Ali realized they loved him. For all of his audacity and lip, he had become the symbol of tolerance and forgiveness. He was hypnotic.

CHAPTER TWELVE

THE STUTZ

O ver the years of celebrity, Muhammad had some great cars, a Roll Royce, a Stutz, and even an Alfa Romeo Spider. He must have been a sight in the tiny Alfa convertible. Billy Crystal observed, "he'd look like a circus bear driving it."

Muhammad stored the Rolls in the old garage surrounded by gardens out front of the main house. The garage had that great smell of ancient wood scented with motor oil and a whiff of gasoline. Layered in dust, the Rolls had not been driven in months.

The Stutz was different. It looked like a nineteen-seventies era Pontiac Grand Prix with a body kit added: a chrome Rolls Royce style grill set between big, round, twin beam headlights. The trunk had a continental spare tire kit built into the lid. Pinstripes ran down the sides with silver paint above and burgundy paint below. While the Stutz may have been an odd-looking luxury car, they were owned by a litany of celebrities, from Elvis to Sinatra.

Most of the time, the Stutz was parked in the old garage alongside the Rolls, occasionally outside near the driveway or on the lawn under the trees. This morning it sat alongside the drive, freshly washed, gleaming in the morning sun.

My partner Joe and I were painting the trim on the garage below the offices. Across the parking area, Muhammad came out of the house, and with a flip of his hand, waist high tight to his side, he waved "hello."

He shuffled up the drive calling to his fifteen-year-old nephew, Jacob, who was visiting for the week. The two met and spoke briefly, then walked to the Stutz, chatting along the way. Joe and I stopped painting to watch the situation unfold.

Jacob and Ali stood next to the Stutz, continuing their conversation. Ali gestured to the passenger door. Jacob walked around the side of the car, said something more to Ali, pulled the door open, and got in. Ali went to the driver's door. He opened it, looked into the car for a quick minute, and then settled into the driver's seat.

"If that engine starts, I am getting behind a tree." Joe quipped.

I thought Ali might be giving his nephew a driving lesson. Maybe he would race the engine a bit, drive a quarter mile up the driveway, and come back. But he did not. The Stutz rolled up the driveway, slowed as the gates opened, then rumbled down the road toward town.

Joe and I looked at each other startled and with dread that Lonnie would come looking for Muhammad. Ali did not have a bodyguard, but it was implicit we all take some care. Ali was so spur of the moment and impulsive that it drove Lonnie crazy trying to manage his child-self.

She constantly worried over him. If anything happened to Muhammad, it would be a tragedy, and I would have to answer to Lonnie.

They had been gone ten minutes when Lonnie came hurrying out of the house. "Where is Muhammad?" she demanded.

"Well, he ahhhh, he went in the car." I stammered.

"He went in the car?!" she exclaimed rhetorically. "Everyone out here stood and watched him go in the car?"

"Oh man," I thought.

We just stood there in silence, looking down the drive. Lonnie muttered under her breath. She exuded worry and comical frustration with Ali and, along with everyone else, considered precisely what we should do. We waited anxiously, everyone staring at the gates.

In a few minutes, the gates opened, and the Stutz rolled in. Ali was still at the wheel, driving slowly back along the winding drive. He stopped a few yards from the welcoming party.

Lonnie stood with her hands on her hips. The driver's door pushed open. Ali put his hand on the top of the open door and pulled himself up from the seat. He turned and walked toward Lonnie. Putting on his best "hopeful face," he held out his hand, offering Lonnie a sip of his large milkshake from the local McDonald's.

"Oh, Muhammad." was all Lonnie could muster. She took a sip on the straw, turned to the house, and said,

"Would someone please take the keys out of that car?"

CHAPTER THIRTEEN

DOBERMANS

In those first weeks, when we settled into the ambiance of the farm, the pace was leisurely. The weather that Spring was clear and cool. Ali spent his days answering mail, reading, and relaxing around the farm. Still, the Ali's traveled several times each month.

Coming home from one of their trips, Muhammad brought the two biggest Dobermans I have ever seen, Champ and Princess. They were beautiful dogs, thick in the shoulders and bristling with muscle.

The farm was perfect for them, and they ran from the house to the river and sometimes along the entire shoreline. It was a happy sight. Ali liked the two so much that he added two more Doberman pups to the gang.

The pups matured quickly. Though just a few months old and not fully developed, they soon showed the emerging physique of show dogs. Each time we walked to or from the buildings, the dogs were there to greet us. The four of them were powerful and intimidating. I thought it was a good idea to be their friend. We asked about the right treats to give them, and I kept a few in my pocket.

One day I had a soft cotton towel hanging from my back pocket. As I walked from the truck, one of the pups snatched it and ran. He dashed past the other pup setting up a game of tag. They chased each other across the lawn and around trees; soon, a tug of war ensued. The pups chased each other to yank the towel away, then chased some more.

A couple of days later, when the pups again ran to me, I thought it would be fun to have them jump for a towel. I held one high. They made running leaps biting at it. After several passes, I let one of the pups snatch it. Juiced up from our game, they each bit into the towel and soon tugged aggressively. The pups pulled and twisted, throwing each other to the ground. Their growls grew loud and constant. It was frightening.

When a house guest heard the commotion, he ran across the drive, grabbed a garden hose, and sprayed the dogs to get their attention. They dropped the towel and whimpered off. From then on, I kept the towels out of sight.

Even when the Ali's were away, there was constant activity on the farm. There were always people around. The gates opened and closed all day long, and we never knew who would come through them: Ali's family, friends, celebrities, foreign royalty, thick-necked wanna-be-boxers.

One afternoon Becky and I worked late to finish a project. Near completion, she left, and I stayed to wrap things up. It was early evening when I finished, and the sun was setting. I gathered our tools and walked down the office stairs to the parking area.

Just outside the door, the four Dobermans stood at attention. I backed away from the entrance to look out at the house. All the lights were off. The cars were gone from the office parking lot too. I was alone on the farm, and my pocket of treats was empty.

With the towel war fresh in my mind, I thought to eliminate as much temptation as possible. I wrapped the tools in a small drop cloth, bundled the corners, and stepped to the door. The two younger dogs were right there. I struggled to remember their names but could not. When I pulled the door open, one of them growled softly.

My neck bristled a warning. I pushed the door closed and took a breath. There was nothing to do but walk to the truck. I opened the door and stepped out. I spoke softly to the four dogs while I walked briskly to the truck, opened the driver's door, and climbed in. I pulled the door closed without even looking at the dogs.

Like other moments at the farm, I felt the tables turn. I found It was impossible to ignore race; in fact, Muhammad liked nothing more than to make white people feel wildly uncomfortable about race. But he did so with love and with humor. His genuine respect for all people made typical tribalism glaringly evident and sad. In the presence of Ali, the struggles of race united us.

I sat in the truck for a minute, looking out at the pack of Dobermans. I felt a sickening moment. "Run!" The moment when Champ set his eyes on my legs when the fastest my legs would carry me would fall a world short of the trees that might be my salvation. How would I cover my neck, hang on if he ripped at my ears? I don't know where it came from, but the moment strained my emotions, and my eyes welled. Sorrow, shame, sadness, the pain rendered by insecurity and ignorance. How else can I explain the misery wrought by skin tone alone?

Ali had none of it. He could have brought painters from anywhere in the world, but he was happy to have us there, and we felt like family.

"Hating people because of their color is wrong. And it doesn't matter which color does the hating. It is just plain wrong." Muhammad Ali

PART FOUR:

CHAPTER FOURTEEN

CHATTEL

The weeks between continents warped time. Culture dripped away; traditions were trammeled. Souls festered in the stench of humans long shackled in the filth below decks.

Still, Zane clung to the memory of the fields, the sweet breeze rolling down from the mountains. He dreamt of sweetbread and the stream at dawn, but he awoke to the blinding ache of his bones against the rough wood floor. Men seethed in anger cursing in words the short-tempered guards did not understand. Whips cracked.Only pain and cruelty broke the monotony of the passage.

For days the gentle swells of morning grew with the afternoon sun to push the ship fast into the troughs where the bow plowed heavily, jolting the struggling men forward and back. The rolling of the ship across rough ocean swells paced their days, which merged into weeks.

On a distant night, deep in his nightmare, Zane awoke. He heard the involuntary moans of men half-awake, their shoulders ground into the fetid hardwood deck, but he no longer noticed the stench of three hundred men packed together in the forward hold, shackled in the murk below the low beamed ceiling. He no longer shuddered when a man within arm's reach gurgled his final breath and died alone in his agony.

Only the dead escaped their shackles. With the iron ring finally severed, their body was tossed over the rails into the open sea. Zane survived in a tiny cocoon, a thin veil in his mind steeled against utter despair. He was just a boy; he should not be here amongst men damned to this passage. He dreamt of the cool water rushing over his feet in the river while Mira swam.

Then, startled from his sleep, the ship scraped against something solid. Men jerked awake. Months had passed with only the rolling motion of the sea, the bow-pounding waves, timbers shuddering in storms, and the decks searing in the calm of a hot, still afternoon.

Now Zane heard feet on the deck above running and men shouting. He heard crates scrapping across the planks. He listened to the side of the ship rub rhythmically up and down, tight against the pier.

Zane jerked up to his knees, his calloused leg twisted against the ring of the shackle; pus oozed from deep under the crusted skin above his ankle. Zane looked up through the grate to the first glimmering light of dawn.

In time, men were led to the ladder and up into the sun. Hobbled by their shackles and long weeks in the hold, the men could only crouch precariously on the open deck. They walked in pairs to the gangplank, their hands holding onto the arms of their mate for support.

Onshore a man in a torn straw hat and an ill-fitting jacket pointed dramatically to the ground. "Stand here." He shouted as the men approached. He measured their height and estimated their age. Zane was the tallest and clearly the youngest.

"Look at you, the prize you are!" The scurrilous man said, pulling Zane to the side. "Sit here!" he pushed Zane to the ground.

The inspection continued. The obviously crippled or sickly were led away. The healthy men were set in a line to either side of Zane. Finally, a clerk sorted twenty men from the others. A grizzled man stooped to pull a chain through their shackles."On your feet, Let's go! This way." He tugged the men to their feet.

Zane stood. He took one step and stumbled. The chain yanked at his ankle as the group struggled to walk in unison. Slowly they made their way a short distance from the docks to a long stack of crates. Zane smelled the awful smell of burnt flesh and heard oddly muffled cries.

A fat-bellied man strutted in crude heavy boots; his shirt pulled open to display his obscenely swollen belly. A fat wad of tobacco dripped brown ooze over a corner of his lower lip. He spat continuously as he paced back and forth, thumbing a short, fat club.

With impatient bursts, he directed the prisoners behind a tall stack of crates. Zane saw coals burning in an iron kettle hung off a tripod stand; next to it, a narrow-faced man with red hair and knotted hands bundled with rags griped a poker.

The fat-bellied man read from a yellowed paper, "You are at this moment the property of Master Isaiah Newhouse and will be marked so." He spat a brownish wad. "I will give you your Christian name at the command of Master Newhouse. Remember your name, or you will get the whip.

Now, you answer, 'Yes, master,' or you will get the whip. Step forward with the line, or get the whip, and quick. Say 'Yes, master.'"

The line of men understood little and stood fearful but responded to the frequent command; in disparate pairs, they mumbled something like, "Yes, master."

Zane trembled. The narrow-faced man barked, "Step forward." Zane despised his crude manner. Though filthy and beaten, Zane resolved to stand erect. He faced the angry men and their whips. The first shackled man stood aside the barrel; greasy water crested its lip.

"Lean to the water. Now!" a thick-armed man ordered. But the prisoner only stared uncomprehendingly. The guard pushed the shackled man's head deep into the water barrel, while in a single motion, the narrow-faced man grabbed his wrist and planted the hot poker hard against his shoulder. Zane heard the poker sizzle and a muted cry gurgle from the barrel.

In turn, each shackled man was pulled to the barrel and dunked while a rough "N" was branded into their right shoulder. Huddled just beyond the barrel, quivering with pain, they leaned into each other for comfort.

Zane stepped forward defiant but still barely able to stand. Sweat soaked his body. He saw the smoking poker hot on the coals. He saw the eyes of the narrow-faced man steeled, vacant, devoid of emotion. His fear sprung to anger in a moment as a thick-armed man pushed his head toward the barrel.

Zane lunged and plowed both men backward. The poker flew hard against the crates. A club crashed across Zane's back, driving him to the ground. Heavy hands pulled at his arms; a boot slammed against his neck and held him. His breath choked in broken gasps.

The first crack of the whip set fire across Zane's back. The second tore flesh from the splice where the lashes crossed. The braided tips ripped into muscle. The searing whip punctuated the taunts of the narrow-faced man spitting rage with every blow.

Zane knew nothing but the pain. He watched from above as the whip lashed his back again and again. He heard a shrill voice call out,

"Not here. Not here, for god's sake! There are children!

The whipping stopped. Order was restored. Zane, dragged by

his arms to the barrel, lay face down in the dirt, a boot back on his neck. He heard the poker sizzle.

"I mark thee, Isaiah Newhouse. You will be his obedient namesake or die with the whip."

The men to either side pulled Zane to his feet. Then hauled him onto a wagon. The enslaved men sat on narrow planks along the sides, their heads low in the unfamiliar city. Zane lay face down between their feet. The hot sun burnt at the oozing slices that crisscrossed his back.

The wagon trundled over the stony road alongside the harbor for a mile before turning north into the low hills outlying the city. They passed brick homes three stories high. Women in hooped skirts averted their gaze as the wagon rolled past. The shackled men stared at the unfamiliar land. Their bodies were gaunt and aching, but the air was sweet under the brilliant sun.

They rode through the city, then over rolling fields. The surrounding forest of White Oak and Loblolly Pines thickened alongside the road as the sun set ahead of them. The air grew sweeter, and the cool breeze gentler. The men leaned against one another in the rough wagon watching the stars brighten in the darkening sky.

Once out of town, the wagon stopped in the forest beyond the houses that lined much of the road. Their feet against the buckboard, the driver and guard opened a trunk they slid out from beneath the seat.

"Here, pass this amongst you, fatten you up for the master. There will be work in the morning." The driver said.

While the guard sat at the ready, the driver passed the men salted meats, biscuits, and carrots. They rolled out a small water barrel and gave them a ladle to dip. After months of gruel and brackish water, the men devoured the meal. An older man seated at Zane's shoulder portioned out food for

Zane and held it in his lap. The wagon moved on while the men savored the biscuits and salted pork.

The prisoners grew drowsy with the food and rhythmic pace of the horses plodding along the sandy path. Some slumped where they sat, others laid where they could, and all slept in the cool night air.

Zane woke to the dribble of water over his back. The man dared not touch Zane's wounds but splashed water to soothe them. Zane felt the slices tear at the thin scabbing with every motion of the wagon. The man put salted meat in Zane's hand, and he ate.

The wagon arrived at the Newhouse plantation in the early hours before dawn. Enslaved workers led the men to a pond where they stripped naked and burned their sorrowful clothes. They stood in the calm waters; mist hid the pond's far shore.

An old woman with her hair bundled in a cotton towel laid Zane across a planked table under the trees alongside the pond. While the men stood waist-deep in the water, Zane quivered at the gentle touch of soft-wetted cotton rags coaxing fresh ooze from his wounds.

The old woman's soothing touch tempered the pain. Zane's back burnt mightily, but he felt hope in the open air. He lay on the planks looking away from the pond toward the gleaming white plantation house.

To one side, he saw a row of tiny, square brick houses with very steep roofs of wooden shingles falling to the front and rear. A fire burned alongside the furthest house. Zane saw women gathered around the fire in the first light of day, then men and children.

Zane fell into a deep sleep. Lying on the planks, his suffering eased. At times sweat rolled down his sides collecting in puddles on the table. Then his dreams carried him, terrified, over men with twisted faces dying with swollen eyes bugging from their sockets. Then just as panic gripped him, threatening, Zane heard his father call. He looked to hold Mira's hand and run up the path to the road, then home to dress for morning lessons.

Peacefully, Zane slept. The morning breeze soothed his burning flesh. Even the planks felt soft under his body, broken but fed.

When Zane finally awoke, night had fallen. He looked to the big house, dark but for a flicker of light near the porch. The tiny houses were black. Moon glade shimmered across the pond, and stars flickered over the water and in the cloudless sky. The air was warm. Hardly a breeze rippled the pond.

Zane gently slid a leg off the table. He twisted to dangle his other foot, then with his stomach flat to the planks, he slid carefully down till his feet met the dew-soaked grass beneath him. Zane put his hands on the edge of the table, pushed himself up, and stood. His head swooned with a flash of pain as the scabs tore at each other. He waited to breathe. Slowly, he sucked in the savory air and resolved to walk---to freely walk across the grassy expanse to the row of houses.

Zane had enough of the pain and the stench. As he rose, he saw he wore white cotton pants and that his body had been washed. The cold, wet grass pumped adrenaline through Zane's weary body. He shivered and burnt. He looked about at the Angel Oaks that reached their craggy branches far into the night. They may have monsters, but Zane was no longer a child. He walked upright under the haunting limbs.

In the darkness, a man sat near a dying fire; smoldering coals circled the track of the shallow pit. In a familiar dialect, the man called softly to Zane. "Good Evening. Sit with me."

Zane nodded, then eased onto a simple stool set close to the fire. "What is your name, son?" the man asked.

"My name is Zane." He replied.

"On no, that is not your name; you better know. You now have a Christian name; that is your only name. Forget Zane; that is only pain. You may heal when you know your name."

On that stool, close to the timeless dying embers, Zane ceased to exist. There would be no spoken trace, chance recognition, or serendipitous kindred reunion. Only his face bespoke his real identity, and every day that changed too. Zane was now chattel, his master's 'Isaiah Newhouse.'

CHAPTER FIFTEEN

PLANTATION

Three days delivered from the belly of the ship, a cosmos from home, and even before the sun rose, Isaiah meant trouble for William, the plantation's overseer. Master Newhouse had returned during the night and would not be pleased that his prime young purchase had been damaged. To him, a whipped slave meant an ill-behaved slave. Isaiah was no longer worth the price the master had paid.

Young and strong Isaiah cost top dollar, well more than the annual wages of a typical freeman. Master Newhouse might cut his losses and sell Isaiah to the Laddle Plantation, where men and women were whipped severely even for the slightest offense, even to prevent them from doing wrong.

William, born into slavery, now tall and lean and hard, but grey at the temples, led Isaiah to a rough buckboard wagon. William helped him onto the narrow wooden seat, then climbed up and sat alongside Isaiah.

"I'm going to get you out of the master's sight." He said in a familiar dialect. "We'll go to the root doctor. This whipping is not good for you; Master will be angry. He might whip me for not having control of you. But what was I to do, you was hardly off the boat, and you was whipped? You crazy?" he exclaimed.

William steered the wagon between two clay brick houses and then onto a two-track path cut into the brush alongside the marsh. The ground was spongy beneath the wheels of the wagon. A bog of cattails and pools of stagnant water spread further than Isaiah could see.

"You are lucky you got just a few lashes. Master won't whip you for small offenses, but if he sees you torn up, he may sell you, send you off to a master who will whip you for looking at him, or your attitude, or not completing your daily task. Thirty-nine lashes.

If Master Newhouse whips you, yeah, thirty-nine lashes, but for an offense that is serious: Disobey 'em, raise your eyes to Missus Newhouse, or run off...serious offenses. Pushing a white man? You are lucky you only got a few lashes."

They rode deep into the brush. The big spoked wheels cracked the limbs of bushes along the path. The horse's hoofs left round puddles in the soft, wet bog. Mosquitos bit at Isaiah, half-naked and shivering in the cool, damp, pre-dawn air.

Finally, the wagon stopped next to a black birch tree at the edge of a small clearing. A thatched hut was hidden by the ferns and mingled branches of saplings all around. A woman appeared in the low opening at the front of the hovel.

"I have a man for you," William said to her. Then he ordered Isaiah to go. "Get out quick; I have to return before the work bell sounds.

Isaiah spent delirious days and nights intoxicated with a concoction the old woman brewed to make his head right. She fed Isaiah elderberry and willow bark tea for the pain and rubbed a salve of Burdock and Asafetida root into his wounds. For the next week, she sang over him, then tied a talisman around his neck to protect him from future whippings.

The Newhouse Plantation covered a thousand acres of marshland with only a small corner of dry ground where the mansion and slave quarters stood. Over decades, slaves pushed the swamp back to create holding ponds filled to flood the rice fields for planting and for irrigation when the rainy season passed.

Long earthen berms taller than a man circled the ponds. A large cypress tree trunk was hollowed out and then set at an angle in the berm between the pond and the rice fields. When the overseer called for water, a thick round plug was drawn from the trunk, and water flowed from the pond to the field.

In a week's time, William again appeared in the clearing to carry Isaiah back to the plantation. He covered Isaiah's wounds with a cotton shirt.

"Never show those wounds to the master." He instructed. "He may add thirty-nine and sell you quick."

For the next several months, Isaiah learned to plant rice in the soft mud of the rice fields. He became family with the men and women who sang in the fields as they worked long, hot days. They stepped to the rhythm of the songs they sang. Push a hole in the soft mud with a heel, drop a seed, and cover it with a twist of the toe. Step on to the next.

The chanting rhythm carried Isaiah's mind away from the heat and mind-wrecking routine. It was summer. The work horn sounded before dawn, eat quick, hurry to the fields. As the sun began to set in the evening, hurry back to the small houses, eat, wash and mend clothes, tend to the garden, and fish; there was not enough time before Isaiah slept, and the bell rang again before dawn.

Day after day, Isaiah felt his consciousness fade into mere existence. His mind dulled. First, he did not think about Mira and home and the river for an hour or two, then for an entire morning, then sometimes all day. He knew nothing more than the work, the rice, and his single pair of shoes rotting with mud. The thick welts on his back no longer gnawed at him when he lay to rest at night on the damp matted floor.

In the blistering summer heat, they opened the trunk to let the pond water flood the rice fields. In a few weeks, they opened the sluiceways to drain the water and hoe the muddy field of tender plants. They repeated the process several times. The heat of August faded in the dry, windy days of early September, then harvest came to the rice fields.

The elders taught Isaiah English interlaced with phrases from other lands. They taught him how to grow rice as they had taught his master. Isaiah learned to cut down the stalks with a short-curved scythe. He learned to tie thick bundles of rice blades and carry them on his head from the fields.

He spent long days thrashing heaps of rice on the hard floor of the storage house. Then they shoveled the seeds into a bowl as wide as Isaiah could reach across, and with pestles as long as a man is tall, they broke the chafe from the seeds.

Finally, they fanned the seeds in woven bowls; the chaff flew off, leaving only the rice for milling. Isaiah learned quickly. The overseer praised Isaiah for his hard work and knowledge.

CHAPTER SIXTEEN

A NEW FIELD

One day William told Isaiah that Master Newhouse wanted him to help the hands open a new field. In the morning, the master himself would carry Isaiah to the field in the buckboard wagon. The new field was a swamp with a few large trees bordering the marshland. Already the men felled one of the trees two meters across. The logs were hacked into sections to be loaded onto wagons.

Isaiah waited at the head of the path, then climbed up to fidget on the wooden seat next to his master. The buckboard rolled along the muddy trail past the plantation house and then crossed through a field planted in sorghum. It narrowed to a two-track and rounded the edge of a broad, flat bog spotted with irregular pools of water.

The two men rode in silence, then Master Newhouse told Isaiah,

"We need a hand to manage the planting of the new rice field; William spoke highly of you."

Surprised, Isaiah said, "Yes, master.

Master Newhouse continued, "You are strong and know the work; do you believe you have the temperament to draw up the daily tasks? You will be responsible for each hand's productivity."

Unsure, Isaiah said, "Yes, master."

"There is responsibility. William will handle the whip, but you will assign the tasks. Each man will complete the tasks you assign, or he will suffer the whip."

Uncomprehending, Isaiah said, "Yes, master."

"If the field is not prepared and planted in Spring, you will suffer the whip. Do you understand?" he asked.

Isaiah said, "Yes, master."

In awkward silence, the two men rode on to the far edge of the bog. The wagon creaked as it bumped over the muddy path; soon, Isaiah heard the sounds of men sawing the trees being cleared.

With their approach, the hands kept their heads down; no one dared look up at Master Newhouse. William greeted them.

"Good Morning Master Newhouse; the men are back to working hard."

The wagon stopped next to a pile of logs near a felled tree. The two men climbed down. William was nervous; he sputtered.

"Master Newhouse, we will do the work of ten men; we are working hard. There will be no delay due to the poor man who got himself dead."

The day before, a man was killed by an alligator lying in wait under the marshy bank. The man, worried at a snake swimming near shore, did not see the gator fast upon him, unseen in the ink-black water. Now the men looked cautiously at the pond as they worked to clear the reeds and cattails.

While Master Newhouse inspected the work, William ordered Isaiah to help the men load logs into the master's wagon. Isaiah had grown more powerful than any man on the plantation. He attacked his tasks. He lost himself in the grueling monotony freeing his mind from the goading cell of slavery. Alone he hoisted logs two men lifted together.

The men fell silent as the master studied their work. He

walked the perimeter of the new field, then satisfied that work was progressing, he ordered Isaiah back onto the wagon, and they turned back to the millhouse with their load.

The wagon was heavy with logs. The wheels squished deep into the muddy track sucking the acrid smell of decomposing marsh into the air as they rolled. For a hundred feet, the rough path followed the open pond.

Isaiah looked down at the iron-banded wheels plowing through the mud under the heavy stack of logs. Master Newhouse sat on the low side of the wagon, talking gently to the horses and nudging the wagon along. As the path tipped toward the water, Isaiah gripped the seat and leaned over into the hill, careful not to bump into Master Newhouse and suffer the whip.

A low tree partially blocked their way as they approached the final bend taking the path up a slight incline away from the open water. The two men crouched down, ducking under the tree's branches that dipped low over the trail.

Still amongst the limbs, a wheel slipped on the wet track; the wagon lurched only slightly, but in an instant, the logs shifted, the sliding wheel caught a root, and the wagon began a slow-motion flip.

Isaiah grabbed at the seat as the pile broke, and logs rolled forward off the rough stack. A small chunk smashed into master Newhouse's back. A great many more followed. Isaiah instinctively grabbed Master Newhouse by the shoulders and rolled away from the tumbling pile. The two men faced each other as they twisted from the seat, toppling backward down the bank. Isaiah made one final grab at the foot box, desperate to hang on, but a log rolled over the back of the seat. It slammed through the bench and crushed Isaiah's fingers.

Isaiah screamed as his fingers burst. Then the horses, the

wagon, and the two men splashed hard into the shallow mucky water. Isaiah struggled for footing. Blood flowed thick from his smashed hand.

The wagon stuck hard in the muddy bank. The harness held one of the struggling horses fast beneath the surface; the other kicked and neighed. Isaiah rolled over to lock his injured arm around the wagon tongue; his smashed hand throbbed with blinding pain.

Master Isaiah Newhouse slid down into the muck beneath the murky water. Gasping, eyes desperate, his head disappeared. Isaiah saw his arms flail wildly. Isaiah stretched his feet to reach his master's hands, now barely above the water's surface. His fingers found Isaiah's shoes. In a panic, he grasped them. Isaiah felt the desperate grip of a man drowning in mud.

Isaiah pulled, and the grip tightened. Then he heaved his knees to his chest. Master Newhouse burst to the surface, gasping, choking out screams of panic. With his strong hand, Isaiah found his master's arm; he clenched it hard, "I got you, master, I got you." He assured. And Isaiah pulled him from the pond.

The muck sucked Master Newhouse's boots from his feet. His mouth filled with turbid water. He spat, gasping for air. Then he embraced Isaiah.

"Thank you, thank you, thank you." He repeated.

"ISAIAH!!!" William shouted. He had heard the screams and ran to the scene.

"Get yo hands-off, Master Newhouse! Oh, you will get the whip. Oh, po'boy, you will get the whip." He lamented. "You will get the whip."

Master Newhouse could not compose himself as he clutched at Isaiah. His eyes scrunched shut, gritty with mud. Wet mud caked the corners of his mouth. He spat again and again, mumbling incoherently.

Isaiah looked at his throbbing hand. Two fingers were flat, the bones smashed, the skin hung loose and puffy with blood, dangling sickeningly toward the ground. Isaiah was nauseous. He clutched the talisman hung around his neck.

"Get water!!!" William screamed to the men running toward them. The men ran back to the wagon. They returned with skins of water "Pour it over, Master Newhouse." The overseer ordered.

Water rinsed some of the mud from the master's hair and face. He took a skin himself and rinsed his eyes. He blinked and poured water, then blinked and poured some more. In time Master Newhouse laid back against the bank. Isaiah held his broken fingers to his chest. He clutched the talisman. He sucked short quick breaths; his heart pounded. In a monotone voice, barely audible, Master Newhouse said to no one in particular, "Isaiah saved my life."

The anxious workers stood in rapt silence.

PART FIVE:

CHAPTER SEVENTEEN

CABINETS

Destiny is a funny thing. On a gentle fall afternoon one hundred and thirty years ago, a maple-tree seed helicoptered to the ground. The seed germinated, the tree matured, and today, the felled tree was being planed at Great Lakes Stair and Case to build paneled doors destined for Ali's kitchen.

The tree survived ground fires, was seemingly invisible to the ax, then to chainsaws, and gave cover to crows and blackbirds, robins, and herons for decades before being selected to grace the Ali home. That maple tree was kiln-dried to six percent moisture, then ripped, planed, and shaped into cabinet doors. The old-growth maple glowed subtle and warm beneath a clear lacquer finish.

Projects on the farm followed in quick succession. We finished the inside of the old offices, the house's exterior, then the garage bays and laundry. By the time we began the house interior, expectations were high.

The skilled tradespeople transformed the kitchen and family room with large format clay tile floors, smooth plastered walls, and new cabinetry. A wall of bookcases in the family room matched the kitchen cabinets---but they were installed unfinished. We were shocked when we saw them.

Brushing on a cabinet-quality finish is right next to impossible. Factory finishes are applied in a controlled environment with filtered air and high-tech spray equipment. We were armed only with brushes and sandpaper.

Lucky for us, the Ali's were to be away for a couple of weeks, and we would have the house to ourselves. First, we applied a thin coat of sanding finish to the fresh wood cabinets so the burrs could be sanded away. Next, we brushed on four coats of urethane wet sanding between each coat. It was an old-school finish; though tedious, it looked beautiful on the clear maple cabinets. The finish was not as perfect as the cabinet shop's work, but gorgeous, nonetheless.

Lonnie was cheered by the completed room, hitherto shadowy and close. The carpenters had removed a wall section and installed broad windows to brighten the space. The new kitchen cabinets and matching bookcases flowed seamlessly from one area to the other. The finished living quarters were open, warm, and inviting, all very satisfying after long hours of detailed work.

A few days after their return, Lonnie met me at the truck when we arrived in the morning.

"Come here; you need to see what your dear friend has done." She said anxiously.

I followed Lonnie into the kitchen. Near the phone, on a cabinet above the built-in desk, Muhammad had carefully written a phone number in ink on the front of a cabinet door. Lonnie looked with disbelief at the carefully written numbers and then at me to assess my reaction.

I laughed out loud.

There was no paper in sight, so Muhammad wrote the number where he could, on a cabinet door—in ink!

"Goodness, Lonnie, what are we going to do with him?!" I chuckled.

It felt good to share the moment, to realize we were all there simply to take care of Muhammad. If he wrote on a cabinet, there was little to say. I copied the number on a piece of paper and set about fixing the door.

The truth was if Muhammad had been told he was to live in a trailer by the river, he would have been happy. As it was, almost everything about the house was small. Muhammad was not. The Ali's could have built a grand, beautiful home, but it just did not matter to Muhammad.

What did matter to Muhammad was the old Huffy-style bike kept in the garage. During the summer months, it leaned against the house near the back door. Mornings, Ali peddled up the lane to his office or to the gym.

When he rode back to the house, he veered off the drive just past the barn to zip down the almost vertical hill cutout to access the lower level of the barn. His face showed determination as he navigated the steep incline, his feet swinging from the pedals; he grinned as he coasted the last fifty yards to the house.

CHAPTER EIGHTEEN

PREPARED

When the crew arrived at the Ali farm, serendipitous as it was, we were utterly prepared for the work. For several years we restored old farmhouses for the founder of Kitty Litter. The farmhouses were the original homesteads in Cass County, Michigan dating back to 1829 when Lewis Cass was governor of the Michigan Territories.

Cass enslaved people and promoted legal slave holdings for all federal territories. Cass became Secretary of War under Andrew Jackson, where he oversaw the Indian Removal Act, which mandated over sixty-thousand Indians give up their land east of the Mississippi River. They were forced to march the Trail of Tears to a western Oklahoma reservation that still exists today.

So maybe the homes we restored were not the "original homesteads" but were so thought by us, white people. Anyway, the Kitty Litter guy was eccentric. He fashioned himself as a larger-than-life capitalist with a vision to create something special. While he fathered Kitty Litter, founding an entire industry, he also built a model farm in Southwest Michigan.

The Litter guy's father had discovered the absorbent qualities of dried clay to mop up spills. Over time the son refined the texture of the dried clay to create a patented product. In the early days, he traveled the country, stopping at gas stations and sucking up oil spills with his clay. The trunk of his car was filled with little bags of the absorbent---he was building the market from the ground up. He joked that he got wealthy selling bags of dirt.

The gas station market for oil absorbents was sound, but the potential was nothing compared to the cat litter business. In the end, it was not little bags of dirt that made him wealthy; it was cat urine. His team figured out how to put fragrance into the clay product and sell it to cat lovers, and the industry exploded. Kitty Litter was a cash cow.

While attempting to revive an old childhood town, he met an interior designer he later married. They were a great match, especially for the crew and me. They began to aggressively buy up property adjacent to their farm. Eventually, the farm encompassed over twenty-five hundred acres of gorgeous rolling farmland, unspoiled forests, and two small lakes.

The farmhouses that came with the land were dilapidated wrecks. Most of the structures were more than one hundred years old. All were unkempt and unfinished. They showed the wear and tear from decades of hard lives farming rocky soil. Often, for economy, the plastered walls and poplar trim on the second floors had never been painted.

The stair treads to the upper floor were often worn so distinctly you could see that the inhabitants consistently stepped first with their right foot as they climbed them. The soles sculpted broad smiles in the treads, right then left, right then left, all the way to the top.

The happy couple hired brilliant carpenters to rebuild the old houses. They added bathrooms, rebuilt windows, and installed crown moldings with materials of the home's era. When the carpenters finished, our crew went in to restore the wall and trim finishes.

We became experts at repairing cracks and chips in hundred-year-old doors and trim. We filled and sanded, primed, and sanded some more. Then we brushed on three or four coats of satin sheen paint on the trim and painted or papered walls and ceilings. It was not unusual for our crew of four workers to spend several months restoring a single three-bedroom farmhouse.

While we worked, the owners traveled the country buying up antique furniture to fill the rooms. Sometimes he relaxed in the car, knocking down a six-pack while she explored the shops.

One afternoon he sat and watched a crew dismantle an old drugstore. He scavenged antique doors and windows and trim. This day he saw the workers cutting out a decorative door system set into the corner of the old drugstore.

The doorway sliced across the corner of the building. Two steps led to the stately door framed with ornate trim and a scrolled header. He climbed out of the car and approached the job foreman.

"Hey buddy, that is a clever entry you are cutting off that building." He offered.

"Yes, sir, they don't build them like that anymore." The man replied.

"How about I give you one hundred and fifty dollars for it?" he asked.

"That sounds good to me." The man replied. "Pay up and come by in the morning; we'll load you up."

He peeled the cash off the big roll he kept in his pocket, paid the man, and they shook hands to close the deal. The next morning, he returned to retrieve his purchase. He found the door and framework and began to load the trim. A tall, muscular man wearing Carhart's with a toolbelt and ballcap jumped off his ladder and ran to him.

"Hey there partner, what exactly are ou doing?" he shouted.

"Well, I'm picking up this door I bought yesterday," he replied.

"Bought?" the mand sad incredulous. "This is my project, and none of this is for sale."

"Well, I bought and paid for it yesterday,' he demanded.

"Yeah, who from?"

"Your guy in the plaid jacket and boots,," he said warily.

"Well, I don't know you, and I don't know that guy. I saw you two talking; I thought you knew him. The both of you walked up at about the same time. I guess if you bought this door from him, he is the smarter of you two."

"I'll be damned," he replied, "I don't know that guy, but I like him. Damn smooth of him to seize the opportunity."

He left without the door----or his one-hundred and fifty dollars.

The old industrialist loved to tell that story, but he was consumed with his wealth and visions of grandeur most of the times we met. In retrospect, he was the antithesis of the grace and compassion we would embrace in Ali.

CHAPTER NINETEEN

THE GYM

Once the residence was updated and the new offices built, Ali added a gym. The facility was a showpiece carved into the crescent hill between the office complex and the small barn.

Gardens of boxwood, ivy, and red impatiens bordered a brick walkway leading to elegant French glass entry doors. Inside, a tiled mezzanine looked over the open gym five steps below. The overlook made for a stunning view. An imposing twenty-four by twenty-four-foot boxing ring rests at your feet, its sterling white canvas deck framed with a bright red top rope and alternating white and blue ropes beneath.

Beyond the ring, the gym flows toward the river, visible through floor-to-ceiling windows lining the rear wall. In the back-left corner, a pedestaled statue of Ali, larger than life, crouching menacingly, arm slung across his body after landing a fierce body blow to his mythic opponent. On the walls are photographs of Ali with boxing greats, Presidents, and celebrities. Everyone wanted a picture with Ali.

There is a workout area with strength equipment and a mat for jumping rope between the ring and windows. Dressing rooms, two steam baths, and a leather-topped massage table head up a spa with loungers and a swimming pool-sized jacuzzi that overlooks the river and forest beyond.

When I first stood on the mezzanine, looking over our just-completed paintwork, I was rattled by the physical reality of

Ali. The immediacy of the ring made me feel very small. My daydreaming led me to imagine slipping between the ropes to do battle with another human being, but I could not.

Yet, in such a ring, Ali did his work. He faced the fiercest human beings on the planet, Liston, Frazier, Foreman, and Holmes, and he did so after taunting them with barbs and name-calling. I was transfixed, looking down into the ring and thinking of the gentle man I knew here at the farm.

It is one thing to see boxers from a safe distance on television, packaged with fanfare, and quite another to stand face-to-face with them. The sheer size of these men makes them intimidating even to greet, broad-shouldered, rippling with muscles from years of training their eyes in locked determination.

Twice I saw a wanna-be boxer come to the gym hoping Ali would judge them a worthy student. Yet, for all their skills and apparent power, Ali did not think they had a chance to be a contender inside those ropes.

We worked for several weeks before the ring was installed to finish the walls, window frames, and ceiling. We primed and sanded every surface. Then we removed the window latches and their closing mechanisms. The complete window frames and sash were primed and finished with three topcoats, even the bits beneath the latches. We strived for perfection. This was Ali's new gym, the reward for decades of hard work in stark, sweaty gyms on the rough streets of Louisville and Miami.

The ceiling presented a real challenge. The trick to a perfectly consistent ceiling finish is a solid primer coat and flowing topcoats that stay wet across the entire ceiling in a swath eight or ten feet wide, so broad areas dry as one.

Anytime wet paint lays against semi-dry paint, there will be a permanent line, a visible "roller mark." Few ceilings are finished without them. It is even necessary that each final pass be rolled in a single direction: always to the right or to the left, but not alternating. The slight tilt of the stipple left by a roller, bending one way then the other, will create a distinct shadow.

The gym ceiling was interrupted by several openings for vents, lights, and the recess above the ring itself. Working around the openings meant getting large areas to each side of the void coated and then bridging the two before the paint began to dry.

After several failed attempts at perfection, we figured out a cheat. We powered up the steam rooms and left the doors open to the entire gym. The steam ran for twenty minutes, and the windows began to mist. In an hour, the room was almost dripping with moisture. Two of us rolled with long extension handles, and we finished the entire ceiling before even the first paint we applied began to dry. We shut off the steam and opened the windows; the warm breeze dried the ceiling perfectly. We gave the contractor the okay to install the ring and fitness equipment.

A cleaning crew polished every surface while delivery teams unloaded a stair stepper, a treadmill, and several upper and lower-body workout apparatuses. The gym was ready for the grand opening.

Three weeks later, soon after the grand opening, I got a call about problems with the ceiling. Stress cracks appeared in two corners of the recessed area above the ring. With an open expanse of almost forty feet, it was not surprising there might be cracks as the building settled in after initial construction. Still, we had to repair them; worse, we had to repaint the entire ceiling, quick touch-ups would be easy to spot.

It was a simple matter to tape and plaster the cracks. But then we had to cover the ring, put drop cloths over the floors and fitness equipment, then paint around trimmed lights and vents not yet installed the first time through. A perfect finish was complex when the gym was empty, now stocked full of equipment and Ali's ring; it was nearly impossible. We brought in help so three could roll while a helper kept our paint trays filled.

The steam cheat saved us again. We finished the ceiling and, with little fanfare, packed up our tools, rolled up the drop cloths, and looked close to ensure there were no tell-tale paint splatters.

While the main workout area was complete, we still had weeks of work to finish the locker rooms and the private spa area. Lonnie was excited to have the gym outfitted. She pushed hard for Muhammad to get into a routine of exercise every day. But, like so many athletes, with his body worn and beaten, the last thing Muhammad wanted to do was a workout. Still, Lonnie pressed. According to the doctors, exercise was critical in Ali's battle with Parkinson's disease.

Lucky for us, most days we worked, Muhammad showed up to "exercise." We loved to see him walk in the door. Everything stopped. Like a kid avoiding his chores, Muhammad spent an hour or two goofing. He always did a couple of magic tricks, usually repeats from the day before, and hit the speed bag.

Speech was difficult, so he answered questions with a nod or a couple of quiet words. Though his face was masked by Parkinson's, his countenance was frozen in a slight but easily perceptible smile. Ali knew joy.

Ali loved to hit the speed bag. He'd tug my arm and gesture to it, and we'd walk across the gym together. I'd watch Ali size up the bag and tag it a few times. Then he set a rhythm. The bag thumped with discipline. The pace increased. The bag slapped rat-a-tat-tat. Ali changed up the rhythm. The speed increased again. The blows echoed across the gym, the rhythms perfect. Ali's hands just rolled to deliver the punishment. Every sign of the disease was gone. His hands were fresh, the blows exacting. The bag was a blur. Patterns in the rhythm sped and slowed.

Then, WHAM! He stopped. And with a slow turn, he stared down at me with an evil eye.

"Holy crap Muhammad, I think you broke it." I said.
"I'm a bad, bad man." Ali declared, and his evil eye transformed to an upraised eyebrow---a comedian's look of dash. There was a playful kid in Ali, and the kid showed up a lot.

CHAPTER TWENTY

FIVE

The completed gym created a new focus for visitors to the farm. The complex was comfortable, with generous spacing and large sunny windows. Most guests dreamt of getting pictures with Ali in the ring, and Muhammad loved to accommodate. At a minimum, Muhammad clowned and always performed magic tricks.

Ali often feigned distemper at a guest's comment or question. He put on his mean face, brought his shoulders up tall, and swelled his chest with gritted teeth while his eyes glared down at an unwitting guest. The act never got old. Even when I knew he was kidding, Ali was intimidating, then he broke into a boyish laugh that warmed the room.

One morning a photographer for a magazine, I do not remember which, came to the gym for specific shots of Ali in his new ring. While the photographer got his camera set, Ali asked me to hold the ropes so he could step onto the canvas.

Here I was with a foot on the third rope, pulling up the second so the three-time Heavyweight Champion of the World could enter the ring once again. I felt privileged.

I positioned myself like I had seen trainers do so many times on tv. One foot pinning the lower ropes, shoulders turned to the boxer. Ali climbed three steps up to ring height, put a foot on the canvas outside the ropes, and swung a foot into the ring. As he crouched, I noticed his heavy black shoes. The sole of his trailing foot looked thick and wider than a shoe should be.

I watched the Champ duck under the top ropes and swing his body through. Almost in, he began rising up. Enthralled in the moment, I relaxed my foot holding the bottom ropes. Ali's toe snagged the rope. Still somewhat hunched, he lost his balance and fell with an echoing thud on the canvas.

I stared down at Ali lying full out on the mat. His eyes blinked, then he looked up at me with a sad, questioning gaze---like, "why did you do that!?" I froze.

I had just tripped Muhammad Ali, and he fell with a body slam in the ring! Ali stared, then his eyes widened comically, and he said, "You're five."

Ali had only been knocked down four times in five hundred and forty-eight rounds. Ignominiously, I dropped him the fifth.

I jumper quickly into the ring and took Muhammad's hand, but he quickly yanked it back. He rolled onto his stomach and pulled his legs up under him. From there, he reached out, and I took his hand.

Ali stood. I said, "I am sorry Muhammad, that was stupid."

"The great white dope, he replied. I put my hands on his shoulders and said, "Sorry champ."

To lighten the moment, I asked, "Muhammad, have you ever just laid down in the ring and looked up to see what it would have been like to be down there?"

He replied, "Man, you really are dumb. I'm too pretty to lay on the floor."

CHAPTER TWENTY-ONE

VIDEOGRAPHER

When our work in the gym was nearly complete, a videographer from the Smithsonian came to the farm to immortalize Ali with photographs and video. The man wore the khaki uniform typical of photographers, a buttoned shirt with double breast pockets, Dockers, and ankle-high brown leather shoes. He worked his way around the farm, snapping pictures of the grounds and the buildings.

We were painting trim in the spa area when Becky saw Muhammad walking from the main house with the videographer alongside; Ali was eager to show off the new facility. We quickly closed up the open paint cans and wrapped our brushes. They were just through the door when we hurried over to say hello.

Muhammad had spring in his step. He was more animated than usual, apparently eager to tour the newly outfitted gym.

The two men entered. Ali saw us and paused mid-step, just inside the door. His eyes widened as though he was immersed in deep concentration. His hands floated up; his arms spread wide to amplify his balance. Ali was preparing to levitate.

We had seen the trick a dozen times but watching Muhammad work the act was still a hoot. He caught each of us with a deep, ponderous stare; the anticipation deepened.

Trance-like, his hands circled mystically in pursuit of perfect balance. Then his eyes opened wide in apparent awe of the power welling within his core. The schtick was on.

Ali gathered himself. He bent slightly at the knees and set his feet squarely beneath his shoulders. Then, with great aplomb, he rose high on his right tiptoe. He gripped his outstretched fists tight in perfect balance. Then, set gracefully on his right toe, he tested his energies. His left heel rose briefly and quickly descended.

Again, he stretched his arms outward and stiffened as he settled down with his full weight. Then with renewed determination, he again balanced on his right toe, raised his left heel, his left toe, and with immense concentration, his right toe drifted from the floor. Just a little bit, and only for an instant, Ali floated, weightless.

Instantaneously he let his body settle back down; his knees cushioned his "descent ." He whipped his glance from a point in infinity to gaze down at his left foot, now firmly back on the floor. With wide-eyed surprise, Ali was utterly convincing.

He looked briefly at Becky, then at me, then peered at the videographer with a look that said, "Can you explain that to me? How did that just happen?" Ali held his stare until his subject submitted, shaking his head, speechless. Muhammad got a bigger kick out of the trick than anyone who watched; truly a showman.

There was a fascinating juxtaposition in Ali. After all the training, two hundred thousand blows to the body, the boxing commission theft of his heavyweight championship title, and the Jim Crow discrimination that dogged so much of his life, how could he be this kind, gentle man who lived on the edge of a smile?

In these simple moments with a new audience, even of just one, he still found deep joy in the performance. The long list of "terrible" things that happened to Ali, things that could have engendered hate and bitterness, were put aside through his devotion to Allah and his almost unique love for people.

Ali descended the stairs and led the videographer, ambling around the ring, pointing out photographs lining the walls: Ali with the Beatles, with Michael Jordan, and my favorite, his chiseled physique in side view, wearing white boxing trunks with a red stripe and white leather shoes, ready to take on Sonny Liston.

As they progressed, the videographer turned back several times to take in the boxing ring. Finally, he interrupted the tour to ask Ali if he could film him inside the ropes. Ali quickly agreed.

While the videographer prepared his camera, I went to Ali and, this time, carefully held the ropes as he ducked into the ring. Becky and I stood ringside to watch the performance.

Muhammad took his time. He circled in the corner of the ring, shaking his arms to loosen them up. He tucked his chin close to his chest and threw a few low jabs into the air. He fell into a rhythm, dancing and tossing punches.

I held the ropes for the videographer while he cradled his camera with two hands and stepped carefully between the ropes onto the canvas. The videographer stood still for a few minutes, filming Muhammad as he shuffled across the ring, punches flying. Then he moved in front of Muhammad and stepped backward as Ali leaned into the camera.

Ali trained on the lens. He popped off a rapid set of punches. He stepped forward; the videographer stepped back. Ali leaned in tighter, "pop, pop, pop" in quick succession. Ali set the pace; the videographer followed.

Soon they flowed in a close duet. Holding the camera low, the videographer mirrored Ali, and he responded moving into the camera, popping off punches. His momentum built; his shoes squeaked as he stepped in and back.

"Pheet, pheet, pheet," his shoes squeaked; his sharp breaths matched the jabs.

Now the videographer moved quickly to stay with him. Ali jabbed at the lens. He moved with grace; sweat glistened on his forehead. He floated like a butterfly snapping off lightning-fast jabs. His face tightened. His breathing was precise; all indications of Parkinson's disappeared. Ali, the athlete, surfaced, and he was glorious.

Ali appeared comfortable in a way I had not seen, clearly happy to be in that moment. His movements were precise, not just the shape of the blows but his very being. There was a willingness, a surrender.

In just a few minutes, it was over. Breathing deep, his arms spent, Muhammad stepped back to lean on the ropes. The videographer looked down at his camera as he walked across the ring. I held the ropes. He clutched his camera hard and ducked back out.

"I hope you have the film in that thing!" I quipped as he passed.

He paused and looked up at me; tears ran down his face. "It was beautiful," he said, "Ali is beautiful," he hesitated, "....that was terrifying."

CHAPTER TWENTY-TWO

BIGGER

Muhammad had a joke that he thought was just so funny. He loved to make the "white man" quiver in his boots. Over time Becky had seen him play it many times; she became his set-up partner. It goes like this.

One afternoon Becky and I left the gym with Ali close behind. We walked the few steps from the entry to the lane out front and waited for Ali to join us. A landscape crew was planting ground cover in the gardens bordering the entryway. These were the final touches outside the newly completed gym.

A scrappy young man knelt at the edge of the sidewalk, planting plugs of ivy. A dozen little seedlings were laying loose amongst the wood chips, ready to plant. Courteous, the worker looked up to say "hello" with a nervous smile as we passed. I noticed he was missing at least a couple of teeth. The young man knelt low, plunging the handle of his gardening shovel into the soft ground and then pushing in a plug of ivy.

As Muhammad approached, Becky hollered, "Hey Muhammad, he said it." Becky looked serious and concerned. "That guy there, he said it."

Muhammad stopped with a startled look on his face. He looked at Becky, then lowered his stern gaze to the worker. Becky repeated,

"Yes, Muhammad, that guy. He said it."

Muhammad pulled himself up tall and took a deep breath.

The worker blurted out to Becky, "What are you doing? What did I say? I didn't say nothing."

Muhammad walked directly to him and stopped just inches from the young man crouching low. Muhammad took a deep breath and pulled his shoulders back, looming. He glared down. Then he thundered, "Did you call me a nigger?"

"Oh god, no. I didn't say that. No! What are you guys doing? No sir, I didn't say it!"

The young man fell back on the sidewalk, positioned to do the fastest backside crab walk ever witnessed.

Ali tipped his head back and roared with laughter. "Oh, you just said I was bigger!"
Ali reached his hand down to help the guy up. Smiling wide, he gave him a big hug. The young man just stood with his arms at his sides. When Ali opened his embrace, the kid walked around the side of the gym. I followed to see if he was ok. I found him leaning against the wall.

"I thought he was going to kill me! I never said that but my dad did; I thought he would kill me!"

I explained the joke, and he calmed down; still, the young guy and his co-worker packed up their tools and left for the day.

Another time Ali played the same joke on Jim, a heavy equipment operator. Jim was on the farm with a giant excavator to take down the old dairy barn.

We had joked for a couple of weeks about the possibility of finding a body buried under the concrete floor when it was scraped away. It seemed far-fetched, but it didn't seem unlikely considering the lore of the Chicago mobster who once owned the farm. Before the demolition, we searched the barn floor for any three-by-six-foot patches, but we did not find any.

Jim unloaded the excavator from the tandem axle trailer he pulled with his Tonka toy-looking dump truck. Becky and I heard the beeping and the engine roar; we left our work in the gym to gawk. We were all excited to see the destruction, as disturbing as it was to lose the storied barn.

Ali walked from the main house to witness the commotion. We met him in front of the barn. Jim was already around the backside of the building in the excavator, dragging shrubbery from the old flower beds in preparation for the demolition. He quickly shut off the engine when he saw Ali and climbed down.

Jim brushed his hands on his heavy work khakis as he walked toward Ali, smiling hard, then his right hand outstretched. Ali shook his hand earnestly, then stopped suddenly. He pulled his hand back, turned his head to one side, and studied Jim through narrowed eyes.

The prank was on. Ali twisted his big smile into a frown; he took a deep breath and pulled up to his towering self. Ali stood over Jim and thundered the earth-shaking question.

Jim considered Ali for a moment, then apologized, "I did, sir. I regret it, but yes, I shouted it when you were on tv with Cosell."

Ali looked surprised. He frowned momentarily, considering Jim. Then he laughed and gave Jim a big hug.

"I've asked that a thousand times and you are the first chump honest enough to admit it!" Ali cheered.

Jim had the barn knocked down in two days, loaded into huge dumpsters, and hauled them away. We were sadly pleased that there were no bodies under the floor.

CHAPTER TWENTY-THREE

MICHIGAN STATE

On a warm Saturday in October, Greg, a family friend, drove Muhammad and Kim, Muhammad's assistant, two hours to a Michigan State football game. It was not unusual for Muhammad to visit the MSU football or basketball locker rooms before a game. He was their inspiration.

On this day, Ali was in good cheer. While motoring along the expressway, he thought it was funny to wait until their car was in the left lane parallel to a vehicle in the right lane. With his window in line with the other driver, Ali would put his face tight to the darkly tinted side glass and push the down button.

Suddenly the unsuspecting driver would see Muhammad Ali staring just a few feet away. Muhammad loved their startled reactions. He would laugh and laugh.

Kim scolded him: "Muhammad, someday someone is going to drive right off into the ditch when you do that. You are scaring those people!" Muhammad made big eyes like he had no idea, then looked down and chuckled to himself.

Ali face-bombed a few drivers on the two-hour trip and worked on an old magic trick. He had a new false thumb and practiced making a scarf disappear. Ali stretched the scarf between his hands, then clenched a fist with his right hand while stuffing the scarf into the clinch with his left. Then, poof, he opened his hands; the scarf had disappeared. The trick was solid until the audience noticed his right thumb, obviously oversized and made of rubber; it was also very white.

Traffic was thick on the expressway and grew more congested as they approached the stadium. On campus, a state police officer signaled Greg to stop at an intersection momentarily closed for pedestrians hurrying to the game.

In the car, waiting for the crosswalk to clear, Muhammad noticed a hot dog vendor at the corner of the street. Ali opened the door and walked across the intersection with the car still in the driving lane. Greg and company could only watch him go.

Muhammad had just made it to the vendor when the crowd closed in around him. It was chaos. Muhammad stood at the cart alongside the awestruck vendor. Then he picked up a hotdog wrapped in foil and handed it to the first guy in line. Then he served a dog to another guest. Soon Ali was throwing hot dog bombs to receivers, "going deep."

The entire intersection filled with fans no longer walking. The State police stood enthralled and a bit confused. A Sargent went to Greg, "Can you folks please get him back in the car?"

Greg answered, "Well, I think that is your job, but I don't think you can do it either!"

When the hot dogs were gone, Ali gave the vendor a wad of bills, a big hug and returned to the car, jammed in by the crowd, right where he had left it.

CHAPTER TWENTY-FOUR

CAREER DAY

onnie tried mightily to keep Muhammad in line, but he was a handful. One year he was scheduled to be at home on career day held at the Dowagiac Middle School. I knew the students would be thrilled and that Muhammad would enjoy the interaction, so I asked if he would like to visit with the young people. Muhammad quickly agreed, and Lonnie graciously asked Kim to make the arrangements.

Lonnie had a last-minute conflict on the day of the event, so Kim alone drove Muhammad to the Middle School. I waited in the parking lot for them to arrive. In those days before cell phones, I had lingering anxiety that a problem might arise to disrupt our plans. But all went smoothly.

I waved to Kim when the black GMC Yukon rolled into the driveway. She parked, and Muhammad stepped out dressed in a black turtleneck and dark sunglasses. He looked oddly formidable in the everyday surroundings of the old school lot. A global icon in a tiny old town.

We shared our hellos and enjoyed the fresh Fall air taking our time walking into the school. I told Ali the building was being replaced with a new school building; this was one of its last years. The excited Principal and office staff met us at the door. They were in disbelief; Muhammad Ali was really there, walking down the hall in the old school building.

The Principal escorted us to the auditorium, where the staff had set up a table on the stage with chairs for Ali, the local newspaper reporter, and Kim. A group of us stood to the side talking until a bell rang, and two classrooms of students were led in to meet Ali and ask a few questions.

The students were in awe of Muhammad. He dazzled them with his magic tricks; he even worked in a bit of the famous Ali shuffle. Then he sat to answer their questions.

"Mr. Ali, does it hurt when you box?"

""Are the gloves soft?"

"Mr. Ali, where did you learn to write poetry?"

Muhammad seemed humored by the questions. His face lit up as he shot back quick little answers, clearly happy to be with the children.

Then one young girl stood to ask her question, "Mr. Ali, if you had not been a boxer, what would you have been?"

In the blink of an eye, Ali leaned back in his chair and held an arm out straight with his hand hung down as if slung over the wheel of a big Cadillac and said,

"I'd a been a pimp. Jive'n and driven. Jive'n and driven."

It took a moment for anyone to realize what he had said. Then the kids screamed with laughter, and the adults just looked at each other, trying to comprehend the moment. The news reporter leaned into me and said,

"The greatest line I will ever hear, and I can't use it!"

Kim blushed beet red and whispered, "If Lonnie ever finds out, Muhammad will never leave the farm without her again!"

Muhammad just laughed in delight at the uproar.

For the rest of the afternoon, every class who came to the auditorium asked the same question, and none got the same answer.

CHAPTER TWENTY-FIVE

RED NECKS

Muhammad never had the security protection that his stature as an athlete and prominence at the vanguard of social justice might indicate. Outspoken and controversial, Ali still did not surround himself with armed bodyguards.

While advocates for equality were being shot with alarming frequency, Martin Luther King Jr., Malcolm X, and Bobbie Kennedy, Muhammad dared to walk freely amongst people. 'A gun for protection would be an insult to Allah; if Allah wants me, what difference would a gun make?' Muhammad thought it would be dishonorable to presume a man with a gun could thwart divine will.

Initially, there was little to no security on the farm either. Even the house had no alarm. Only an ornamental fence ran along the west property line from the river at the southeast corner to the river at the north corner. The fence delineated the peninsula that was the farm. Only that simple decorative ironwork guarded the farm against threats that might come looking to take down the Greatest of All Time.

The six-foot-tall black wrought iron fence was anchored at intervals with handsome brick columns. At any point, an intruder would have an easy time climbing over. In Capone's day, they would have been met with a couple quick rifle shots. But for Ali, there were no security personnel and no rifles.

As we came and went, the only active consolation to security was to be sure the gate closed when we passed, that was the extent of protection for the most recognizable and possibly the most controversial person alive.

One late August afternoon, Joe and I sat against the shaded side of the garage, escaping the sun's blazing heat. That morning we had begun work on the laundry room built into the first of the four garage bays beneath the old offices.

Painting the laundry was as glamorous as it sounds, and as the afternoon wore on, the low afternoon sun beat against the building while the industrial-sized washer and dryer churned away. We sat in the shadows to let the dryer finish its cycle, hoping the room would cool to tolerable.

It was a lazy day in August. We had not seen Muhammad since early morning and wondered if he was still around. Then Lonnie appeared and called out, "See you tomorrow." She waved and drove off for an appointment. Soon after, the office staff left for the day.

Still enjoying the shadows, we heard the rumble of an engine thumping through its broken exhaust pipe. We sat low against the garage and could not see the drive except the final leg, which dropped down to the parking area between the house and garage. Joe stood to look up the lane. A badly rusted pick-up truck rolled slowly along the drive.

"Hey, look at this gem." He said

I stood to look. We did not recognize the old red truck; it was dented and rumbled like there was no muffler at all. There were two men in the cab. They twisted in their seats, looking at the buildings clearly unfamiliar with the farm. They followed the lane to the cul-de-sac.

When they drove around the circle, we saw a confederate flag draped across the rear window and the chrome silhouette of a reclining woman on the mud flaps.

"Whoa, this does not look good," Joe warned

"I don't recognize them; think Muhammad is here?" I asked.

"It looks like everyone else has left. Let's see if they stop," Joe replied.

The driver slowed and pointed to the door leading into the kitchen. I saw the inner door standing open; only the screen door was closed.

"It looks like the house is open. I hope Muhammad is not alone in there." I said.

The old truck stopped and idled while the driver spoke; he pointed at the screen door and then back at our truck parked at the far end of the garages. Then he turned back to the house. The passenger crouched low, looking up to survey the third-floor windows.

Finally, the driver shut off the engine, and the two men climbed out. Both were gangly and walked somewhat hunched and unsteady. The driver had thin hair, reddish and wild. His passenger, though skinny, showed his round belly hanging beneath his partially open shirt. They wore ill-fitting blue jeans that hung precariously on their stove pipe hips. We could hear their southern accents and smelled stale cigarettes even at a distance.

"This is some fuckin' place!" The driver said.

"Bang on that door; see if he is in there." The other instructed.

Joe said, "Man, I don't like this. Who are these guys?"

"I don't know," I said, "let's walk to our truck so they know we are here.

We walked across the parking area and fumbled in the back of the truck for tools. The two men went to the screen door. One of them hollered, "Muhammad? Muhammad, you home?"

If he was home, we hoped Muhammad would not answer. We did not hear him respond, but the driver opened the screen door and looked in. I remember my hands felt sweaty, and we did not have much that would work as a weapon if these two were armed and set to harm Ali.

"Okay, let's go," Joe said.

I grabbed a club-like paint scraper, and Joe picked up a short extension pole. We started toward the house. We saw the driver stroll inside; the second guy followed. We hurried to the door and stood tight to the wall on either side. We could hear them talking to Muhammad.

"How are you, Champ? This is a nice place," one of them said.

Ali mumbled a reply we could not make out. It seemed clear they only wandered onto the farm; they did not know the place and were not invited. Everything about them seemed threatening.

I took the scraper and banged it against the siding as if we were working.

Joe said aloud, "Go ahead with that. I'll get the caulk."

O stood next to the door as if I was inspecting our work. I could hear the muffled conversation. Joe waved me back to the truck.

I think we just go in and get them out of there.

"I'm just worried if we start something and they have a gun..." I replied.

"Muhammad is alone; we can't just stand here with these guys just walking into the house!" he said.

Then we saw movement just inside the screen door. Muhammad came out first. The two men followed. Muhammad looked relaxed. He crouched and juked, and he tossed a few soft punches. The passenger put his arm over Ali's shoulder.

"Well, you was one ass-kicker, Champ," he said and shook Ali's hand.

Then the driver reached over to shake Muhammad's hand. Muhammad gave each of them that big Ali hug. Then they climbed back in their truck, fired up the engine that revved wildly, then drove slowly up the drive. Ali stood near the screen-door waving goodbye.

Joe and I only watched. It seemed impossible that Ali had survived all these years with every knucklehead in the country able to simply walk up and say hi---even to walk right into his house.

"I'll drive up to make sure the gate closes," I said as I walked to our truck.

Joe walked to Ali, bumped against his shoulder, and together they walked back inside the house.

PART SIX:

CHAPTER TWENTY-SIX

WHIPPING

Thirty years before the drugstore in Dowagiac was built, Isaiah awoke in a room off the kitchen, across the yard, away from the plantation house. For the first time in his life, he laid on a mattress of horsehair covered with white sheets. His head rested on a pillow of rolled cotton cloth. His oddly shaped hand was wrapped in blood-stained cotton. He studied his hand, throbbing heavily to the pulse of his heart. He felt for the talisman still around his neck.

In the yard, he heard William plead,

"You have got to whip that boy! He grabbed hold of you! If you don't whip him, there is no respect. No respect, Master. I cannot run the fields with no whip."

"The boy saved my life." Master Newhouse replied in a low tone. "I cannot whip a boy for saving my life."

"Well, Master, it makes me shudder in my bones, but then you got to whip me. I lost control of that boy, and he grabbed you; you got to whip me for it. There has to be a whippin'. No work will get done."

"William, you have been a faithful servant, a good man. I will be troubled all my life if I have you whipped. I brought this trouble on myself; I was careless. I will not have you whipped. I will not have him whipped."

William backed a step away from Master Newhouse as his head sank to his chest. He fidgeted, wringing the tips of his finger

"Master, I made a mistake. A bad mistake. I cannot overseer your plantation, Master."

"William, what are you saying?" the Master replied.

"Master, I told the men I was coming to the house to get Isaiah to whip that boy 'cuz none of them can ever touch Master Newhouse. I was wrong to do it, but that is what I have done. I created a contradiction."

His voice shook, and tears filled his eyes. "I am scared for it." He pleaded.

Master Newhouse exhaled a heavy sigh. His head fell back. He stared at a single cloud floating across the sky for a long minute.

"William, go to the fields. Things have to be made right."

"Yes, sir, Master Newhouse, things got to be made right."

For twenty years, William had done all the whipping that had to be done on the plantation. Now he faced the scourge. Master Newhouse felt anger well up inside. Though he had witnessed a thousand lashes, he hated the sight of the whip tearing at the bare flesh of a man.

He had no stomach for the whip but told himself he was forced to it. He had to protect his family. He had to keep order. He told himself that without the whip, the men would not work.

Master Newhouse walked into the kitchen. He opened a narrow cabinet above the wood bin next to the stove and pulled down an amber bottle of rum. He twisted out the cork and drew a long drink of the flaming liquid, then another.

He gripped the door handle to Isaiah's room, hesitated, then pushed the door open. Isaiah sat on the bed, terrified. The crack of the whip across his back filled his mind. Master put the bottle in Isaiah's hand. "Drink, drink deep, Isaiah." He warned.

Isaiah first tasted the rum; its flame burned down his throat. Then he guzzled a long drink. His hand clutching the bottle shook with dread; the other throbbed.

Master tied a cord around Isaiah's neck and led him out the door and across the yard toward the row of brick houses. Two elderly women were still at the morning's fire, slicing bean pods, beets, and turnips for the midday stew. Isaiah saw their eyes follow him stumbling behind Master Newhouse, quick-stepping to the fields.

At the head of the path, on a knoll above the rice fields, an old gate hung from a length of tree trunk. Master Newhouse put his hand on Isaiah's back, pressing him against the post. He wrapped the cord around the post and then cinched it tight to the loop around Isaiah's neck.

Master turned to face the men in the field below. They were still chopping into the mud with hoes turning out weeds and carefully smoothing the soil to support the seedling rice plants. One by one, their song fell silent as they looked up to see Master Newhouse gazing at them, stoic.
William rode his horse from the field to face his Master. "Stand at the gate." Master Newhouse ordered.

William swung down from the horse and walked to the gate. He positioned himself three paces aside Isaiah, ready to flog the boy when the whip was presented. Master Newhouse took the whip from its sheath alongside William's horse's saddle. He also took a rope spooled over the horn.

He threw the length of rope to William, "Tie him." was all he said.

William pulled Isaiah's hands around the post. Then he tore

the shirt from Isaiah's back. Master Newhouse stood in front of Isaiah; he saw his eyes fill with terror; Master turned away.

"Go to the post." He ordered William.

Master Newhouse nodded to the vacant post at the other side of the gate. William hesitated. He turned back to his Master to verify with his eyes what his ears had heard.

He saw his Master's tight lips quivering, his narrow stare hollow. William walked to the post and wrapped his arms around it. He held th column close. He thought of the wires he had sewn into the tips of the flogger tails.

"Tie him." The Master ordered.

A man from a gathered cluster of workers stepped forward to tie William. Master Newhouse walked five paces behind Isaiah and William, now strapped to the posts at either side of the old gate. He raised the whip to flog Isaiah when he saw the thick welts crisscrossing his back. He turned to William.

"You have deceived me!" he shouted. "This boy is damaged. He has been whipped, yet I paid prime for him; did you keep the difference? How many times have you lied and deceived me?" he shouted louder, enraged, the rum incensing his ire.

The whip cracked with fury. The first bits of flesh flew from William's shoulders as his Master's aim was not well-practiced. The next blow tore at his buttocks, searing through his legs. Then the rhythm quickened, and the aim narrowed to a tight swath across William's broad back.

Master Newhouse did not even shout out his count. He just thrashed and thrashed at William. He hated the whipping. He hated the thick humid air that hung over the bog. He hated listening to the dozens of men just across the yard who might slaughter his family in the night.

In time his arm ached, and the lashes lost some of their

fury. Still, the leather seared William's torn flesh. The bits of wire chipped at his ribs with each blow. William hung by his hands, his legs bent lifeless to one side.

"Get vinegar to wash him, clean those wounds, cleanse him!" Master Newhouse roared.

Master Isaiah Newhouse stepped toward Isaiah. "Damaged... Damaged," He repeated faintly under heavy breath. His arm ached as he again raised the whip.

The long leather whip cracked across Isaiah's back, but Master stood too close. The whip's tail wrapped around Isaiah, so the wired tips bit into the post.

Though he had vowed not to make a sound, Isaiah screamed wildly across the bog. The whip burned but did not tear. Quickly Master Newhouse lost interest. His fury subsided into drunken self-pity.

Master looked to the men, their eyes to the ground. "Go work," he said.

Then he dropped the crusted whip and walked toward the plantation house. "Bring me Isaiah," he commanded.

Back in the room off the kitchen, laying on the horsehair mattress, the rolled cotton pillow cradling his cheek, tears mingled in the sweat-soaked white fabric. Still shuddering, Isaiah listened to the unearthly screams resounding through centuries as quivering hands rubbed yellow vinegar into William's slashed flesh.

CHAPTER TWENTY-SEVEN

KNOWLEDGE

Master Newhouse ordered the pantry servants to care for Isaiah and called the surgeon to remove Isaiah's smashed fingers; with only one good hand, he would not return to clear the bog; Isaiah became a house servant.

Missus Newhouse understood he had saved Master Newhouse. She was careful that the house servants nursed his wounds, then she ensured they fed him an extra portion as his stature grew to a powerful chiseled physique.

William almost died from his beating. His torn muscles never healed. One shoulder sagged as he limped to the fields. From that day on, he was assigned tasks like every other common slave, but he was rarely able to complete them, so he suffered more beatings at the hands of the new overseer.

Master Newhouse saw to less and less of the operation. He was sickened at the pitiable sight of William's failing condition, but he looked away with confused emotion.

Isaiah had few tasks in the household, so he often became a companion for Benjamin, Newhouse's ten-year-old son. Every morning, Missus Newhouse taught Isaiah to speak "correctly" and read right alongside her Benjamin. Isaiah learned quickly and soon coached Benjamin as well.

Within a year, Isaiah was able to read the newspaper and struggle through books. He spent hours in his room studying, plodding through every written word he could find.

One Spring morning Missus Newhouse was at the table teaching the boys penmanship. Master Newhouse came into the kitchen looking for Missus. He saw the papers and Isaiah forming vowels in neat rows on lined paper. Master Newhouse glared at the table, then took Missus by the elbow and walked her out into the yard.

"Don't you understand? It is one thing to allow that boy to read, but if you teach him to write!? I will send him back to the fields; if he learns too much, he will never again be a good slave. It is time to cease these studies. No more!" he shouted. "He will always be trouble."

Isaiah sat at the table, listening through the thin wall of the kitchen. Then he went quickly to his room to think about what he had heard. Why did Master Newhouse raise his voice to chastise Missus right there in earshot of Isaiah?

'If he learns too much, he will never be a good slave.' Played over and over in Isaiah's mind. What is a good slave? What would change if he learned too much?

Isaiah thought of his father and the elders who met in the village. He knew they had met, but as a child, he had no idea what they spoke about. Now he realized they shared knowledge and that knowledge could change things.

That day the studies with Missus Newhouse ended. There was even less for Isaiah to do, so he did his best to be cheerful and helpful to the other hands. He also stayed out of sight as much as possible.

For the following years, Isaiah kept the yard clean and watched over Benjamin when Missus Newhouse called. But most days, before Master Newhouse awoke, Isaiah slipped into the library behind the parlor to trade out a new book.

In the early afternoon, when his tasks were completed, and for long hours into the night, when the house went silent, Isaiah read beneath a single lit candle.

He made notes explaining words he did not know and wrote out phrases that seemed important. He kept a file of quotations and definitions in a box beneath his bed.

One morning he found a pamphlet, "The Declaration of Independence." He read, "We hold these truths to be self-evident, that all men are created equal, that they are endowed by their Creator with certain unalienable rights, that among these are life, liberty, and the pursuit of happiness."

Isaiah lay in his bed, tears welling in his eyes. For the first time in what seemed a very long time, he thought of Mira and his mother and father. He thought of the life he would have known in the village and what happiness really meant.

A few nights later, Master Newhouse came looking for him.

"Isaiah, I had a pamphlet with my books that I referred to in a letter to our governor. I know you have had books, and that is fine, but I need the pamphlet."

"Yessir," Isaiah answered. "I do have that pamphlet. I did a study of it. Do you believe in it, Master?"

"You should leave that alone, Isaiah; war is coming. Say too much and you may be hung." he warned.

"War Master?" Isaiah asked.

"Men in the north do not believe the Southern Confederacy has the right to form its own union. The Republicans want to tell us, Southern businessmen, how to run our affairs, and we say hooey." Master Newhouse explained.

"You will serve yourself well to keep your thoughts private until this unpleasantness is passed," he warned.

Master Newhouse took the pamphlet from Isaiah's night table and turned to leave the room. He stopped short; his gaze fell to the box half-tucked under Isaiah's bed. The Master's sudden appearance interrupted Isaiah amidst concealing his file.

"I see you are keeping possessions under my roof Isaiah, open that box and show me what you have collected."

"Well, it's just things about my reading, sir." Isaiah feigned. "I don't think it will interest you."

"That is fine, Isaiah," he answered, "hand me the box."

Isaiah did not know what in his notes might be offensive to Master Newhouse, but they were all written with his pen. With little training, Isaiah nonetheless discovered he had the hand of an artist. He took great pleasure in forming small letters with precision and capital letters with flourish.

Master Newhouse opened the box and leafed through the first few notes, stopping to read several. Then he sat at the edge of the bed, a pack of notes across his knees. His eyes fixed on them. He slowly turned the leaves, then halted at the entry for "slavery." It began:

"Slavery: a condition in which one is completely subservient to a dominating influence."

Isaiah saw the note. He saw Master Newhouse take a deep breath, sigh, then stare, eyes fixed on the letters Isaiah had formed.

"Master Newhouse, I believe I am no longer fully a slave." Isaiah dared, "I am not completely subservient to you. Though you are my Master, we both are men. You could not whip me terribly that day because we share something. We were in that muck together, and we climbed out of it together. I care for

157

you, Master Newhouse, and I think you care for me. You trust me here with your Missus and with your children. I mean no disrespect, but I do not think I am completely subservient any longer."

Master Newhouse sat in silence while Isaiah fidgeted, thinking of what more he could say. He began to speak, but the words left him; he began softly and halted again.

After several minutes, Master Newhouse simply stood and said to him:

"Isaiah, I am sending you away. I wll make arrangements and inform you in a few days."

Isaiah watched him go, then heard the door latch quietly shut.

PART SEVEN:

CHAPTER TWENTY-EIGHT

THE RING

Several decades after the Emancipation Proclamation, but before the days of mobsters and prohibition, there was a sweet simplicity to the old farm. Cows grazed on the lush grass of the floodplain; horses pulled wagons over the gravel lane that began where the road to town ended. Four white barns were a sign of wealth and a bustling operation.

The largest structure was the hay barn, stocked in the Fall to feed the livestock through a snowy winter; the barn had to be big to hold an entire season's feed. In Winter, the farm glistened white. Lake effect snow from Lake Michigan fell almost every night.

A smaller barn was stocked with scythes to cut hay and wagons to haul it. There were tillers for planting and carpentry tools to build whatever needed to be repaired to support the farm.

The third barn housed the cows. It sat at the end of the lane, almost centered on the expanse of grass that covered the floodplain.

Finally, there was the milk barn, where the real work of the farm began early morning before dawn. The barn was bright and cheerful, painted white inside and out with long windows under the eaves, but the cows were hand milked before sun-up, so the farmer may have rarely enjoyed the sweet light of a Winter's morning in that building.

The barns anchored the farm in another century but still

functioned well for Ali. The hay barn was packed on two floors with accumulated belongings and Ali's memorabilia. The smaller barn served as storage for mowers and tools to support the modern-day farm. The old cow barn had been converted into the main house.

It was the old, picturesque milk barn that fell into disuse. Ali had set up his gym equipment and a boxing ring in the barn, but it became defunct at the end of his storied boxing career. Still, the glistening white barn was a gem.

I was saddened the morning we heard the barn was scheduled to be demolished. Ali needed the ground to build professional office space to host dignitaries and organize his wide-ranging charitable work as an emissary for human rights. The barn would have to go.

With the demolition pending, questions arose, especially what to do with Ali's old practice ring that was dismantled and stacked along a wall in the old barn.

At the time, I worked with the Downtown Development Authority, the DDA, commissioned to restore the central business district in Dowagiac, Michigan. The city had fallen on hard times, and like so many small towns, there were few recreational opportunities for young people. The community needed an anchor for youth activities. At committee meetings, we often discussed what we could do for kids.

During a morning work break, when Ali's new gym was under construction, we sat with the carpenters, talking about the coming office project and what to do with the dismantled ring

We lamented the loss of the barn and scoffed at the thought the ring might be scrapped. It was Ali's ring! There was no way it could be tossed out as scrap iron. Sipping coffee, we casually discussed how the ring might be sold or how we might help find a local place to donate it.

This was during my first weeks on the farm; I was not yet close with Muhammad and Lonnie. Thinking of the DDA and the need for youth activities, I casually mentioned using the ring to create a boxing club for kids. Almost simultaneously, Lonnie walked into the room.

One of the carpenters hollered out,

"Lonnie, Larry wants the old ring to start a boxing club for kids."

Lonnie responded without hesitation, "Well, you just take that old thing; Muhammad doesn't need it anymore."

I squirmed. Besides being called out, this was an imposition. I could not just take the ring, and really, what was I going to do with a boxing ring? But there it was, that smart-aleck carpenter set me up, and the story stuck; I was going to start a boxing club for kids.

The paint crew talked about little else as we worked for the next few days. Becky, Joe, and I discussed the logistics of putting a club together and the positive impact a club could have on kids. It would be a boxing club, a study hall, and a center for service to the community.

Within days the Dowagiac newspaper called for an interview. Since the resulting article mentioned Ali, it was picked up by the Associated Press, and the story went worldwide.

Reading her local newspaper at breakfast in Clearwater, Florida, my mother saw that Muhammad Ali had given her son a boxing ring. Family from England to Washington State sent notes of congratulations. The project was real. Events moved very quickly, and Muhammad wanted to help!

CHAPTER TWENTY-NINE

OLD BUILDINGS AND
A BOXING CLUB

Dowagiac was a wealthy town with a solid manufacturing base in the 1800s. It was the home to Round Oak Stoves, wood burners that heated homes from Dowagiac to California. Two massive warehouses on either side of the railroad tracks were loaded with stoves all Spring and Summer. In August, salesmen armed with brochures and miniature model stoves rode the train west. They took orders from Kankakee to California. Train cars loaded with stoves followed in September to fill the orders.

Downtown Dowagiac flourished. The two city blocks of the central business district were lined with two-story buildings that housed a bakery, dry goods, clothing, and hardware stores. On the second floor were apartments and offices: two doctors, a dentist, and even a second-floor funeral parlor.

When we arrived in the 1990s, the town was a sorry shell of its past. Storefronts had been covered with corrugated aluminum from the sidewalk to the cornice. These "Kawneer" storefronts were meant to modernize the old buildings but destroyed the town's ambiance.

The second floors were abandoned, their windows covered with the aluminum sheets. Cornices were removed; grand entryways were ripped out and replaced with flat-stock commercial doors with modern self-closing hinges. The business district all but died.

On a whim, we bought a building that housed the worst bar in town; it was terrible. The storefront was speckled aluminum with tiny metal frame windows fogged over with years of accumulated filth.

Under the floor mats behind the bar, holes rotted through into the basement. The only running water in the men's room was in the sink. The toilet and urinal flushed with a garden hose that ran up through a wall from the basement. The building was a mess, but the price made it a gift. Paradoxically, a renewal notice form the Health Department was in the mailbox.

Young and strong and naïve, our paint crew had a grand time tearing the aluminum from the front of the building. In the basement, we found the discarded entry doors, eight feet tall, and reconstructed the old storefront. We restored the original tin ceiling, salvaged three-quarter-inch cherry paneling from the walls to lay as flooring, and pounded the remaining plaster from the Chicago brick walls.

Outside, we refitted the original windows with thermal pane glass, painted the new storefront sterling white, the second-floor brickwork dark red, and the cornice deep green with gold accents. To finish it off, we installed historically correct canvas canopies. We opened an interior design studio to support our painting business when complete. We had no idea of the impact on the community.

Townspeople stood across the street gaping at the showpiece with tears welling in their eyes. No one knew Dowagiac could be beautiful. Ours was the first building to be painted in over twenty years, much less be fully renovated.

The restoration began a firestorm of renovation anchored by the nascent Downtown Development Authority (DDA). The DDA came with incentives to restore the original storefronts and second-floor apartments. Encouraged by the success of our first renovation, we bought some other awful buildings.

One of them was a double storefront that once housed Rose's dance studio on the second floor. The studio was filled to the ceiling with old fixtures and inventory from the defunct first-floor businesses. The windows above the alley in the back had been broken out for years; much of the riffraff was coated inches thick with pigeon droppings. The pigeons paid no rent but had a full run of the place. Beneath all the mess, we found a Thomas Dewey for President poster pasted to the floor.

Following renovations, the space was once again leased as a dance studio, then a gymnastics center, and ultimately, it would house the Dowagiac Boxing Club.

With news of Ali and a boxing club, people from town and surrounding communities came forward. Muhammad asked how the club progressed, and I told him we had some funding and held organizational meetings Thursday evenings.

"Pick me up." He said.

"...Pick me up?" Like I would drive out to the farm, load Ali in my car, and drive to a meeting in Dowagiac? I went to Lonnie.

"Muhammad asked me to pick him up for the boxing club meeting Thursday night," I explained

"Well, that's not going to happen. Muhammad does not remember he has a plane to catch Friday morning at 6 am." She declared.

I understood there was probably no plane to catch, that Ali was a national treasure, a global treasure. But he did not see himself that way. To him, he was just a guy that wanted a ride. To the rest of the world, he was Muhammad Ali.

There was a vast divide between Muhammad's self-perception and the reality that he was a national icon. I think Muhammad had moved well-passed celebrity. He had a disarming ability to be in the present and find joy in quiet moments and in the people he met. While we all treated him with reverence, he put on no airs.

One afternoon Ali and I watched tapes of a few of his fights. He enjoyed showing off the highlights. In one fight, he danced on his toes, taunting his opponent with his arms hanging at his sides, letting the flummoxed boxer take seemingly unguarded shots at his head. Ali infuriated his opponent, smiling and talking trash until he was worn enough to let his own guard down. Then in a flurry of blows, Ali pummeled the boxer to the canvas.

I looked from the screen to Ali, "Do you remember those moments? Can you put yourself back in that ring?" I asked. even know that guy,"

Ali responded, "I dont even know that guy," then, tipping his head to the side, "he was craaaazy!"

CHAPTER THIRTY

THE OPENING

Over the next five or six weeks, the club's organization began to take shape. We applied for non-profit status, elected a Board of Directors, and I knocked on the doors of three well-known community angels and collected over twenty thousand dollars to outfit the club. It took less than thirty minutes of discussion for each angel to offer help. All asked to be anonymous and told me to come back if we needed more.

In a small town, even a little splash sends big ripples through the community. The club won the support of City Hall, the Dowagiac Schools, and most of the community at large; the club was rolling!

(Initially, some folks thought a boxing club taught violence, in fact, it taught respect and engendered a strong sense of community in its members.)

Volunteers worked with our paint crew to build and carpet a study room and install several used computers. They built two dressing rooms with lockers donated by a local school district. There were two tiny showers barely large enough to turn around in; we aimed to thwart future hanky- panky. The club had to be safe and wholesome. Our first rule was that no adult could ever be alone in the presence of a minor---any violation meant an immediate dismissal from the club.

We were fortunate some of the dads had experience with boxing and the training equipment. First, they helped us organize what equipment we needed. Then, when it seemed obvious to me that we would anchor the practice equipment directly onto the brick walls, they knew better.

Our building was constructed in 1865, and the brick was soft. Besides that, the side walls were common to the neighboring buildings. Boxers hitting the speed bags and the heavy bags would create near-constant pounding. The thumping would travel through the adjacent buildings and would destroy the soft brick. An independent structure was the only way to isolate the noise and keep the equipment securely anchored.

A week later, one of the dads showed up with a truckload of old industrial racking and a welding torch. He and some volunteers cut and welded all weekend. By Sunday night, they had assembled what looked like a long u-shaped set of monkey bars.

The framework ran down two sides of the sixty-foot room and across the back. There were stations designed to hold speed bags, heavy bags, chin-up bars, and sit-up stations. The club began to look like the real deal.

Overall, the building was forty-four feet wide and one hundred feet long. There were two large rooms to the rear which overlooked the alley. A hallway intersected the building toward the front. Opposite the hallway, the general office, study room, and locker rooms overlooked Front Street. We put workout equipment in one of the large rooms and the boxing ring in the other.

The old boxing ring was a beast. I had no experience with boxing and knew nothing about the structure of a boxing ring. I saw the rings were bright and white on TV and had ropes strung through corner poles. Until Ali built the new gym, there was no assembled ring on the property.

Just before the move to the club, we piled all the parts in the center of the room, and reality set in. Initially, the side rails looked long but not particularly heavy, and the inch-thick plywood floor looked tidy stacked against the wall.

However, the assembled ring was twenty-four feet square and weighed 3,500 pounds. Beneath the top canvas, there was a layer of heavy canvas that took two men to lift. Beneath, eighteen sheets of inch-thick plywood covered an I-beam structure held taut with cables and turnbuckles. The corner posts themselves stood almost six feet tall. They were heavy gauge six-inch metal pipes.

We might have rented a flatbed trailer to haul the ring but used the best no-cost option available, the trailer for an inboard ski boat.

On the morning of the move, we pulled the trailer to the farm with my baby blue 1953 GMC pick-up. Ali met us along with the carpenters. Together we loaded the beams onto the trailer, stringing them along the bunks which usually carried the boat. Then we stacked the plywood on top of the beams and tied it all down. The ropes, canvas, and hardware went in the back of the pick-up, and we were on our way.

The fifteen-mile drive from Berrien Springs to Dowagiac took about thirty minutes. The sweet old truck and funny-looking load turned heads all along the route. In town, a small army of teens collected to help carry the ring up the two flights of stairs to the former dance studio. It seemed the entire city buzzed with excitement.

A local policeman walking his beat pulled me aside to point out the delinquents we had helping unload the ring. It seemed every young man arrested in the past two years was there working.

"Be careful they are not just casing the place," he warned.

But I did not see thugs. I saw boys and girls struggling to navigate the stairway and landings as they lugged the awkward i-beams up to the club. Eighteen times teams of two stumbled up the stairs carrying a thick sheet of plywood. Then they hustled for position to run the bolts through the rails and leg brackets and wrench them tight.

Joe and I stood against the wall to watch. With little supervision, the newly assembled team figured out how all the parts went together and built themselves a boxing ring.

While construction went on, we wrote a job description for a coach to work six days per week with the young boxers. We worried about finding someone willing to work with dozens of kids daily for very little pay. A wise man on the Board set our worries aside,

"Every non-profit organization needs donors; without them, nothing happens. We need directors and a Board; that is us; we put the pieces in place. The organization also needs volunteers, these folks may not have a lot of time or money, but the club could not exist without them. Finally, the club needs a director, a coach who is here every day doing what he loves to do---- working directly with the young people. This will be a dream job for the person who is looking."

Sure enough, a veteran boxer in the community was eager for the job. As the weeks flew past, enrollment in the club soared. We hoped for thirty boxers. In the first month, we signed up sixty. In the first year, we would have over two hundred and forty young people signed up as USA Amateur Boxers.

For thirty-five dollars, members received a mouthpiece, hand wraps, a Boxing Club t-shirt, and an official USA Boxing fight book to record their bouts. Members had access to the study room with tutors and counselors.

They could hit the heavy bags, speed bags, and the real prize, working out in Muhammad Ali's practice ring. Being proud of the club and boxing also meant taking care of schoolwork.

We long debated the membership fee, but in the end, we figured kids had the money for sodas and movie rentals; we would redirect some of that money to earn a commitment from them. We wanted youth to dedicate something of themselves to the club, and they did; most days, the club looked more like daycare than an athletic club, but kids were there in a place of their own, building community.

Before members could hit the bags or pull chin-ups, they had to sign off on completing their homework. Their good standing in the club depended on positive reports from their teachers and parents.

The club's biggest problem with the schools was the young boys wearing their hand wraps to class. We celebrated the pride they felt but counseled them on the expression of it.

From a distance of years, it seems audacious that we charged for membership and required an hour of community service each week from club members, but it worked. If a young person said they could not find the money for membership, we quietly waived the fee.

We created opportunities for members to fulfill their community service. Captains organized pop-up cleaning projects gathering a dozen boxers wearing their boxing club t-shirts to sweep sidewalks and mow lawns for the elderly. Individual members visited their grandparents at the nursing home or volunteered at school. Each week they signed off that they had completed their community service. "Honor Yourself, Honor the Club."

For the two weeks leading up to the grand opening, groups of boxers thoroughly swept downtown sidewalks and the gutters along Front Street. Crews worked in the alley behind the club, gathering up decades of broken glass, cutting out scrubby little trees that pinched through cracks in the pavement, and shoveling out mounds of dirt pushed up against the buildings.

They loaded two pick-up trucks with refuse and hosed the rest down the storm drains. The crews swept, rinsed down the alley, and washed all the windows they could reach. Every week the local newspaper ran front-page pictures of the boxers in their Dowagiac Boxing Club t-shirts sweeping the town.

In a moment of inspiration, we checked with the City Clerk, who confirmed the alley behind the club, though 150 years old, had never been officially named. Joe suggested the City designate it: "Muhammad Alley." Muhammad grinned; he thought the homonym was perfect. City Council approved the resolution by unanimous consent.

With "Muhammad Alley" sparkling clean, all was ready for the day Muhammad Ali came to town.

On March 31, 2007, I climbed the two flights of stairs to the Boxing Club. "Honor Yourself" "Honor the Club" emblazoned in gilded letters adorned the top step of the first and second flights of stairs. We had just signed our eightieth amateur boxer to the club, boys and girls from twelve to eighteen years.

In my excitement, I bounded up the stairs, greeted by a swirl of t-shirted boxers, volunteers, and parents. The club sparkled. Today was the Grand Opening. Ali was coming to town!

With a thousand details finalized, the club was ready. Floors were swept, office windows washed, and all equipment was wiped down. Some older boys upholstered a big cushioned chair in black and gold fabric solely for Muhammad. On the wall just inside the entry, a long column listed community donors on the club's twelve-foot-wide bulletin board. Across the bottom of the six-inch frame, gold letters boldly read:

"Look What We Can Do Together!"

CHAPTER THIRTY-ONE

THE DEDICATION

The Boxing Club was on the second floor in the middle of a long block of buildings. We planned to have Muhammad park in a lot behind the Club, just off Muhammad Alley, for the Dedication Ceremony. Rather than walk Muhammad around the far end of the block and then back to the middle, we planned to have him cut through the pizza parlor below the Boxing Club.

The entrance to the Club was on Front Street, alongside the pizza parlor. We were in the center of town and across from a small park. For our grand opening, the City had set up the Mayor's grandstand, usually reserved for Memorial Day and Christmas Night parades, in the street directly in front of the building.

Anxious to be underway, I waited upstairs with an eye out the second-floor windows at the back of the gym, looking for Muhammad and Lonnie. The alley was quiet; a small crowd had formed around the grandstand on Front Street. The air was electric. Suddenly a half-dozen young boxers ran up the stairs shouting for me.

"Larry, Lonnie is out front. She doesn't know where to go!"

I hustled downstairs. Lonnie had driven alone. Muhammad and Kim were to follow. I met Lonnie on the sidewalk and made our way up to the Club. I was torn while showing Lonnie the facilities knowing Muhammad would arrive at any minute.

Our plan was already in disarray. Within minutes a lookout came running; Muhammad and Kim were in the alley, looking up at the buildings, bewildered. I excused myself and ran to the emergency door at the back of the Club, then scampered down the narrow fire escape and ducking under a vent pipe halfway down, long waiting to knock me out, then half leaped to the alley below.

Muhammad and Kim had walked from the parking lot behind the building to the far end of the block. I hurried to them.

I hollered, "Hello," then, hurrying closer, said, "Sorry, Lonnie came to the front; we got turned around for a minute."

"No problem," Kim said with cheer. "Is this Muhammad Alley?" "Yes, it is a first; Muhammad Ali is walking on Muhammad Alley," I replied.

Muhammad surveyed the narrow alley tucked between the old 1800's era buildings. He quipped, "I look old and skinny."It did not make sense to walk back down the alley and through the pizza shop to the grandstand, so I led Kim and Muhammad the short distance from the alley entrance to the sidewalk leading around the end building to Front Street.

A nearly blind octogenarian, Mr. Klepter, clattered toward us as we rounded the building. He tapped his cane back and forth across the sidewalk as he approached, then struck Muhammad on his foot. Mr. Klepter jolted to a stop, surprised, then wobbled into Ali.

"Hello?" he stammered.

Ali reached down to steady the old guy as he regained his footing. Mr. Klepter looked up, squinting at Muhammad.

"Do you know this guy?" I asked.

Mr. Klepter turned his head from side to side, gathering an

image of the man towering over him.

"Haaaah!" he squealed. "I know you! You're Muhammad Ali!"

With that, Ali wrapped his arms around old Mr. Klepter. I don't remember that Ali said a word, but the two seemed to be buddies together again after a long time apart. With a look of satisfaction, the two men bade farewell and shuffled in opposite directions along the sidewalk.

At the corner, we turned onto Front Street. I suddenly worried that we had to walk a city block. This was my first time in a public setting, more or less alone with Muhammad. But few people were in sight, and the mid-afternoon sun shone warmly. I assured my worried self it would be a pleasant introduction for Ali to Dowagiac.

By the time we walked sixty feet from the corner, past a small parking lot to the China Garden storefront, merchants had begun coming out of their buildings along with staff from the restaurant. There had been no formal announcement, but they all knew Ali had arrived.

Ali stopped to greet the Chinese cooks in their caps and long white aprons. The kitchen crew spoke little English but smiled so hard they would not have been able to say much anyway. Tears filled their eyes. Each of the cooks, in turn, hurriedly shook Muhammad's hand, nodding several times, repeating, "Thank you. Thank you."

I looked up the street, anxious to see how we might progress to the grandstand. In just a few minutes, two long rows of people lined the sidewalk all the way to the Club. Townspeople looked on with faces glowing. The moment they would meet Muhammad Ali was upon them. We ambled up the sidewalk. Ali gave time to each of them.

Some people said they had seen him fight or met him at an event; others smiled hard with tears running freely down their cheeks, unable to speak. Ali signed a few autographs, but most people just wanted to shake his hand, though that was not enough for Ali. He hugged every person he greeted.

When we arrived at the grandstand, the street, the central intersection, and the little park filled with Ali fans, especially students. Right there, when everything came together, I remembered an omission. It occurred to me that we had not put up posters announcing the grand opening at the schools.

The Boxing Club looked out over the park with statuary and an octagonal gazebo. A short one-quarter block street ran along one side of the park; on the other, a two-story, red-bricked restaurant. In minutes onlookers jammed the streets and park, excited to see Ali.

Finally, after thirty minutes of hugs and handshakes, we climbed the stairs to the grandstand. Muhammad, Lonnie, the Mayor, our boxing coach, four dads, a mom, and my buddy Joe, our Master of Ceremonies, sat in folding chairs on the small stage.

We began the Club's formal dedication:

"Heaven on earth can be found in the heart's endless capacity to care for others. Indeed, our happiness can be measured by the care we share. Hate, bigotry, and greed are windows to our malnourished souls. No money, fame, or success can make a bigot happy. In the end, the only joy that can sustain us is the joy of giving and caring and sharing with others. Find a friend, then do a kind thing for someone ... Just Look at What We Can Do Together!"

Togetherness was the vehicle, and it was the message. During the months that followed the Club's opening, the police chief told us incidents with young people dropped significantly--- to almost zero. In the schools, fewer students acted out. Eighty young boxers were registered by the day of the grand opening, just over a month since the Club had opened. By the end of that first year, we would sign-up more than two hundred and forty registered amateur boxers.

With Muhammad at her side, Lonnie spoke:

"When he (the author) told me there were 80 kids signed up for this boxing club, I was astounded that there would be that many people interested. But it really shows there is a need. Children want to be somewhere where they can produce and do something positive and be productive

This particular project here, I think, will be a focal point for Dowagiac. I hope it will be something surrounding communities in southwestern Michigan can model. It's a start, and I think you have something great here. It's such an honor for all of us to be here. Thank you."

Then Joe lightened the moment. Speaking in the shadow of Ali, Joe announced.

"Please understand, if I seem really nervous up here, that one semester of high school speech class hardly prepares you to give a speech with someone as famous as the Mayor of Dowagiac sitting next to you."

Ali took the queue and hit Joe with a stink eye.

Speeches followed then young orators took the stage. One by one, they came up to quote Ali.

"This is the legend of Muhammad Ali, the greatest fighter there ever will be. He talks a great deal and brags indeed of a powerful punch and blinding speed. Ali's got speed and endurance. If you sign him to fight, increase your insurance. Ali's got left; Ali's got right. If he hits you once, you're asleep for the night," said Schuyler File.

"If you think the world was shocked when Nixon resigned," continued Michael Lamb, "wait 'til I whip George Foreman's behind.

Float like a butterfly, sting like a bee, his hands can't hit what eyes hands can't see. Now you see me, now you don't. George thinks he will, but I know he won't.

I done wrestled an alligator, I done tussled with a whale. Only last week, I murdered a rock, injured a stone, and hospitalized a brick. I'm so mean; I make medicine sick."

"The greatness or smallness of a man does not depend on his education or wealth. Regardless of how wealthy a man is, regardless of how educated a man is, if his heart is not great, he cannot be great. It is the heart that makes one great or small," said Molly Seurynck.

"If I say a cow can lay an egg, don't argue with me. Go get the skillet," said Ricki McNary

The youngsters looked as if they had won a prize. Muhammad smiled, and the crowd in the street cheered. Then we moved on to the official ribbon cutting. Lonnie and Mark Gourley, our boxing coach, held the banner while Muhammad cut the ribbon, officially dedicating the Dowagiac Boxing Club. Then, with a policeman in the lead to prevent chaos, we descended the grandstand and climbed the stairs to the Club.

Inside the Club, we first walked the hallway that ran across the front of the building. We showed off the central office with file cabinets, a conference table, and the study room with three long tables with computers for students and tutors. We showed Ali the library with big soft chairs for reading and a small wall of books. Then the two small dressing rooms. Young volunteers and their parents that helped build everything clamored to show Ali their work.

The rear two-thirds of the building was split to create the two long rooms. The workout equipment was on one side; on the other was Ali's old practice ring and his chair. Ali inspected the equipment and tried out the speed bag. He tagged it a few times, made it pound the rat-a-tat rhythm for a minute or so but hurried to see the ring.

We crossed through an arched doorway into the long room with the ring set to the front. A dozen folding chairs shuffled to the rear, and a square array of fluorescent lights hung tight to the ceiling above the ring. The lights glared. Ali pointed to Ricky, the biggest kid in the Club, "C'mon, let's go!" he challenged.

Ricky climbed into the ring. Muhammad danced back and forth, playing for the crowd. The jam-packed audience cheered and whooped when Ali popped off a flurry of punches ripping the air. Then he set Ricky up for the photo, Ricky's big right square to Ali's jaw.

Ali welcomed every child who climbed into that ring. The kids laughed in awe of this towering man, this powerhouse, who gave each time to have a special moment. Ali clowned, he posed for pictures, and he laughed. It was almost two hours when the last young boxer had their moment with Ali.

When we finally got Ali out of the ring, he was spent. A young girl took his hand and led him to his chair. Ali plunked back in the seat, looking like he had gone twelve rounds. The children continued to play with his hands, climb on his lap, tease him and scream when he made big mean faces. I went to Ali and leaned to his ear.

"Do you want to get going home, Champ? You have to be getting tired," I said.

"Leave?" he said, kids pulling at his hands. "I am in heaven. I am in heaven.

I stood for a long time watching all the children that just wanted to be near Muhammad. Very few had ever seen a heavyweight fight or understood anything about a heavyweight champion. Still, Muhammad generated electricity. He filled the room and everyone in it with warm affection.

A man who made himself the most famous boxer in history, with audacious braggadocio backed up with skill and ferocity, now able to settle into a big soft chair to simply wallow in the affection of young children in our small town. Ali was a powerful man.

Epitaph: DOWAGIAC BOXING CLUB

That glorious year, the Club flourished. At one point, it was the largest amateur boxing club in the country. The reason was simple, the only way we could insure the Club was to have each member sign up as a registered USA amateur boxer. All the young girls and boys had official USA amateur fight books to record their rounds, wins, and losses. But only a handful ever put on the gloves, and far fewer got into the ring. The Club was a place to belong, to hang out after school, and the t-shirts were cool.

When it came time to renew all those memberships, the Club collapsed. We just did not have the administrative smarts to keep it going. At that point, the City stepped in to form a Police Athletic League. In one form or another, the Club survived for over ten years.

CHAPTER THIRTY-TWO

VANITY FAIR

It was a busy morning at the Boxing Club. The coach was trying to give two young boxers a lesson on the speed bag when a new boy arrived with his mother ready to sign up. I watched Coach hurry from one task to the other and back again. Then the phone in his back pocket rang. It was apparent that we did not have enough staff to handle the sign-ups, boxers, and phone calls.

I took over the sign-up. The young mom told me her son talked about nothing but the boxing club. He was desperate to get his block-lettered Dowagiac Boxing Club t-shirt emblazoned with a pair of dangling boxing gloves.

Amid the paperwork, I got a call from Kim.

Vanity Fair proposed a photoshoot with Muhammad teaching young boxers the craft. They suggested that Kim find fighters in Chicago, from very young to high school. Staff photographers would come to Ali's farm to work with him and his students to build a photoshoot.

Rather than travel the distance from a club in Chicago, Kim asked if we could bring our boxers from Dowagiac. "Sure, I am certain we can make that happen," I told her.

As soon as she hung up, I called a couple buddies with boxer children. "Hey, would you like your daughter/son in a Vanity Fair photoshoot with Ali?"

It took a minute to absorb the reality of the opportunity coming at us, Vanity Fair, Ali, and our kids. Over the next few days, we put together a roster of ten boxers, six to sixteen years old, that we would take to the shoot.

Of course, Joe's son, my son, and two daughters were among them. We let Kim know we were all set. Vanity fair set the date of September 15, 2001, for the shoot.

The Fall day was clear with a bright sun but a cool breeze that made me hurry. I painted the doors on a new garage next to Ali's offices. They had finally decided to build a garage large enough for a modern car.

I still remember the paint stroke, one-third of the way up the lower left-hand side of the door frame, when I heard Kim calling me to the office. Her voice was sharp and anxious. "Larry, you need to see this."

I dropped my brush into the paint tray and hurried to the office. Kim sat on the edge of a desk; Howard Bingham sat in one of the overstuffed chairs.

On television, the North Tower of the World Trade Center sent a plume of smoke into the sky. "A plane hit the tower," Howard said. At that point, like the rest of America, we had no idea what was unfolding.

The tower had a big chunk knocked out about the 95th floor. The three of us sat in silence, listening to the newscast, trying to sort out the events. Within minutes the second plane appeared and crashed into the South Tower. It was clear this was not an accident.

There, in Ali's office, we watched the towers fall. The same blue sky over the towers softened the sweet morning on the farm. Muhammad and Lonnie were due home later in the week. But they were grounded along with the rest of the United States and the Vanity Fair photographers stuck on assignment in Toronto. A trivial loss in the face of national events, but there would be no photoshoot with Ali and our young boxers.

I had only met Howard in passing one time before. He was a hero to me as Ali's long-time photographer, known to be the only person in Ali's circle who, over the decades, had neither begged, borrowed, or stolen from Ali. Muhammad was generous to a fault. He had casually given away millions and lost track of his championship belts. None of it mattered much to Ali. It did matter to his good friend Howard not to be one of the many who took from Muhammad.

I emulated his resolve. I tried never to ask for anything but to visit Ali; it felt good to just be there.

CHAPTER THIRTY-THREE

BARN TALK

Great men bring comfort to others, even in simple encounters. Their ears hear while their eyes draw a person closer. The most straightforward give and take becomes a profound validation of oneself. Muhammad gave that gift endlessly. The talent does not grow out of celebrity but arises with genuine engagement. True greatness follows compassion, empathy, and a heart open to accepting and loving each person.

The more time I spent on the farm, the more I felt part of a family. Even though Ali's celebrity was global, the pace at the farm was leisurely. He traveled to palaces and villages. He performed his magic tricks for kings and kids on dusty streets. When Ali left the gates, he was The Greatest of All Time.

I only saw him when he returned to the farm to take a little time back from the world. There seemed an entire lifetime between the global treasure and the quiet, gentle man I knew on the farm.

One day a long-time friend from Ali's boxing days came by. I was introduced but quickly forgot his name. We were in the gym talking. The man showed me the Heavyweight Championship ring Ali had given him. The ring was heavy and gaudy, bigger than anything I could wear on my hand. He told me he wore it every day, always honored, grateful for his friend and the gift.

The man asked me, "How long have you known Ali?"

"Just a couple of years," I replied.

"Oh, you should have seen him in his prime. He was the most beautiful human being. Majestic. The way he could move. He was awesome and beautiful, I don't mind saying. There has never been anyone like him."

I would have been lost if I had met Ali then, unable to connect with the man, simply overwhelmed by the celebrity.

The following morning, I sat on an old concrete retaining wall alongside the big white barn just up the lane from the house and garage. I had our tools and three boxes of paint in gallon cans unloaded from the truck. We were set to paint the barn, and I waited for the delivery of a boom lift to get us up to the peaks.

The barn, built into the hill, was towering and challenging to access. Big double doors opened to the driveway. Inside, the barn was cavernous, the first floor tall with a loft above. The gable ends rose forty feet above the cut-away hill. Oversized sliding doors at the back of the lower level opened to the floodplain.

A long gentle hill ran from the barn down to the house. The ground was cut away from the shoulder of the driveway, and a retaining wall ran along the front of the barn, then tapered off down the hill.

I sat against the barn, closed my eyes, and felt the warm fall sun. The farm was almost silent but for the birds and the sounds of insects chirping in the bushes.

I may have fallen asleep, but I was startled to hear the creaking of Ali's bicycle creeping up the low incline at my feet. Ali on the old Huffy smiled in the sunshine. "Good Morning, Champ," I said. Ali was a gift before my eyes; I cherished every moment in his presence.

Ali stopped and stood straddling the bike; he hesitated momentarily to catch his breath. "Good Morning, praise Allah." He replied softly.

Ali climbed from the bike and pushed it to lean on the barn. "Looks nice." He said in a whisper, checking out my little spot in the sun. He put a hand against the barn and eased down to sit on the stack of boxes next to me. There were no selfies then, but we were posed there for my ultimate selfie. Ali and me sitting with our backs to the bright white barn. The sun warming the crisp morning air.

"This is beautiful, Muhammad," I said.

"Yes, yes...it is nice." He whispered, forming his words with his lips stiff and mouth barely moving.

We sat silently for a minute or so, "You can hear the birds." He said. "Blessings from Allah."

I think that is what he said; I did not hear clearly and did not want to ask Ali to repeat himself. I leaned hard into the wall and looked over at Ali. His long shins, his wide feet in clunky black leather shoes. I thought about how he ducked and danced.

"Muhammad, how did you find the courage to get in the ring with all those terrifying boxers who just wanted to knock you out?"

"I worked hard." He said, then paused. "I had to fight...It made me brave."

I looked at his hands. I thought his fingernails were oddly oblong. I contemplated the right hand that sent Liston to the mat in their second fight. I remember being confident Ali would take Liston down in the rematch, but not the first time. Before that fight, Ali could only trust his skills would stack up against the dangerous heavy-weight champ.

As we quietly sat, I hesitated to question Ali because it took so much effort for him to speak. His hands continuously trembled. His body bobbed back and forth as if leaning in to stand up, but he still sat.

We shared the silence, then he said, "I was going to work out, now I hear the birds." He chuckled---Ali embraced any excuse not to work out.

"How much more can you work out?" I asked. "You've spent your life working out."

"I worked hard, haaaaard." He replied.

"Do you miss it? Do you miss the lights?" I asked.

"No, no. This is a gift from Allah." He replied.

"It is a beautiful day," I said.

"Not the day; everything is Allah," Ali instructed.

Up the drive, the gates opened, and a big tractor-trailer rolled in with the boom lift.

"What's that?" Ali asked.

"It's a boom lift to get me up to paint the overhangs and peaks on the barn," I said.

"You're craaaazy," Muhammad chided.

While the truck chirped its "beep, beep, beep" backup warning, Muhammad climbed back onto the Huffy and pedaled a hundred yards to the gym. It seemed an odd choice: I could go hang with Muhammad in the gym or get to work painting the barn. It was only right that I get to work. I wonder what I missed.

PART EIGHT:

CHAPTER THIRTY-FOUR

SAINT LOUIS

In a week's time, Master Newhouse came to Isaiah. Speaking in low tones, he said:

"Isaiah, your head is full of dangerous ideas. You are of little value to me, laying around all day and night reading books. War is coming, and in time your thoughts will have you hung.

You hanging from a tree will bring me more grief than your daily tasks can account for. I am sending you west to Saint Louis."

Master Newhouse spoke with finality that signaled Isaiah dared not protest. Yet he knew nothing of Saint Louis or the conditions of his servitude or in what house he was to go. Silence filled the small room. There was something more. Master Newhouse, his hand shaking, handed Isaiah a thick envelope sealed with the wax stamp of the plantation.

"Isaiah, take this envelope and present it to anyone who causes you great difficulty, then to Professor William Greenleaf Elliot at the Benton School in Saint Louis. These are documents of manumission. The documents have been signed and witnessed by the county magistrate. When you get to Saint Louis, you will be a free man."

Isaiah did not understand. He heard the words, but he went hollow inside. In a whisper, he asked,

"How can I be a free man Master Newhouse? If I just walk away from here, they will put me in jail and sell me to who knows what plantation."

"The documents of manumission free you of your duty to me. They declare you are no longer chattel, no longer the property of this plantation. But you must leave now. Gather your things. There can be no word of your circumstance beyond this room. A wagon hired from the Laddle Plantation will take you to the train."

"Oh, Master Newhouse, I cannot go in the Laddle wagon. They will whip me regularly. I can go back to the field. I can do a day's task for you. Don't make me go." Isaiah pleaded aloud

Master Newhouse took Isaiah's forearm and said in a hushed voice,

"Isaiah, I am delivering you a free man to Saint Louis. The documents are in your hand. The municipality of Saint Louis recognizes manumission. Present the documents to Professor Elliot; he will see to the legalities. Nobody will suspect you will go to your freedom in a wagon from the Laddle plantation; there will be no speculating."

He handed Isaiah a rough burlap bag, twenty dollars, stage, and railroad tickets to Atlanta and west to Memphis.

"Go, Isaiah, leave now. Open the bag when you are alone at the river. Take the riverboat north to St Louis."

Master Newhouse reached for the doorknob; he paused as if there was something more to say, then briskly opened the door and walked off through the kitchen. He did not look back; he did not bid farewell.

Isaiah whirled. Tears filled his eyes as he put his few things in a seed bag and pulled the string tight. He stepped into the kitchen. The kitchen hands turned to Isaiah, their tears flowing,

"We are sorry, Mister Isaiah; we heard the master. You do

not deserve this wrong. You have been lazy, but you do not deserve the whip. There is a wagon from the Laddle plantation in the yard. Say our goodbyes; we will not hear of you from Laddle."

Isaiah hurried out, uncertain of his fate and unable to speak. He walked out into the morning sun and across the yard to the waiting wagon. He climbed up to sit alongside the driver dressed in field rags without a word. With a click of the whip, the wagon rolled along the fence line toward the lane leading away from the Newhouse plantation.

As the horses pulled the wagon up the long hill out of the lowlands, Isaiah mulled his fate. He would not survive on the Laddle Plantation. Did the master play a trick? Isaiah had never heard of a slave freed by his master.

Though trembling, he was resolute; he had to know his destiny; he might well jump and run to the woods if the wagon was headed to Laddle. He looked to the driver, summoned his courage, and asked,

"Do you know the road to the stage livery?"

"Why, yes, I do." The youthful driver responded. "At the main road, we turn easterly; our plantation is across the road a mile. The livery is six miles east down fine road. I go there every month with a wagon of rice. Master Laddle stores rice and keeps it dry. It doesn't rot. Master Laddle is mean as a snake, but he knows about rice."

At the main road, the driver turned east. Isaiah turned away to face the passing fields; tears filled his eyes and streamed down over his scarred cheek. For the first time in years, he closed his eyes and saw Mira smiling.

Isaiah feared every rider on horseback, every wagon that approached. He had the envelope from Master Newhouse, but he was still a slave.

The driver spoke, "When you are in the city, don't take drink from any of those men. Don't go friendly with them. Master Laddle told me I do not want to know your business, but nothin' you can be facing is as bad as those slavers who will steal you to the south. They load them stolen slaves on boats daily, going to work in New Orleans."

Isaiah sat hunched against the wooden bench, his arms folded between his knees, the rice sack and burlap bag between his feet. He pulled his hat down low and let his eyes close to the steady rhythm of the horses plodding along the smooth, hard road.

He thought of William and Benjamin and Missus Newhouse. He thought of Master Newhouse and felt for his fingers that were no longer there. He had no idea how long his journey would be, but he would stay to himself, careful, until he was in the hands of Professor Elliot.

The driver stopped the wagon in an open lot next to the livery, bustling with activity, "This is the end for me. I have to hurry on back to Laddle; that whip'll be itching to tear me up if I am late."

Isaiah picked up his bags and climbed down from the wagon. He made his way to a coach loaded with passengers under a sign reading: "Charleston." The driver showed Isaiah the ladder up the back of the stage, where he would ride with three other men, jostling over the sandy roads.

CHAPTER THIRTY-FIVE

SOJOURNER

At the end of the long carriage ride, the warm evening air smelled of coal and the sodden dirt of the corral where the horses milled. Isaiah laid back on the rice bag while the coach emptied and the luggage was hauled. He watched the crowd of passengers climb three steps into the train cars.

When he heard the conductor bark, "All aboard," he put his anxiety to the side and hustled to the foot of the platform.

Clutching the ticket, he climbed into the train car for the long journey west. He kept the two sacks over his shoulder and the envelope tight under his belt. With his eyes down, he crouched against the hard wooden seat, giving a wide berth to white people, fearing every man a slave trader.

The train chugged up the low mountains and through towns no more than a cluster of houses. Each day the increasingly unfamiliar landscape deepened his anxiety. Sitting alone, an ancient-looking woman with pear-shaped cheekbones drawn beneath her bright round eyes leaned in from the aisle and spoke directly to Isaiah,

"Mister. You all scrunched up there. Yo' mind if I take a seat here?"

Isaiah looked up, startled. Her motherly countenance washed over him, his anxiety lifted, and he smiled,

"Yes, Ma'am, yes, sit here," he said, his hand on the vacant seat next to him. The old woman sat.

She reached her knotted hand to greet Isaiah, "Thank you, a gentleman. I have said that I am a woman, and I deserve to sit in the best seat and be re'spected. I es'pect you too have felt the whip, and that influences your kindness."

"I have felt the whip," Isaiah replied, "but I don't think it has added to my kindness."

"I will tell you somethin'." She replied. "I was born Isabella in the year of 1787 or there' bouts. My father and mother, James and Betsy, were good people that won the favor of our master, Charles Ardinburgh. He gave them a spec of land that they farmed ev'nins and Sundays after they prayed. Their work and that land kept us fed and clothed."

Isaiah leaned into her warm rambling words learning of a life as sad and troubled as his own.

"But th'os days numbered but a few. We were mov'd to the new house, a cellar with no light but a couple small panes. Ev'ry body in there, men, women, little children. All sleepin' on those damp boards with a little straw, like horses. But horses have some space; we were all 'an top of one another."

"My mother, I called her Mau-Mau, bore ten or twelve children; most were gone b'fore I was born. My father, tall and straight as a young man, wore hisself out fretting over all those children, all of them sold off. My next older sister and brother, just five and seven years old, were taken off in a big ugly wagon when snow was freezing on the ground. They put her in the box at the foot of that wagon and closed it on her. My brother, jus' five, was held to by the driver. Mau-Mau and Papa clung ahold of each other, watchin' that wagon go.

Isaiah thought of his mother on her knees sobbing for Mira and in her heart asking Zane what happened to her children.

"When Master Adinburgh died suddenly, Mau-Mau cried more every day. She did not care that Master Adinburgh passed, though she was sorry. She knew it meant we would all be sold off. Our family would only be t'gether under the same stars and the moon. She told us God was there to hear our prayers and give comfort in the worst times of our troubled lives. Oh, she gave me a deep well of relief when trouble came."

"The family sold us all off. Separated me and all da' children. They all went a separate way, some to Alabama, a child to New York. And wid' father too old to work, they let Mau-Mau go to care for him. I heard Mau-Mau died suddenly, and I tried to get back to father in his grief and decrepitude."

Isaiah listened to the old woman go on for hours, sharing her story. Again and again, he thought of his mother and father, their grief, and he wondered if he could ever find them again.

"Father lived on blind and destitute." The old woman continued. "And the way this world works, he lived for some years alone in a tiny cabin set way back in the forest, out of sight of those who enslaved him. When another winter came, an old woman looked for shelter, and she found him alone and cold as the wind with a thin cover for protection that couldn't save him no more."

The old woman stopped for a moment. Isaiah felt her hand on his arm. She squeezed his forearm and said, "I see I've caused you sadness with my long story." She began again. "I have lived for so long and seen so much trouble, but now I am a free woman. I am speaking everywhere I can because other people are speaking too.

They throwed me off this train two days ago because I was speaking. I had to wait for this train to come by again to carry me the rest of the way to Memphis."

"I used to speak only when it happened that I was spoken to. I addressed all the men' yessir 'my master' and let on with the husbands they put to me. Now I don't wait for no invitation to speak. I show up and tell them what they need to hear. There is trouble coming for all those men that have men as their 'prop-per-tee.' And I don't mean physical. They are goin' to meet the Lord, and that day will not be a day for their joyousness.

Didn't the Lord make their skin white? And didn't the Lord make our skin black? How is there a difference? We are both children of the Lord. But they treat us worse than the horses they ride. Do you think the Lord will be pleased with them? Oh, they are coming to some trouble!"

The old woman brought comfort to Isaiah yet worried him so. He needed to think, to sort things out. He remembered her name,

"Your name is Isabella?" he asked.

"Now, that is another story," she replied. My master told my momma she'd name me Isabella when she bore me. Now that the spirit came to me, I had to travel forth, not strikin' out in that slave mentality but to teach the truth of the Lord to every person.

I am the traveler. I am Sojourner Truth."

PART NINE:

CHAPTER THIRTY-SIX

JESSE

Not every day at Ali's was filled with story and excitement. Much of the work was meticulous, and we took great pains not to stumble. We spent hours sanding and cleaning in preparation before finishing with coats of urethane and satin enamel paint. Often the projects were big, and our crew was generally just the two of us, Becky and me; Joe taught third grade most of the year. Some days I worked alone while Becky kept our other accounts happy.

The interior of the new offices was a big project. The building is four thousand square feet on one floor. The walls were painted a warm cream, the ceilings white, and the clear maple cabinets finished with satin urethane. The desks and tables were of the same maple as the built-in cabinetry. We finished the cabinetry on-site once the carpenters completed the installation.

We spent long days seeking perfection. We applied the skills we had developed over the years, but most of the work was simple physical labor.

One morning I had finished sanding a base coat of urethane on a large wall cabinet in Lonnie's new office. Before wiping down the cabinets, I vacuumed most of the dust with a large shop vacuum. It was mundane work, sucking up dust and then wiping every inch of the cabinets with a tack cloth. The entire process was repeated four or five times until the finish was solid and dust-free.

I was hunched down with the shop vacuum roaring when I

noticed people in the doorway. As I moved to shut off the vacuum, I heard Kim shout, "Hello."

Standing next to her, Jesse Ventura looked on. He was flanked by three uniformed police officers. It took me a second to get to the vacuum to stop its roar. Kim asked."Larry, do you see ho this is?"asked,

"Larry, do you see who this is?"

Well, of course I recognized Jesse Ventura. He had just been elected Governor of Minnesota. "Hello Jesse!" I offered.

It's weird how even a short distance across a room can make a moment awkward. Kim was giving a tour of the new offices, but Jesse was in a rush to get to the house to see Muhammad. Even though I walked directly to them, they moved on before I could cover twenty feet.

The entourage looked dignified and very official; the police officers wore their dress uniforms, and Kim and Jesse were stylish in business wear. They lingered for a moment in the vestibule of the main entry while I caught up and again said, "Hello." I had just an instant to shake Jesse's hand. I felt poorly placed in my painter whites.

In seconds, they left to see Muhammad. I went back to vacuuming, wishing I had been more collected and able to engage with Jesse.

At the time, Jesse Ventura was one of the great stories in American politics. Jesse was a national hero and a true badass. Today, Jesse's reputation is steeped in twenty years of controversy and sodden with conspiracy theories.

Still, he began his career as a Navy SEAL, a member of the Underwater Demolition Team deployed to Vietnam. Following his tour, he returned to Minnesota, rose through the ranks of the Mongols motorcycle gang, and spent time as a bouncer at a local dance club. That progression led to his storied career as a pro-wrestler, Jesse "The Body" Ventura.

Jesse won bouts across the country. His strong opinions and colorful elocution won him the handle, Jesse "The Mouth" Ventura. The moniker bit back when he lost three consecutive matches to Hulk Hogan and retired from pro wrestling. Still, Jesse was colorful and infectious.

In 1991, Ventura re-invented himself and tapped his notoriety to defeat the eighteen-year veteran Mayor of his hometown, Brooklyn Park, Minnesota. Following that success, Jesse ran for Governor of Minnesota in 1998 as the Reform party candidate.

As a wrestler, Jesse had learned how to get a crowd's attention---there were no contracts. To be successful, wrestlers had to fill arenas; to fill arenas, wrestlers had to stand out from the crowd; what Jesse used that skill to fill arenas as a politician too.

On January 4th, 1999, Jesse became the 38th Governor of Minnesota. Three days later, as one of his first acts as Governor, Jesse snuck off to Berrien Springs, Michigan, to meet his hero, Muhammad Ali.

In those first days, Jesse was only warming to the fact that he had won. He was the first and only Reform Party candidate to win a significant campaign. Few prognosticators thought he had any chance of winning the election, but he did.

When Jesse and the small entourage left the building, I did not feel much like vacuuming cabinets. The Boxing Club was going great guns, and I thought it would be good to get a picture and an autograph from Jesse to hang on the wall for the boxers.

I walked down the lane to Lonnie's office, still above the garage. She was working at her desk. I had an Ali picture I thought Jesse could sign in the unlikely event he did not have one of himself in his shirt pocket. I asked Lonnie if she could have Jesse sign a photo I could pick up later.

"Now, don't you be silly. You just walk right over to the house, and YOU ask Jesse to sign it. They are just hanging around." She scolded.

These moments were overwhelming: Ali, his celebrity, his world threw me off. But Lonnie laid the lumber; I could slink off to vacuum cabinets or march in to interrupt Jesse and Muhammad to ask for Jesse's autograph. Ouch.

I thanked Lonnie and went down that narrow stairway to the parking area. I felt a bit queasy crossing the parking area to the house. But I took a breath and opened the door. I looked in and said hello to one of the police officers, who rose quickly from the sofa when I entered.

It was an odd group. The officers sat close together on a small sofa. A State Police sergeant from Minnesota was dressed in his formal uniform, a dark brown jacket, and medium brown pants with a yellow stripe up the side. He sat with his broad, flat-brimmed hat in his lap, his lapel glistening with medals of recognition.

Next to him was a female State Police sergeant from Indiana. She, too, wore her formal uniform, dark blue, with a light blue tie and flat-brimmed hat.

The third officer, still standing, was a State Police sergeant from Michigan dressed in his formal deep blue attire. They were an intimidating trio but seemed strangely inconsequential in the company of Jesse and Muhammad.

Since Jesse was a Governor, each state was required to provide a police escort as he entered and traveled within that state. When Jesse left Minnesota, flew to Indiana, and drove to Michigan, he gained an escort in each state.

I took a couple of steps into the room and told the group I hoped Jesse could sign a picture for me. "Hey, no problem." Jesse offered.

Muhammad waved me over. Jesse sat on a kitchen chair between the sofa to his right, with the three officers, and Muhammad in his big comfortable chair to his left.

Muhammad tugged my arm; I leaned down, and he whispered, "Stay with me."

I remember the genuine sense of elation at that moment. "Stay with me." Played in my mind.

At this point, Parkinson's made it difficult for Muhammad to speak and make himself understood. I pulled a kitchen chair over and sat close to Ali to listen closely when he spoke.

There was a television with a VCR on a credenza beneath the stairs. Muhammad had just gotten a few new VHS tapes of his early fights. He shuffled across the room to put a video in the player. Jesse was clearly excited to be there with Ali. He sat on the edge of his chair. As Ali strode away, Jesse looked at me and said with pride,

"Meeting Muhammad is the first thing I've done as Governor."

I laughed at Jesse's larger-than-life "sing-songy" voice and "Yaah-suuure" intonation.

"Man, you sound just like Jesse Ventura," I remarked. His voice was unique, a thick Minnesota accent that boomed with excitement.

While Muhammad fiddled to get the tape queued up, Jesse told his story.

"When Muhammad beat Sonny Liston, I was the only one in our family to bet on Muhammad! My dad loved boxing. We watched matches together since I was a kid. Dad thought Ali

was all gas; a big tough guy like Liston would knock him out. I knew Muhammad would win. Then, when Muhammad beat Liston, which nobody thought he could do, Muhammad shouted, "We shocked the world!" And you did, Muhammad.

Do you guys know what Muhammad did when I won the Governor's race? He sent me boxing gloves he signed, "Shock the World." No one thought I would win either!

Muhammad, you are my hero. This is the greatest day of my life."

Jesse exuded awe. He seemed proud of the very fact Muhammad was his idol. He was pleased to express his admiration. His eyes welled with emotion. It was an epic moment, and there I was in my white pants smeared with paint and my speckled work shirt.

I saw the three officers sitting stiffly in their starched uniforms, their hats in their laps. I heard Jesse Ventura's voice booming, "it was the greatest day" in his storied life, and Muhammad Ali, the world's heavyweight champion, had just asked me to stay with him.

To this day, Jesse tells that same story with tears in his eyes. He was honored that Muhammad sent those boxing gloves. And, it was so like Jesse to slip away without telling his staff.

Jesse was still in a basement office while the previous Governor vacated the official second-floor facilities. Telling almost no one, Jesse ordered a plane and left to meet Muhammad. He was found out when a reporter following another story for the South Bend newspaper spotted him at the local airport. Still, Jesse did not reveal exactly where he was headed.

We settled into the afternoon, watching fights. Ventura roared with laughter when Sonny Banks caught Ali off guard with a crushing left, square to the face. The punch clearly dropped Ali for an instant.

Ali leaned into Ventura and said, "Slipped."

Jesse roared. Even when the punch was so obvious, Ali would not admit he got decked. Ali danced with his hands at his sides in a later video, seemingly a wide-open target.

I teased Ali, "Right there, Muhammad, if you had learned to keep your hands up...."

Ali glared at me with a mock stink eye as if his next move would teach me a lesson. He leaned in to stand, scowling. Across the room, all three of the police officers drew a breath, tense with apprehension. Ali settled back and smiled side-eyed. He never missed a queue.

We watched Ali's matches and listened to Jesse's commentary for a couple of hours. He explained Ali had a name for each of his opponents. Sonny Liston was the Bear, Joe Frazier the Gorilla, George Foreman the Mummy, and George Chuvalo the Washerwoman.

The names were a way for Ali to get the fighters off their game, angry or insulted. Either way, they entered the ring looking to do damage rather than strategically win the fight.

I sat in the kitchen chair tight to Muhammad. I leaned in over the arm of his chair to listen as he spoke. Jesse, too, moved in closer; finally, he sat on the arm of Ali's big overstuffed chair. I said something directly to Ventura; he responded to me, then he leaned back to talk to the police officers sitting on the couch.

For a moment, Ali was not the center of attention. I heard him begin to snore, and his fists clenched. Jesse looked at Muhammad, bewildered. What do you do when your host falls fast asleep with guests all around?

I told Jesse, "Man, I have seen this before. This is the

Parkinson's. He just falls asleep, just like that." I clicked my fingers.

"Sometimes, he starts swinging like he is in one of his fights. Must be all these movies have his head back in the ring." I continued.

And right on queue, Ali mumbled under his breath, then threw a couple of slow-motion punches.

"Oh, he is swinging!" Jesse exclaimed. He put his hand on the arm of Ali's chair, leaning in to stand. Ali tossed off a punch that sent Jesse stumbling backward to avoid a thumping. Ali opened his eyes a crack and grinned.

"Jesse, you are as dumb as you look!" he chuckled. Everyone hooted with laughter.

For one of the few times in his life, Jesse Ventura was speechless. He still backed away, laughing hard. Ali got him good.

Jesse walked past us to sit at the island in the kitchen. I touched Ali's arm and stood to visit with Jesse. Muhammad folded his hands and leaned back in his chair for a quiet minute.

"Congratulations, Governor." I offered.

"Thank you, I am so privileged to finally meet the champ. Do you get to see him often?" Jesse asked.

"I do; I am on the farm several days a week. We are re-doing each building, and they built the gym and now the new offices."

"He has earned every bit of it," Jesse commented. "I have learned so much from him. He taught me how to fill stadiums."

"How do you do that? I mean, I hear about you in the national press all the time. Do you plan out a strategy? How do you come up with that stuff?" I asked.

"Well, it's pretty easy," he replied, "like when I go to Dallas. I get an interview with a sportswriter a few days before the event and trash their manhood. Like I tell them, Dallas is nothing; they're just a bunch of miserable goat ropers."

"Oh jeez, that must get some attention."

"Yaaaah, when I walk into the arena, they are on their feet booing. Everyone wants the guy to kill me. Muhammad did the same thing, but he ended up with everyone loving him. I don't think a man has ever been more courageous."

"It is amazing to be here with him," I said.

"Yaaaah," Jesse replied, and he went back to sit on the arm of Muhammad's chair. The officer from Minnesota stood and stretched a bit. He walked over to say hello.

"Well, this is quite a day," I said.

"It will be a unique four years." He replied. "We got the call about ten minutes before the Governor had the plane scheduled to fly. He didn't tell anyone."

"It's great he is here. I can't believe he sounds just like he does on television. That big voice and Minnesota accent. Do you get these details often?" I asked

"Yes, I am one of the escorting officers. One of us accompanies the Governor and his family anytime they leave the capitol grounds. It can make for an interesting day. This is certainly one of them." He said.

Then I went to visit with the other two officers. We chatted about the farm and my good fortune to work for Ali. Since Ali's big joke on Jesse, the room relaxed. It felt like we were all part of the same thing. Indeed, everyone was in awe of

Muhammad, and he was enjoying the company---at least, that is how he made us feel.

CHAPTER THIRTY-SEVEN

NEVILLE

In 2001 the Dowagiac Fine Arts Festival hosted the Charles Neville Quartet as part of its Dogwood Fine Arts Festival. The Quartet performed in the auditorium one evening and had a performance scheduled at the high school as part of the festival outreach. I asked Kim if Muhammad might like to visit the school to listen to the Quartet perform with the high school jazz band. Kim knew Muhammad already had a busy schedule that day, but she would let me know if he could make a date.

Sadly, a young man in high school was losing his mother to cancer. Her situation was grave. She was so very ill and desperately concerned about the son she was leaving behind. One of the school's office staff knew the family and also knew Kim. Together they quietly made arrangements to ask Ali if he might visit her.

On the day of the Neville event at the high school, Muhammad asked Kim to reschedule his morning obligations, so he could meet the young man's mother at their home. With Ali's school visit tentative, I went to work in my painter whites but took dress clothes just in case. Kim said she would let me know if Muhammad's schedule opened up. I had no idea they were going to visit the ill mom.

Kim drove Muhammad to the house. The woman was indeed gravely ill, barely able to speak. She took great relief just to visit with Muhammad. He laid his hand on hers, and they prayed together. She said she was so worried about her son and his education that she would not be there for him.

Muhammad told her to be at peace; he would see to it her son went to college. It may have been Ali's reassurance, and though it had been a very long battle, the mom was finally able to let go. She passed away just two days later.

She was frail, so the morning meeting was brief. There was plenty of time to visit the high school, so Kim called to ask that I meet them. I was working twenty miles from the school and was already late. I drove too fast and changed into my dress clothes while doing so. When I arrived, I ran to Kim and Muhammad, who were already walking to the entry.

Charles Neville set up his Quartet in the center of a large music room. Students circled around on folding chairs, their feet tapping to Neville's saxophone slinging "Summertime" in his distinctive New Orleans funk.

We were late to the party, so we slipped in and sat on folding chairs behind the students. The music was enthralling; no one noticed Ali. The Quartet rotated high school musicians in and out of their ensemble. As the music flowed, a musician nodded to a student standing at the ready. Then the drummer stopped to let a student pick up the beat. The young percussionist played with such exuberance that Neville's drummer sat on the floor to brace the drum kit. The audience was on their feet.

Ali was clearly enjoying the time as one person after another finally noticed he was there, sitting quietly in the back. The Quartet rocked, and students clapped as the room filled with whispers about Ali. When the song ended, Charles Neville, too, noticed Ali. His jaw dropped.

"My goodness, people, Muhammad Ali is in the house!" he announced.

Muhammad stood and nodded humbly, then sat back on the

folding chair, and we listened to the rest of the hour-long performance. When the music was over, Muhammad signed autographs for everyone in the room.

CHAPTER THIRTY-EIGHT

BUKK TEEF

li loved to clown, tell jokes, and perform magic tricks.
The best part of each trick was the wide-eyed
expression that followed each scheme. No one was
more amazed at the deception than Ali.

Ali routinely honored requests that he redo a trick---
anathema to most magicians. Muhammad believed the
Quran forbade deceit, so he willingly repeated tricks over and
over, even to flat-out show how he did them. He revealed the
quarter stuck between two fingers, the silk scarf tucked up
his sleeve or in his thumb, and roared with laughter when he
pulled the white rubber thumb from over his brown skin.

For those of us around the office, the simple tricks were
ofttimes repeated. Ali performed them for each new guest
and sometimes just because he loved to do them. His manner
and feigned concentration to complete the "magic" made the
moment a delight. Even though I had seen the scarf disappear
a dozen times, Ali performed it like he had spent the previous
night working on a mysterious experiment in the dark arts.

One year, for Ali's birthday, the paint crew presented
Muhammad with a set of Dr. Bukk Teef. These were pretty
sophisticated gag dentures marketed with names like "Final
Four" and "Cow Catcher." We got Muhammad "Leon's Grill."
Big white teeth, a couple in the front blacked out, with an
oversized gold tooth replacement. Muhammad immediately
put them in his mouth and took on the role.

Ali set off explosions of laughter as he walked from office to office, showing off his new look. His upper lip bulged with the gold caps stuck in over his own teeth. When he tried to talk, everything he said was a mumble.

He walked into the main office to greet the staff struggling to close his lips over the dentures; then, with all the seriousness he could muster, he asked a question, gesturing and turning his head inquisitively.

Ali went to everyone on the farm for approval of his new look. The paint crew trailed him, holding our faces because we hurt so much from laughing. And Ali would not stop.

The office staff was in an uproar, everyone but Lonnie. We talked about Ali showing up at events, the White House, a Cubs game, or a speaking engagement while playing up Leon's Grill as his natural teeth. Who would have the nerve to say something?

"Aaaah, Muhammad, have you had dental work done lately?" Ali would play it to the limit.

Then Muhammad laughed so hard the teeth fell out. He leaned against the wall laughing out loud. I saw him smile many times; this was the only time I saw him completely break down laughing.

Lonnie let us know those teeth would never be seen outside the front gates; in fact, after that day, we never saw them again inside the gates either. Lonnie knew Muhammad, given a chance, would have worn them to meet the Queen.

Alas, the opportunities gone by.

CHAPTER THIRTY-NINE

BIRTHDAY PARTY

Marie searched the faces around her for hints of a joke. In front of her was a table set for ten, a platter stacked with sandwiches, and a huge green salad heaped atop a fan-shaped bowl. Marie was one of the staff, and today was her birthday.

We all gathered in Muhammad's office then Lonnie led Marie to the celebration. Marie smiled with thanks and humility. Each of us had our role, and it was sweet to celebrate Marie. We were just a circle of workers, along with the greatest heavyweight champion of all time.

The conversation began with niceties, but by the time we finished eating, there was chatter up and down the table. Lonnie was at one end, talking and laughing aloud with Marie. Kim sat next to Muhammad, conversing with a young man at her side. I sat across from Muhammad. I noticed him look to his left and then to his right; no one was paying attention to him.

Muhammad pounded both fists hard on the table, leaned back and roared, "I am theeeeeee Greatest!!!"

The group fell silent. Ali grinned.

Lonnie said, "Right there, Muhammad, that is what the doctors are telling you. Speak from your throat, not the tip of your tongue."

From deep in his throat, Muhammad repeated, "I am the Greatest!" His eyes widened as he rose tall in his chair.

Lonnie said, "Would someone please pay attention to Muhammad." And she quietly continued her conversation with Marie.

Ali looked over at me and showed a devilish little grin. His whole face smiled. He loved the attention, and he loved to tweak Lonnie.

As the party continued, the conversations grew noisier as everyone unconsciously spoke louder to be heard over an ever-increasing thump, thump, thump. Muhammad was making one of his signature "Rumble in the Jungle" drawings on the inside flap of a hardcover book.

Muhammad had been working on the drawing for twenty minutes or so. He was finishing up a descending circle of fans around a roped boxing ring with the two ill-proportioned boxers in the center, one drawn tall and thick, the other drawn with fat squat lines. Ali would point to the squat little character and whisper, "Foreman."

Ali continued to thump, thump, thump, pounding the marker on the book cover.

"Muhammad, can you stop that right now?" Lonnie asked, "And look what you have done to that book. Your greasy fingerprints have ruined it!"

Indeed, Muhammad had worked on the book through lunch, and traces of mayonnaise stained the hard fabric cover. Muhammad sheepishly gestured an "Oh well," that gently blended into a big-eyed look of "I am the Greatest," and he smiled. He closed the book and pushed it across the table to me.

"Thank you, Muhammad; I will treasure this," I said.

Muhammad leaned back and smiled wide. He looked around the table and glowed in the good company of his extended family. It was a happy day.

CHAPTER FORTY

WOODFIRE

Over the years I worked on the farm, we watched the progression of Parkinson's take away Muhammad's facial expression, diminish his speech and add visibly to the tremors in his hands. Lonnie led the defense with guidance from Muhammad's doctors.

She knew exercise would help Muhammad, so she had the gym built. But Muhammad was a bad patient. He had no interest in working out. Lonnie tried to modify his diet to help combat the disease. But Muhammad still found ways to enjoy his hamburgers and milkshakes.

Finally, Lonnie hired Mike, a well-established chef. Mike was to prepare gourmet foods with the most beneficial ingredients possible. He often broiled fish or chicken on an outdoor grill and packed meals with balanced nutrition. The idea was to serve Muhammad good foods he would love to eat.

I first met Mike at the outdoor grill station at the back of the house; the sweet smell of dry-rubbed chicken filled the air. Smoke rolled from the heavy iron grating as Mike tended the cutlets with a long-handled fork. I parked across the lot and walked over to say hello.

"Man, that smells great! Cooking an early lunch?" I asked. It was about 10 am.

"No," Mike replied, "I am grilling the chicken with a savory rub, letting it chill, then working it into an avocado salad for lunch at twelve-thirty."

"Sweet, I want to be there!" I prodded.

"Yeah, we have a full week of gourmet planned for Muhammad." He offered.

"I hope it helps; I know Lonnie has fits trying to get Muhammad to eat right. Is this your full- time job now?" I asked.

"For now, yes. I am in-between restaurants. My partner and I are working on a concept to develop when we find a building."

As a Dowagiac Downtown Development Authority member, I was ever vigilant for retail opportunities. A restaurant would be a great addition.

"You should see the building we are painting for the City of Dowagiac," I told him. "It had been in a state of collapse, so the City took it over. They have done a vanilla box treatment to the interior, but the outside is gorgeous."

The roof had partially fallen in on a long-neglected building right in the heart of town. The building was constructed in 1865, historical, like all buildings in the central business district.

"I heard Dowagiac is a pretty little town; maybe it could work," Mike replied.

Over the next couple of weeks, Mike and I chatted when we met up on the farm. He had a lot of energy. His upbeat attitude and skills in the kitchen won over Muhammad, who looked forward to a grilled lunch more and more often. He even liked Mike's marinated zucchini.

We did not have a big project underway for Ali, so I worked almost full-time trimming the exterior of the building in Dowagiac. The City had rebuilt the cornice that hung from the second-story roof, the six arched windows stretching across the second floor, and the lower storefronts, all restored according to photographs taken in the 1920s.

The building had separate entryways, one for each twenty-foot-wide facade. I was painting the eight-foot doors into the south entry when Mike jumped from his car and shouted, "Wow, this is awesome."

He loved the charm of the Victorian-era buildings. Our crew had restored most every building in town; this City-owned building was the icing on the cake.

"We have to put a restaurant in here." Mike declared.

Late that afternoon, Mike brought Kevin, his business partner, to meet the City Manager and me to tour the building.

The four of us walked through the space, planning how we could knock out walls to make the two buildings one large restaurant. I took a broom handle to poke out a couple tiles in the drop ceiling to show off the old pressed tin panels hidden above.

"There are a lot of holes in the tin, and some sections are missing, but we can restore the ceiling." I explained, "It's not difficult to fill the small holes and order replacement panels where the areas are destroyed."

We were seduced by the concept of a modern, high-end restaurant nestled in the romance of brick and mahogany interior. An old wooden elevator still hung from the ceiling at the rear of the long room.

The City embraced the idea. They offered the buildings for meager rent and gave us license to do what we wanted to build out the restaurant. I agreed to manage the restoration while Mike and his partner organized the restaurant operation. Soon, we were underway.

I took my twelve-year-old son and the paint crew in to tear out the drop ceilings and false sheetrock walls that the City had just installed. Large sections of plaster had fallen from the old brick walls. We pounded the remaining plaster from the brick, scrubbed away the remaining debris then sprayed on a few coats of urethane.

We re-cast broken sections of the two-foot tall decorative cornice that topped the inner walls and ordered new tin panels to replace about one-third of the ceiling.

Then we dismantled twenty-five feet of the brick center wall to open the kitchen to the main dining area. In the front section of the building, we took out ten feet of the center wall to create an arched doorway for a semi-private dining room. Our carpenter built a bar and booths along the walls in the back half of the one-hundred-foot-long room.

Meanwhile, the plans for the kitchen and menu took shape. Mike was excited about the project; his energy re-fueled my enthusiasm daily. Then, one Tuesday morning, I got a call. Mike had quit his job at Ali's and would move to a town on northern Lake Michigan. He did not want to work at the restaurant in Dowagiac after all.

I was numb. The City's renovations were destroyed. We had demolished one restroom and roughed in two others. We had cut out the entire entryway in the south building and punched big holes in the center wall. The electric service was joined; the two buildings were now one. There was no going back.

I saw no option but to continue alone. I did not bother to ask why they lost interest and soon forgot about Mike and his partner; there was too much to do.

We had a brilliant carpenter for the project, Olin, a friend I met working for the Kitty Litter guy years before. Olin was an old-school craftsman who showed up each day with a skill saw, a hammer, and a square. He was a woodworking genius.

From the arched doorway to the side dining room to the maple and mahogany dining tables, Olin knew how to lay out the project, and his ego was solid enough to let me and the crew do the repetitive work. The physical side of the project progressed quickly.

Founding a restaurant seems so romantic, at least to a dreamer like me. I knew we wanted a wood-fired oven from the very start. We found a source to import the stone oven itself from Italy. It came in thirteen pieces packed in a crate that the shipper simply dropped off on the sidewalk out front.

We lugged the heavy stones inside and hired two local masons, brothers, to build the oven. They began with a footing in the basement, then laid block up to a concrete and sand platform on the main floor upon which sat the oven.

The top of the stone burn chamber was encased in firestop mortar two feet thick. We had the masons design the face of the oven reminiscent of the arched brick over the second-story windows out front.

The coming restaurant was big news in the small town. Naysayers challenged, "There is no place to park. There is no parking lot and no space on Front Street; the City lots are too far away." they repeated. Finally, frustrated, I announced, "We will have valet parking."

The rumor did not take long to spread through town and in the newspaper. Soon the entire county was abuzz, 'the new restaurant in Dowagiac is so fancy they will have valet parking,' the first such service ever in our rural county. We never intended to have valet parking, but the publicity was incredible. The project steamrolled.

Some weeks later, we opened the WoodFire with an abbreviated menu, two pizzas, and spaghetti with marinara. Even with few offerings, the rush of guests was overwhelming. The kitchen staff calls it "being in the weeds." Times they are so busy they can't look up; it's like running in tall weeds. Then, the rush suddenly passes, but no one can say precisely when. We had those nights that first week and every weekend that followed.

The business was as breathtaking as the bills. It seemed like we were making money, but there were big expenses, payroll taxes, credit card processing fees, wages, food, and even royalty fees for playing music in a commercial setting. A friend called managing it "drinking from a fire hose."

Every day there were new issues. The demands on my time finally made me quit the paint business altogether. I continued to care for our work at Ali's, but even that commitment suffered. Restaurants are a lot of work. A fellow owner had a sign over his desk that read: It Never Stops.

The WoodFire opened in 2003. These were heady times in Dowagiac. The downtown enjoyed a renaissance not seen in one hundred years. The main street and underground infrastructure were completely rebuilt. Most every building in the central business district had been restored to approximate its appearance when built in the mid-1800s.

Dowagiac's crown jewel in those years was the Dogwood Fine Arts Festival. Two weeks in May, when the town hosted visual and literary artists from around the world. The authors' series brought us Gwendolyn Brooks, Kurt Vonnegut, John Updike (who came to "see the small town that had the audacity to invite him"), Joyce Carol Oates, and many, many more. Each of these brilliant authors came for a reception at the WoodFire.

Meantime, we began hosting music on Friday and Sunday nights. It quickly became difficult to accommodate even the most talented players. The core of the music was the great American songbook, deeply romantic. A few times each year, we hosted special performances with Leon Redbone, Dan Hicks and the Hot Licks, and stride pianist Paul Asaro.

A friend always wanted to open an art studio, so we lent him the walls in the dining rooms to display regional artists. The WoodFire became an ever-changing expression of American art and music, and the food was phenomenal. More than half of the meals we served were cooked in our applewood-burning oven. We were a destination for diners an hour's drive away.

CHAPTER FORTY-ONE

ALI AT DINNER

While I could not work at the farm, I stayed in touch with Lonnie and stopped to see Muhammad whenever I could. Several times Lonnie and Muhammad came to dinner at the WoodFire.

One bustling night, Muhammad came to the door with a party of eight. Lonnie was there along with guests I did not recognize. I hurriedly asked the staff to prepare a table while we stood talking at the entry. A second group of diners came in right behind Ali's. They were stunned to see Muhammad waiting there too.

I sat Ali's party and returned to the host station. The second group peppered me with questions. "Will Muhammad sign autographs?" "Does he come here often?" "Is that his wife with him?" I joked that Muhammad would not only be receptive to autographs, but he would probably come to their table for dinner. I sat the group at their reserved table happily adjacent to the Ali's and went to be sure the kitchen staff had everything under control.

In five minutes, I was back in the dining room. Muhammad had indeed moved his chair over to the second table. Everyone was either on their cell phone telling friends they were at dinner with Muhammad Ali or taking pictures of him. Muhammad loved it.

I went to Lonnie to apologize for the disruption. "Oh, that's

Muhammad." Lonnie opined. "He is not happy if he is not the center of attention making jokes and doing magic tricks for people." Lonnie had such a nonchalance for Muhammad. The contrast between her matter-of-fact perspective and the awe from everyone else was amusing.

While Muhammad was in the restaurant, I kept an eye on the sidewalk outside. There had never been any trouble, but I felt the need to be vigilant. Passersby might see Muhammad and stop to look for a minute, then move on or they would linger and call on their phone to announce the news.

When Muhammad finished dinner, I noticed an entranced group of teenage boys and girls collected on the sidewalk. I went out to invite them in.

"Hey, come on in. Would you like to meet Muhammad?" I asked.

The boys in the group kind of shuffled away, "Nah, Nah, we are good." One of them said. One of the girls stepped right up to me, "I would love to meet Muhammad!" she bubbled.

With a broad swing of my arm, I ushered them in. The four girls walked past me and through the open door. The boys held back, fumbling back and forth, unsure.

Muhammad was sitting in the middle of the side room off the entry. He saw the group of girls all giddy and staring at him. When Muhammad stood, the girls walked a few steps toward him.
With cheerful eyes and a tight smile, Muhammad walked over. In typical fashion, he asked their names and shared hugs all around.

To this point, the boys were still only halfway through the door. I asked them again to come in. With hesitation, they stepped just inside. From the dining room, Muhammad looked over at them. They froze.

"Hey." Muhammad gestured to them.

The boys did not move; they stood just inside the open door. Muhammad stepped toward them. As a group, they took a step back from his approach. Muhammad kept walking toward them, and they matched his steps backward. Within a few paces, they were against the side wall of the dining room. Muhammad stepped to them.

The boys stood, oddly frozen, gazing in disbelief at Muhammad. He made his mean face and feigned a couple punches at the cowering group. Then he laughed and took the shoulders of the young man closest to him. He gave him a hug. The boys smiled in unison; now they were loose, bobbing around, hanging with Ali.

The entire restaurant buzzed with excitement as Muhammad left the teens to walk amongst the tables stopping at each to say hello. We had an empty table near the front of the room. I asked the teens to sit down; we had pizza coming. Again, the girls spoke up,

"Are you sure? We don't have money." They warned.

"Hey, it's just pizza; sit down and enjoy," We practically had to push the boys to their seats. They were so far out of their comfort zone; the night was pure joy.

Ali sat with tables throughout the dining room. He did magic tricks, and he levitated for the delighted crowd. The oven chef whipped up a few pizzas for our young guests, and three minutes later, a server delivered sodas and pizzas to the awestruck group.

Dean Martin sang, "Ain't that a kick in the head," while I stopped to look over the room and thought, "How di this happen?"

In time the night slowed down. Muhammad came to me

at the bar to ask for one of our linen napkins. Neither he nor Lonnie drank (Lonnie said she had never even tasted alcohol). Muhammad sat at the bar, resting his elbows on the varnished mahogany top. I presented him with a brilliant white napkin, starched and pressed. He carefully spread it open on the bar and smoothed it with his hands.

"Do you have a marker?" he asked.

I went to the wait station and found a black and green felt marker. I took them to Muhammad. For the next half-hour, Muhammad drew the Rumble in the Jungle. The picture comprises a small ring in the center of the scene with one thick, powerful-looking boxer and another twiggy- looking figure. Around the ropes are hundreds of dots in rows descending to the edge of the ring. Naming the obvious, Muhammad wrote in tiny letters "Frazier" next to the scrawny boxer.

Muhammad sat in deep concentration, tap-tap-tapping all those people in the crowd, some black, some green, all witnessing the Rumble in the Jungle.

At the bottom of the napkin, he drew a big heart and filled it in with black and green. Next, he wrote "To Larry" and signed Muhammad Ali. Then he smiled and pushed the napkin across the bar to me. Pure kindness, I don't know what other words to say.

I tried hard not to take advantage of Muhammad; it was enough to be there with him, to spend time in his presence. But Ali gave and gave. He made every encounter seem like it was his good fortune.

The following day, I saw black and green dots all over the corner of the bar where Muhammad sat. The markers bled through the linen to stain the bar top. Perfect. I hoped they would never fade.

CHAPTER FORTY-TWO

ALI AND ME

I settled into opening the restaurant seven days a week, moping floors, balancing books, and running just ahead of the freight train packed with everyday issues. I worked as a host in the evenings, welcoming guests and maneuvering the odd celebrity role. My kids laughed, "Dad, you are famous in Dowagiac."

One morning, somewhere between stocking Stella Artois and Clausthaler, my sister, one of 588 dentists in Ann Arbor, phoned from her dental office.

"Hey Lar, one of my patients has house guests staying with her between side trips to photograph boxing clubs for a book project. They are here from Portland, Oregon. I told them they should call you."

"You have a patient writing a book about boxing clubs?"

"No, my patient has a houseguest writing a book." she replied.

"From Portland? They just happen to be visiting from Portland? And your patient happens to mention them and their work?" I ask incredulously.

"Well, you know I love to pry!" she admitted.

"Anyway, they are probably going to the Kronk gym in Detroit and some in Chicago; I don't think Dowagiac fits the profile," I said.

"Well, they are going to call later when they are on the road. I told them you would be happy to show off the club and that you know Muhammad," She responded.

Turns out Jim and Cindy Lommasson were on a photographic journey for a book, Shadow Boxers: Sweat, Sacrifice and the Will to Survive in American Boxing Gyms."

They traveled the country photographing famous gyms and hole-in-the-wall gyms and interviewing the people who inhabit them.

The next day, Cindy phoned from the car as they made their way to their first destination in heavy downtown Detroit traffic.

"So, my friend Andrea called me yesterday all excited even though she was sitting in a dentist's chair! That was weird, but she said you have a boxing club, though you have never boxed, and that you know Muhammad Ali," she said.

"Yup, we have a club. It usually looks more like a daycare than a gym, but..." I began.

"Maybe we can visit the club on our return trip from Chicago in the next day or so. Any chance we could also meet Ali?" Cindy ventured.

"Well, the club is not a big-time boxing center, but it would be fun to show it off. I can call to see if Muhammad is around; I have not seen him in a few weeks. When are you available?"

Cindy held the phone against her leg and turned to Jim. With a roll of her eyes, she dashed his hope of meeting Ali this time around. Muffling the phone, she whispered, "Sure, he knows Ali but hasn't seen him in a few weeks," and laughed. "Yeah, uh-huh....and he is good friends."

Later Jim told me that in almost every club, some old gym rat would offer that if he ever wanted to meet Ali, just let them know. Jim always replied clearly, "I'm letting you know now that I very much want to meet the champ."

Then there would be a little snag, and after fumbling around in their wallet or shirt pocket, they wouldn't be able to find Ali's phone number. Well, that happened so many times that it became a running joke.

I turned the conversation away from Ali. Cindy and I chatted on about the book they were writing, my paintwork for Ali, and the restaurant that grew from meeting Ali's chef. Then the call dropped.

Cindy summarized our conversation by telling Jim, ' this guy had just opened a restaurant and was no longer working for Ali and had not seen him in weeks.' Like so many others, this serendipitous hook-up didn't look like the ticket to meeting "the greatest of all time" either. And the small-town boxing club certainly did not fit the profile of a legendary boxing club; still, the next day, Jim made the obligatory call.

Riding along on I-94 from Detroit heading to Chicago, he called to talk about the boxing gym in the unlikely event he'd want to schedule a side trip to Dowagiac on the return from Chicago. The discussion went well, so Jim ventured to add, "So my wife told me you know Muhammad Ali."

I answered, "Yes, I'm honored to say we are good friends."

Jim smiled silently and nodded, "Yeah, sure." to Cindy, skepticism was an understatement.

He pressed on, "So, do you think we could meet him?"

"Sure, I'll call the farm to see if he is in town," I replied, "what day would work for you?"

Now Jim is thinking, "no problem," right, it's that easy to meet the most famous person on the planet, and this housepainter come restauranteur, who's never heard of us, is going to help us do just that. Right. No problem!

Mid-afternoon and still working through a list of chores, it was easy to leave a beer cooler half-filled, so when the call ended, I walked to the dining room, sat in a comfortable chair, and called Muhammad's office. Thoughts of Ali and the Farm were a pleasant distraction.

"Hello Kim, it's..." I began when Kim interrupted.

"Hello Larry, it's nice to hear your voice; how are you?" Kim asked with typical cheer. I told Kim about the serendipitous acquaintance and book project. She said, "Of course, Muhammad would love a visit, but call Monday morning to be sure he is home and feeling up to a meeting."

Jim told me later, "We had pretty much put the possibility of meeting Ali out of our minds (or we would have gone out of our minds). We had to be realistic and didn't feel like getting our hopes up. Muhammad Ali's struggle with his health and the ravages of Parkinson's disease were well-known. Too many things could go wrong. So, we concentrated on our work in Chicago.

There are boxing clubs for youth tucked behind steel doors on the mean streets of cities across the United States. Those two inch-thick doors separate a place of discipline and self-esteem from the violence of a broken society.

Young men and women find solace and inspiration in the safety of boxing clubs. Training brings order to their lives, though few intend to enter the ring for actual combat. Jim told me he often needed help from the locals to escort him to and from the clubs for security, but inside there were strict rules of behavior. "No cussing and No spitting" signs were not merely wall decoration.

For Jim and Cindy, the Chicago club turned out to be a major force in boxing, even though the glory days of the sport were long gone. Like gyms in Detroit and Philadelphia, the club was an excellent photo opportunity; their book was coming together.

Before leaving Chicago and scheduled to fly from Detroit to Portland in the morning, Jim and Andrea discussed the apparent opportunity. Jim told me. "The story was so unlikely, but the opportunity so exciting, we decided to postpone our Monday morning flight home until Tuesday night."

Monday morning was a slog at the restaurant. We were jammed all weekend, and I needed a break. The morning came too early, and mopping restroom floors only added to the drudgery. Luckily, I had an excuse to call the Farm, and Kim was excited to tell me Muhammad was home, and we could stop out any time after 12:30. I called to share the news with Jim and Cindy.

The moment was unreal. In disbelief, they turned from I-94 for the thirty-minute side trip to Dowagiac. Cindy later told me their real-world enchantment began when they arrived in Dowagiac. The historic building restorations and renovated streetscape created an aura of comfort. The feeling grew as they peered into the wood-fired oven just inside the WoodFire while the staff hunted me down.

I cannot deny my warm sense of accomplishment, showing off the antique brick walls and hand-turned balusters around a second-floor balcony. Ultra-modern appointments counter-posed the antique building. For most guests, the beauty of the space was wholly unexpected. We enjoyed a quick lunch and then left for the Farm. As we crossed the river heading into Berrien Springs, I pointed out the tree-lined bank downstream where the Farm began.

"Ali's property begins just past that bend," I said.

Jim considered the Saint Joseph river; the current sent whirlpools spinning off the bridge pilings, disappearing into the swelling flow. He turned back to me, looking a bit startled, "We really are going to Ali's, aren't we?" he mulled, turning again to look at the passing hillside.

"Yeah, it's just another mile or so," I assured him.

It had been too long since I had seen Muhammad, so I, too, was excited to visit, and Jim and Cindy were so agog I could hardly wait for the introductions. We turned onto Kephart Lane, approached the gates, and stopped at the keypad. I punched in my code. The gates rolled open. I thought I heard Jim mutter something like, "No way."

I parked alongside the G.O.A.T. sign announcing the Ali offices, and we stepped into the warm autumn sunshine. The concrete pad gave way to a bricked walkway and manicured gardens. Inside, soft cream-colored walls in the foyer backdropped the hard maple trim and cabinetry. Subtle and warm, the room exuded a welcoming glow.

Kim hurried to the entry when she heard us arrive. Her energetic smile melted our anxieties. While arranging a visit seemed wonderful, I worried this time, just like every time I had scheduled a visit with Muhammad, that I was taking unfair advantage of our friendship. After all, he was just back from a whirlwind tour of meetings and book signings, and he struggled every day with Parkinson's.

Kim put us immediately at ease. "Muhammad wanted to skip lunch so he could be waiting when you arrived." She said. "But you know his diet is important."

Then she laughed aloud and told us how she came to the office early that morning.

"When I walked through the door, Marie told me Muhammad had left a note on my desk. It was urgent, and he needed to speak with me asap." She said. "I hurried into the office, but the room was dark. I switched on the lights and went around to my desk. When I pulled out my chair, Muhammad popped up from under the desk! "Booo!" he shouted.

"I screamed, and he laughed so hard he had trouble getting to his feet. Kim smiled her big, sweet smile, "That's Muhammad!"

Still milling in the entry, we stopped to admire a life-size etching of Muhammad in frosted glass, backlit from the edges. Ali glowed in the beveled tracings.

We made our way to Muhammad's office. An arch of overstuffed chairs circled a fireplace set into a paneled wall flanked with bookcases. Like kids, we hurried along, checking out each photograph and trophy elegantly displayed. Then we noticed Ali standing silently in the doorway.

"Good Morning, Muhammad," I called, startled by his sudden appearance and an unlikely mustache that would have gone well with red plaid pants and a white vinyl belt. He looked strange like someone had disfigured an iconic painting. He stroked the growth self-consciously and smiled broadly.

"I coulda been a pimp." He quipped hoarsely.

The comment passed so quickly that I don't think anyone else heard it. Jim and Cindy were frozen, staring. Right there before them, Muhammad towered, awe-inspiring. Every expectation was resolved. Of course, there was that mustache, but it was really Ali.

On queue, Muhammad locked eyes with Cindy. With his arms outstretched, he moved his fingers hypnotically.

"Leeeeave him. Leeeeeave him." He chanted.

Cindy just stared, still frozen. Then she melted into the moment, "He is the man I love, but if I left him, it would be for you, Muhammad!"

Muhammad gave her a big hug, then turned to Jim, "Man, she

is too pretty for you!" he scolded.

"True enough, Muhammad," Jim replied. "We are so happy to meet you."

I could see Jim's eyes had teared up. I felt joy and privilege to be Muhammad's buddy. "Good Morning Muhammad." I said, "Good to see you."

He mumbled a hello and turned to Jim and Cindy. He pulled a scarf from his pocket and pushed it between his clenched fists; then his eyes went wide in wonder. Kim and I stood back while Muhammad performed the schtick he loved for the thousandth time. Still, we could not help but look on with big stupid grins. Muhammad was a master.

When the tricks were over, we all sat in the big comfortable chairs and relaxed a bit. Jim opened a box of photos. He handed Muhammad the stack of images bound with two big hoops. Muhammad flipped through the pictures with indifference.

I had not seen him in a down mood, but he was clearly feeling low. He gave each image no more than a glance, then skipped to the next. Jim interrupted.

"Muhammad, I don't think you are seeing something in these pictures," he interjected.

Ali raised his eyes without moving his head. His thick mustache interrupted his "pretty" face.

"Muhammad, you are in each of those images. Each of the clubs memorializes you and what you mean to these kids."

Muhammad sat back in his chair. He reconsidered the first image. The picture showed a couple of young boxers wearing head padding, reaching out, and touching the tips of their gloves before a practice bout. Beyond them, beyond the boxing ring and a row of folding chairs, a rough mural of Ali covered a wall. Ali ran his fingertips over the image.

"That's me." He whispered.

"Yes, Muhammad. You are in every gym we visited. You are an inspiration to the boxers and the trainers. They believe in you."

Muhammad looked up at Jim. "How many pictures?" he asked.

"Thousands Muhammad. We have thousands of pictures of dozens of gyms." Muhammad gently turned to the next picture in the binder.

"See Muhammad, there in the corner, you can see the poster of you towering over Liston."

"Ali chuckled, "I'm a bad man."

But his eyes welled. He blinked and turned to the next image. Again there was a rough mural painted on a cement block wall, "Float like a butterfly, sting....." the words angled across outstretched hands in red boxing gloves.

I looked at Jim; he wiped tears from his eyes. Muhammad turned to image after image, studying the backgrounds of the photos, surveying the posters, the murals, and the altars of hope built in the gyms, inspiring kids to make a life, to survive. Ali wiped a tear from his cheek.

Again, in a moment with Muhammad, wildly disparate thoughts collided. We drove to the Farm, sharing light-hearted tales of Ali. It was a hoot to know him, to have a code to the gate, to be the guy who could make Jim's dream come true. Now, in the presence of Ali, I was once again on terra firma unknown. How to reconcile the complexity of this man sitting beside me, humble, leaning forward in his chair, thumbing through pictures of kids, and weeping at their validation of his life?

A kid from Louisville who invented a hero who inspired the

world, here with hands that float like a butterfly and sting like a bee, now with tears running over his cheeks, wetting that ridiculous mustache.

The audacity of his taunts, so far in the past, the thunderous blows that staggered the most ferocious boxers on the planet, juxtaposed with his moment lighting the torch in Atlanta.

I realized that looking into Ali was like peering into a bottomless well, its waters a magical swirl, where strife and determination, fairness and joy, violence and peace, and humility and greatness all tumble to soften into the flesh and power and humor and love of one great man, the greatest of all time.

Jim leaned toward me with a forearm outstretched. "Pinch me. Honest, pinch me. I want to be sure this is not a dream."

To this day, Jim reminds me that was the greatest day of his life, and I understand what he means. The days I shared some time with Ali brought with them a vision of a world beyond politics and tribalism. Ali seemed to care equally for every person on the planet in a way I have not yet witnessed apart from him.

And still, he appeared surprised and humbled by the affection others felt for him.

CHAPTER FORTY-THREE

WALK AROUND

Muhammad bought the Berrien Springs farm in 1975 while training for the "Thrilla in Manila," his third fight with Joe Frazier. Safe to say, the property was not the focus of his energies. The farm served as a retreat, but Ali was rarely there. Years later, the buildings were sound but well-worn when we began our work. Lonnie brought new energy and a clear vision. Just updating Muhammad's tiny office above the garages was a start.

We were honored and did our best work with great attention to detail. The result was a little bit of perfection. The rooms looked impossibly clean and well put together. Every chip was filled, every seam caulked shut. The trouble was, as we progressed, everything that was unrestored screamed louder for attention. Once Lonnie saw the transformation of the old offices, she was on fire to get to the rest of the buildings. From open rooms to storage closets, every inch of the farm fell in line for restoration.

While we worked, the farm itself was reborn. New entry gates were installed, and the lane was repaved. The gardens were revived with new plantings and ground cover. In all, the farm became a jewel.

The path in front of the house wound through the gardens that had matured over the decades. Tangled plantings were removed, and the old stone wishing pool came alive with a peaceful waterfall tumbling over the rocks holding back a tiny ivy-covered hill.

A lawn swing for two sat in the middle of it all. It was fine to stop for a long minute on cool summer mornings to listen to the waterfall and the babble of the little stream wending its way through the stones. One morning I saw Ali there, hunched forward, silent. He seemed far from the roar of thousands of fans celebrating his victories. The farm was a gift to Ali from everyone who surrounded him.

Lonnie was behind it all, orchestrating the contractors, the doctors, and the masseuse, pushing Muhammad to exercise and control his diet. Lonnie ran the business that was Ali. All the while, she simply spilled over with love. Affection was obvious just in the way she pronounced "Muhammad." It took her a moment to say. It took time to reference his whole being.

Muhammad was audacious and humble, courageous and kind; most of all, he was sincere and loved the way Lonnie watched over him. Nothing was more apparent than the twinkle in his eye when Lonnie caught him in mischief.

Now, it was late Fall. The morning was cold, with the sun low in the eastern sky. I slowed when I passed the road sign announcing "Berrien Springs." With the windows down, a shiver ran over me. I was headed to the farm to look over the exterior work we had completed the past few years to see if anything needed attention before Winter. We had finished our work on the carriage house, the main house, the two old barns, the new gym, the new offices, the new garage, the gazebo, and the pool house.

I passed over the St Joseph river, turned right at the top of the hill, and then drove one mile to Kephart Lane.

I turned slowly onto Kephart, jumbled in thought. Lonnie was talking about moving Muhammad to Arizona for his health and to Louisville to be near the new Ali Center. I would lose my special time with the Champ. I rolled down Kephart Lane, then let the car coast quietly across the cul-de-sac to the gates. The stone columns softened the look of the entry. The elegant black iron fencing disappeared into the lush greenery across the peninsula's eastern arm.

I pushed my code into the pad and watched the gates swing open. I drove slowly up the narrow boulevard bordered by mounds of evergreens, and flowering bushes splashed with colorful Impatiens and Walkers Row. The boulevard narrowed to a single lane as I approached the GOAT Offices (Greatest Of All Time). I parked casually; there were no other cars at this early hour. The farm was peaceful and quiet.

I walked past the gym to the single-story barn at the edge of the lane. Around the back of the barn, I saw the lower siding was stained where the mower threw cut grass against the white-painted wall, and there were a few places where the mower deck scraped the wood siding.

My feet wetted with dew as I walked. The barn smelled old and stately. I thought of the mobsters in an old Packard rolling in from Chicago with a "rat" hog-tied in the boot and spirited into the barns, the double doors closing quickly behind them. The farm seemed to have been rescued from the perversion of the mafia thugs. Still, the history was always there, a juxtaposition to the quiet calm of Ali's golden years.

I strolled in the grass fifty yards past the small barn to the taller barn with the second-floor loft packed with memorabilia. The big sliding doors showed wear; we would have to coat them.

Around the side, the slope fell away quickly. I slid down the hill on the wet grass. The side wall was exposed from the base of the foundation up to the first floor, level with the lane, then up two long stories to the peak that towered forty-five feet up.

When we painted the barn, we brought in a sixty-foot boom lift. Parked tight to the front corner of the barn, the boom stretched across the side and up to the peak. To reach the far upper corner, I had to gently edge the lift's front wheels onto a crib of four-by-four posts we stacked to reinforce the lip of the cutaway hill.

With the boom fully extended across the sidewall, I leaned hard against the work cage railing to paint the corner trim. The bucket bounced gently with every move, then lingered at the low point and held there. I looked back at the ten-ton behemoth, with one tire smashed into the crib, daylight showed under the rear tires---I was at the absolute balance point, and the lift threatened to tip down the bank. I gently finished my work and drew the boom back into its sleeve.

I had great affection for that steep little hill. There, I saw Muhammad swing off the lane to whisk down the incline on his Huffy bike. There he was some years after ducking angry fists bent on delivering temporary brain damage, grinning gleefully, feet off the pedals, streaking down the dangerously steep little hill. Ali never gave up his innocence; he just packed it in a corner while he got on with the business of being the heavyweight champion of the world.

I walked down the drive from the barn to the four-car garage with the offices above. The backside needed cleaning. The ground was always soft beneath the thick grass that flourished, semi-shaded, under the trees. It was difficult to beat back the mildew that crept over the lower half of the building.

The view swept out to the river from the rear of the garages, left to right, almost one mile of riverfront. Across the river, the bank rose high, covered in bushes with trees swaying above. Somewhere under the lawn, that tunnel snuck from the pump room to the St Joseph river.

I finished with a walk around the main house. It functioned well for Ali, except for the climb from the entry-level up two stories to the bedrooms. But it was convenient to park just outside the door to the kitchen.

A walking path to the left of the house led up through the sloping wall of boulders and flowering bushes to the front gardens and past the cobbled stream and waterfall.

The patio and swimming pool were on the far side of the house. The pool was an amenity that got little use. It was a maintenance nightmare for years, with cracks opening in the bottom and sides. The water dropped slowly through the week; Friday afternoons, a garden hose ran lazily to bring it back to level.

I noted a few places on the main house for touch-ups, then walked up the lane back to my car in the office parking lot. Soon, the kitchen crew would be arriving at the WoodFire. I hoped to find time to do the touch-ups myself, to spend another afternoon in the realm of Ali, but I would probably have to ask Becky. Life had moved on. I was busy, now a restauranteur.

PART TEN:

CHAPTER FORTY-FOUR

C.J. CAFFREY

The long train ride to Memphis came to an end. Isaiah held Sojourner's satchel while she climbed unsteadily from the train. Two women waited on the platform. They hurried to greet her.

"Missus Truth, we have waited on every train for two days. The preacher will be so relieved to see you! Our wagon is just there." One of the women said, pointing to the far side of the depot.

"I am sorry, I got throwed off that train for speaking ideas too loudly. I had to wait for things to settle so they would let this old woman back on." She explained.

"Where is your trunk?" one of the women asked.

"No, evr'ything I got is in that satchel." She replied. "I am ready to go. That train has been a terrible long ride; fortunate I had our new friend Isaiah to pass the time."

The women greeted Isaiah and then offered a ride to the riverboat. They all climbed onto the wagon for the short ride to the docks. Alongside the river, Sojourner embraced Isaiah and hoped to see him again. He climbed down from the wagon, and the three women rode off.

Isaiah watched longingly until the wagon was out of sight, then he opened the rice sack. Master Newhouse had sent him a bowler hat and a gentleman's jacket of fine material with four buttons and a flat collar.

Isaiah shaped the hat and pulled it over his short-cropped hair. He had never worn fancy clothes and felt awkward but smart, like he was no ordinary slave. Maybe he would have less trouble if he was dressed fine.

Alongside the pier, a paddlewheel steamboat with three decks beneath a windowed wheelhouse blew a long whistle. The C.J. Caffrey had unloaded a brigade of Confederate soldiers moving north in anticipation of the coming war. Isaiah walked along the wharf, his head down, wary of every man he approached.

At the base of the walkway onto the C.J. Caffrey, glistening white and pulsing with energy, a red-faced man in a tight white jacket stopped Isaiah to ask for his ticket. Isaiah leafed through the documents in the burlap bag and found a ticket with an image of the boat reading, "C.J. Caffrey Passage."

The man looked over the document and bellowed, "Rooftop to Saint Louey. Climb aboard!"

He pointed Isaiah at the gangplank to the rear of the boat. With the coming war, the ship was overbooked. Even the lower decks were jammed with cargo and extra passengers.

A boy of about fourteen, barefoot and hurried, led Isaiah to makeshift quarters on the open roof behind the wheelhouse. Isaiah stood atop the steamer and watched as cargo was wheeled aboard. He watched the fancy passengers in black jackets and hooped skirts led to staterooms on the second level.

By late afternoon the bustle slowed, then the big whistle on the wheelhouse roof blew three times, and the deckhands cast off the lines. The paddle wheel spun backward for a minute, then reversed forward. The C.J. Caffrey swung from the pier out into the main channel. Isaiah was on the final leg of his long journey to Saint Louis.

The boat bristled with activity as the crew tied down cargo and arranged the loose crates that covered the foredeck. The big steam engine chugged rhythmically. The entire ship shook with the pulse of the steam piston pounding back and forth, driving the paddle wheel.

By nightfall, they had steamed twenty miles north of Memphis. Isaiah laid back against his rice sack, exhausted by the excitement and anxiety of his long day, then he slept.

Isaiah awoke to the rolling of the ship. The deep scar at his ankle tugged against the shackle that bound him. Sweat rolled from his forehead. He dreamt of standing, but the low ceiling beneath the deck above him crept down. First, there was no room to sit up, then the deck pressed against the tips of his outstretched hands, then smothered against his chest. Isaiah fought to breathe. In his final desperation, Isaiah shouted aloud, "Oh Lord, have mercy!"

The steamboat approached a bend in the river, and the whistle sounded. An elderly man shook Isaiah's shoulders.

"Son, wake up. We're here with you, them's nightmares."

Isaiah smelled the black smoke rolling from the stacks of the steamboat. Burnt and oily, the constant wisps of the sooty discharge coated his lips and filled his throat. He looked around. Anxious sweat trickled in sporadic droplets down his neck as he lifted up on an elbow. He saw the clear starry sky reflected in the ink-black river steely in the darkness.

"Oh, I had the awfullest dream." He said. "I felt the shackle on my leg, and the ceiling crushed against me."

"You're here now. You're strong. You're are gonna fight till you're truly a free man." The old man declared. "Let your heart soar beneath this spectacular sky. You rest; tomorrow will bring freedom."

Isaiah laid back down. He pulled a kerchief from the jacket Master Newhouse gave him and wrapped it over his mouth and nose. He closed his eyes but didn't sleep. He waited to feel the steam boat roll like the ocean ship, but it glided over the flat water, the big paddle wheel sloshing rhythmically alongside.

Freedom was coming. He had his papers of manumission, and Lincoln was elected the new president. Soon, the war would come, and the North would quickly defeat the South. Everywhere there was talk of the nation being reunited. Then Lincoln would free the slaves. No man would again work under the whip.

During the day, Isaiah sat against the back of the wheelhouse, chatting with the other men bunked out on the roof. They shared stories of hard work and babies born. They avoided talk of shackles and whips; better to embrace the clear, bright sky and take leisure in good company.

He had spent two days aboard the C.J. Caffrey listening to the men when finally, the discussion turned to the politics of the day. Some men wanted gradual emancipation; others wanted the states to make rules. Everyone expected Lincoln to pass a Federal law to free the slaves. But first, the war had to unite the country. Every week since Lincoln's election, another state seceded from the Union. Soon, they speculated, even Missourians would have to spend Confederate money.

Isaiah took comfort in the circle of men. With his journey almost over, he slept well that third night. He awoke in the wee hours when the moon was high. The steamboat whistled loudly; two long blasts echoed down the river. Isaiah saw the outline of Saint Louis just visible above the low trees lining the bank. He stood to see the city.

A stack of smoke sank over Isaiah in the cool night air, and he choked. He wiped his mouth, but he tasted the soot all the more. Isaiah rose, walked to the ladder, and climbed down to the main deck. He longed for sweet air.

He walked along the deck toward the front of the ship. Along the way, Isaiah stopped to watch the swift water roll under the low sides of the riverboat. He could almost reach down to cup a handful to rinse his mouth. He walked further past the cabins and stowage. As the deck swept up to the bow, a row of large traveler trunks lined the way.

Then they steamed fast under a trestle bridge; the big boat barreled the last miles to Saint Louis. Isaiah sat, feeling the air speed past on this windless night.

"Hey, you! Boy! What the hell are you doing!? Where'd you steal that jacket? Think you're gonna get more out of those trunks?" a gruff voice charged at Isaiah. He stood and faced the man.

"No, sir, I am just breathing some sweet air." He replied.

"Yah and I were captain but got tired of the view from the wheelhouse. You thievin' liar!" the man seethed.

He grabbed Isaiah by his shoulders. Isaiah smelled cigars and stale whiskey.

"Sweet air!? You need a sweet bath, too, ya filthy thief!" He pushed Isaiah up against the railing then the brute took hold of Isaiah's waistband and lifted him, thrusting him backward.

Surprised, Isaiah grabbed at the man and swiped for the rail, but he rolled over the railing and into the frigid water. He felt the hull churning over him pound against his legs. The current pushed him hard against the boat; the suction held him under, and he rolled up against the crusty hull. Isaiah kicked and pushed. Then he slammed into the thick wooden rudder at the stern. He grasped at it then the boat was gone.

Isaiah thrashed in the swirling water. He kicked off his

clumsy shoes, desperate to swim. He sank under as he wrestled out of his fancy jacket. He felt the fine fabric tangle eerily at his feet, a demon pulling him under. He looked to the shore, and he swam.

The current drug Isaiah back downstream away from the docks of Saint Louis. He kicked; his arms pinwheeled a chaotic stroke. The deep water in the middle of the channel moved in a quick swirl. Isaiah struggled to stay afloat. Shore was in the far distance. The only sound was the engine of the steamboat chugging upstream.

All Isaiah could do was float along in the black water. He struggled toward shore but tired quickly. He laid back to catch his breath. Suddenly the looming shadow of the trestle bridge blocked out the stars. Isaiah spun forward. A great pile of rocks buttressed the column where the foot of the bridge split the river. The current pushed Isaiah into the stones. He jammed his hand between two large boulders. The fast water wrenched his arm, but he held on.

Isaiah pulled up on the rocks and laid back, listening to his heart pounding. He gripped the talisman, thankful for his good fortune. When he regained his breath, he stood barefoot, soaking wet in the cool air. He looked to the shore a few hundred feet away. With a start, Isaiah realized he had lost his shoes, coat, and the dollars in his satchel. He felt for the soaked envelope still under his belt, pasted against his stomach. The thick paper was intact, but the ink was smeared across where "Professor Greenleaf Eliot?" had been written.

Somewhere above him, Isaiah heard the sound of a heavy timber saw grinding away at a tree trunk.

"A tree trunk on a bridge in the black of night?" he thought. He stood breathless, listening. The sound was distinct.

Isaiah climbed the broad timbers that angled up to a low catwalk leading across the trusses. He stopped to listen again.

The sound was clear and seemed very close; it bounced over the river's smooth surface. Isaiah walked a narrow catwalk toward the western shore. Then, just overhead on a wide beam, Isaiah saw a man hacking at a truss with a long shiny blade. A second man looked away, studying the distant shoreline.

Isaiah inched closer. He could see the man straddling the cross piece sawing an angled cut into a timber that ran directly up to the roadway above. The man cut almost through the beam, then stopped. He pulled the big saw from the cut and slid down the support to where the lookout stood.

"Seen anybody?" asked the man with the saw.

"No one. Let's get that last support and go. Them Yankees will hang us if we get found out. This whole thing is coming down when the troops march across. Hurry up!" he whispered.

The two men hustled in a low crouch along the catwalk to a single brace that crossed to the far side of the bridge. The man with the saw stood straight and walked carefully across the narrow timber. The lookout scanned the shore. Isaiah stood behind an upright, his arms tight to his sides; his heart raced, and he shivered in his wet clothes.

In five minutes, the work was done. The man slung the saw out into the river. It landed with an eerie splash. He hurried back across the narrow timber, "Let's go." He whispered. Then the two men turned to the east bank and ran, crouching low over the long catwalk.

Isaiah watched until they leaped onto the clay bank pounded flat above the stones at the base of the bridge. They disappeared into the low brush. Then Isaiah climbed onto the catwalk and ran to the western shore.

CHAPTER FORTY-FIVE

ARRIVAL

In 1858 Saint Louis was in conflict. Riots broke out, and shots were fired. The civil war was imminent. The strife pitted brother against brother; alliances were hard to discern even within families. With the election of Lincoln, both the north and the south could see the coming end of slavery. People felt it in the air.

Isaiah made his way along the road from the trestle bridge to the beginnings of the town. He found a footpath through the brush along the river where the forest gave way to rows of houses and shops. He followed the narrow trail along the bank, invisible to anyone traveling the roadway.

Isaiah did not know who the saboteurs were, but he needed to warn somebody about the bridge. He ran a mile along the path, then onto the long commercial wharf. Isaiah hurried along amongst the stacks of crates and boxes lining the docks.

Two rows of gleaming steamboats moored side by side against the wharf stretched as far as he could see. In the distance, he saw a long-coated policeman strolling alongside the ships, Billy club in hand. Isaiah realized he looked like a runaway with bare feet and clothes still wet from the river. He hurried from the wharf onto a cobbled street, vanishing behind three-story buildings.

Isaiah moved like a thief. He kept to the shadows, cautious he would not be seen by the random drunks wobbling home before dawn. Isaiah found a cathedral in a large open square surrounded by tall buildings and smaller shops. The towers reached higher than anything he had ever seen. Outside, a spindly old man swept the broad stairs leading up to the vaulted doors of the grand entry. Not to startle him, Isaiah called out as he crossed the street.

"Good morning, sir. The sun will shine upon us soon. The man looked up from his sweeping."

"Yes, the sun will shine on us soon. What are you doing in those muddy clothes and barefoot in this dark hour?" he asked, looking Isaiah up and down.

"I am looking for Professor William Greenleaf Eliot. I have an important message for him."

"You'll see him at first light walking to the Benton School three streets that way," he said, pointing north. "Professor Eliot is a University man. Keep away from any pair of men; they'll be slave traders looking to ship you south for sure, all barefoot and looking like a runaway."

"I'll be careful, thank you," Isaiah said and hurried up the street.

Isaiah shivered in the damp morning air. He hurried along the dark street; the cobblestones were cold under his feet. As the old man promised, he soon found the big red brick building with a sign in the yard, "Benton School."

The courtyard was quiet. Only birds moved in the still morning air. Isaiah sat against a small tree behind a neatly trimmed boxwood hedge alongside the walkway.

Looking up from his little hideaway, Isaiah watched the sun crest the tops of the buildings all around. He contemplated the patchwork of gleaming roofs warming in the early sun and thought of the lush green valley so far away. His heart ached for home while his mind exulted in the fresh morning air; soon, he would be free.

Isaiah listened to the clip-clop of a few horse-drawn carts passing on the cobbles. He dozed lightly. In time he heard the rhythmic gait of hard boots echo along the street. The steady rhythm grew louder until Isaiah could see the outline of a man dressed in a long coat, bare-headed and hurrying toward him. His grey beard, thick yet neatly trimmed, lent an air of formality to his already severe features. His apparent stature was confirmed by jacket tails fluttering with his hurried gait.

Isaiah stood quickly, brushing his hands down his shirt,

"Good Morning, Sir." He blurted. "Are you Professor Eliot? My master sent me to you."

Professor Eliot stopped an arm's length from Isaiah. He looked with concern at Isaiah, much bedraggled by his long trip and unceremonious arrival in Saint Louis.

"You are safe here, be assured." Professor Eliot said in a pleasant tone that belied his stoic appearance. "Who is your master? Is he here in Missouri?"

"No, no, I came from Master Newhouse in North Carolina, but first, sir, I need to tell you there is trouble. Two men sawed the bridge. They aim to stop the Union soldiers from getting into the city." Isaiah blurted, breathless.

Professor Eliot calmly reached to put his hands on Isaiah's shoulders. "Ok, what, men? What bridge? How do you know?" he asked. "We have some time. The soldiers are not marching until midday. Tell me what happened."

Isaiah told the tale of his long night. Thrown overboard, finding the bridge, the man with the saw, and his dash into the city.

"Ok, I know the trestle bridge just south of the city." Professor Greenleaf assured him.

Then, with a single finger gently over Isaiah's lips, he said,

"Don't ever mention the bridge or the men or anything you saw to anyone. I want you to wait here for me."

Then he turned from Isaiah and climbed the stairs to the tall paneled doors at the front of the building. He pushed a thick key into the lock and looked back over his shoulder, "Isaiah, come quickly." He turned the key and swung the heavy door open.

"Rest here on the bench; I will be back shortly."

The big door settled against the stop, and Isaiah heard the key turn in the lock as Professor Eliot closed the lock. Even through the heavy door, Isaiah listened to the sharp rap of his boots hurrying up the street.

Isaiah settled down on the thick wooden bench. The building was unlike anything he knew, but the warmth of the close vestibule gave him comfort. He laid back, fulfilled by the attention Professor Greenfield offered. He was safe in his hands. Finally, exhausted, he settled back on the bench and slept.

PART ELEVEN:

CHAPTER FORTY-SIX

FUNERAL

Some years had passed since I had seen Ali. He spent less and less time at the farm and more time in Arizona. His battle with Parkinson's continued to take its toll. On the first day of June 2016, I heard Muhammad had been hospitalized. For a week, the family knew he was passing. Ali had spent years preparing for his funeral. He wanted it to reflect his devotion and to share the event with his fans and the people of Louisville. Ali died on Friday, June 3, 2016.

I was traveling for work when the family announced that Ali's funeral would be held on Thursday, June 9, in Louisville. Tickets would be distributed, First Come/First Served on the morning of the 8th at nine am. I had to be there.

My daughter's lifelong friend lived in Louisville. Sweet girl, she offered to get in line at six am to get a ticket at ten am. She was there at 5 am, and because of the long line, the ticket office opened early at 8 am. For all of her efforts, she missed tickets by about one hundred people.

Still, I drove through the night from Youngstown, Ohio, to Louisville for the funeral. I arrived in the early hours before dawn and found a parking lot along the river just a half block from the Yum Center where the celebration would take place.

I parked and then took a walk to soak in the atmosphere. Even in the wee hours, the streets were bright with Ali fans all around the Arena. I saw camera crews with trailers of equipment for networks worldwide. Reporters lined the sidewalk conducting interviews broadcast live across oceans.

Far from a mournful scene, I felt a sense of anticipation, comradery, and excitement to pay tribute to Ali.

As I walked through unfamiliar streets, people nodded with familiarity. I asked for directions to the Ali Center. Once headed in the right direction, I followed a motley procession of well-wishers.

Near the Center, a makeshift memorial of flowers, messages written on boxing gloves and greeting cards, and handwritten wishes on plain cardboard grew by the hour. Even in the dark hours, small groups of mourners clustered around the memorial. Each seemed to have a story about meeting Muhammad in an airport, at an event, or of a brother or aunt who had met him. Each could remember the very moment.

I lingered in the still cool night air, languorous with the scent of flowers spread all around the memorial. I remember the police and volunteers on patrol; all had their guards down, there was no tension. People milling in the shadows at four am were there for Ali. Everyone was there for Ali.

From the start, I was uncomfortable hawking for a ticket. I walked around the Ali Center and then several blocks back to the Yum Arena. I did not see anyone with extra tickets to sell or simply give away. I went into a diner to get a coffee and get online, so I could post an ad on Craigslist.

First, I offered to buy a ticket. I immediately got a note saying tickets should not be bought or sold. It was disrespectful to dishonor Ali by using his service for profit. In fact, volunteers from the Ali Center followed up with people who posted tickets for sale to ask they return them to the Center without charge.

I understood. I took my ad down and walked another hour, hoping to find someone with an extra ticket. Finally, I posted an ad offering to share a story or two about Muhammad in exchange for a ticket. I got some screwball responses, typical of Craigslist, but no tickets.

The sun rose, and the crowds thickened. I milled around the Yum Center, still hopeful of finding a way in for the event. The atmosphere was charged with an unusual mix of excitement and reverence.

At an intersection adjacent to the Arena, crowds of pedestrians spilled into the streets, but cars jammed the roadway. A police officer in the middle of the intersection motioned for the vehicles to stop. Then he waved to the pedestrians and shouted, "It's all you folks! Cross however you like."

The intersection was filled with people walking in every direction. We were all there together, for one purpose, filled with the hope Muhammad left us. As the crowds moved past him, the officer repeated, "Enjoy this day. Ali, the Greatest of All Time."

On a crowded street alongside the Arena, a tented entry was erected for social royalty. Limos stopped under a canopy, and sports stars, presidents, and Hollywood legends slipped quietly into the guarded entrance.

I continued my walk, stopping to ask people from time to time if they knew of available tickets. I made my way back to the Ali Center, but the box office was closed. My anxiety grew. The crowds collecting on the sidewalks thinned. I saw people hurrying and realized the funeral procession had begun. I followed a group of young men hustling south toward the route. We arrived as the procession passed. I missed the lead; I missed Ali.

The air was thick, the sun was Louisville hot, and I began to sweat. I hurried back to the Yum Center to get in position to witness the procession. I rushed through almost empty streets. I thought of Ali and how far I was from him and the days we were together in our private little world. I knew him in the quiet confines of the farm when on a cool June morning, he rode the old Huffy down that short little hill next to the barn. I did not know him here in this unfamiliar city where he was shared with the world.

I crossed an intersection, saw a thick crowd a few blocks off to my right, and hurried that way. I could hear the procession coming toward us. Well-wishers chanted "Ali, Ali." Then, the ominous black hearse rolled up the street.

People tossed flowers; shirtless young men ran alongside. Police officers gently swiped flowers off the windshield so the driver could see the road. Emotions tossed inside of me. My eyes welled with tears. I could not distinguish if my feelings were for his loss or the joy in seeing, once again, the power of Ali in regular people.

The procession passed. I walked with the crowds assuming the flow would be back to the Yum Center. My cell phone rang. It was a young man named Brent who said he had extra tickets. He wanted to meet at McDonald's about 20 minutes south. I was skeptical.

Brent said he had five tickets, so he was giving away two pairs and had a single ticket he could give to me. He said his uncle died the night before, and his family was to meet at McDonald's and then drive to Cincinnati.

By this time, the doors to the Yum Center were within an hour of opening. If I drove 20 minutes south and then back, there would be very little time to find a ticket on the street, but I considered I might never see one if I stayed either. I agreed to meet Brent at Mcdonald's.

I hurried to my car, parked in the shade beneath the overpass. As I pulled out, I realized the lot might be full when I returned. Still, I set my GPS and drove. Along the way, Brent called. He said that when I got to McDonald's, I should go through the drive-through and tell the cashier she had a wonderful son who would be there in just a few minutes. He said she could not use her cellphone at work, and my message would let her know her family was on their way; their hasty arrangements were complete.

Then Brent asked me what stories I would share. I told him I would write about meeting Ali, about the farm, and some of the funny things Ali did to people. The arrangement was odd, and I felt desperate.

At McDonald's, I went through the drive-thru and ordered a small coffee. I told the cashier she had a wonderful son who would be there in ten minutes. She looked at me like I was from Mars and said, "What?"

I repeated, "You have a wonderful son. He will be here in ten minutes."

She stared at me, then laughed, "No one has ever told me I have a wonderful son. Thank you!"

I parked and waited ten minutes. I had thoughts of just hurrying back to the Yum Center. My sense of desperation was unbearable. I knew a Craigslist rendezvous was chancy at best, and this was a goose chase, probably for a cruel laugh, and I was going to miss Ali.

I quickly composed a couple of stories on my phone that I could email to Brent, still hoping he would show. Minutes passed. I wrote about the farm and the river and rows of flowers. It was calming to envision the time I spent there.

A half-hour passed then a dented-up minivan packed with people stopped right in front of me. A lanky teen jumped out of the sliding side door.

"You Larry?" he hollared through the glass. "Yes, I lowered the window. "You Brent?"

"Yup, I'm the wonderful son." He chuckled. "Here is your ticket."

I took the ticket and got out of the car to say thank you. I shook Brent's hand as his mother came around the back of the van.

"You must think we are all a bit crazy to miss the funeral, but we have one of our own. My husband's brother passed last night, so we have to hurry to Cincinnati."

"I am sorry for your loss," I said. "I am very happy to get this ticket. It means a lot to me."

"Well, you are very welcome. Please let us know how the memorial goes. Brent says you knew Ali."

"I did. I will share some stories." I replied.

I asked Brent for his email, thanked him again, and we left out of the parking lot in opposite directions.

I set the GPS for the Yum Center and drove. I read the ticket front and back, hoping it was authentic. When I got near the Center, I turned out of traffic toward the river. I followed along service streets and came to the same parking lot I had left earlier. It seemed a secret lot because it was still half empty. I parked in the shade and opened the trunk to get fresh clothes.

I changed in the car, wishing I could shower. It was cool under the overpass, but the sun was hot with little breeze. With a sports coat over my arm, I hurried up the sidewalk alongside the Yum Center.

The celebrity door to the Arena was jammed with limousines and sightseers. Police officers kept a single line open for pedestrians to squeeze between the masses. I hustled through. As I passed, I glimpsed Katie Couric and Bob Costas. It occurred to me I was going to see a U.S. President, Billy Crystal, and Bryant Gumbel. Since meeting Ali, I would have been comfortable having any one of them over for sandwiches. I could be star-struck no more.

It was only minutes until the ceremony began. A flood of people converged on the plaza in front of the Arena. I felt a wave of excitement and walked quickly to the entry doors. The crowd at the door was genteel making way for one another with obvious care for decorum. A man to my right held a ticket in his hand that looked much like mine; I took a breath.

Once inside, I found my seat on an aisle on the first balcony. The stage was to the left. Below, the arena floor was filled with chairs. A steady murmur of voices softened the atmosphere. Though much relieved, my anxiety had not passed. The strange journey of the night and uneasy desperation of the morning left me a bit sickened. I realized that I had remembered coffee but had forgotten breakfast. I left my seat to wander the Arena and maybe find food.

The Yum Center is a beautiful glass-front building with the entrance lobby open to an elegant ceiling sixty feet above the floor. Long escalators crisscrossing the facing wall lead to the balcony level. I stood at the railing, looking down at the crush of people entering the gates. I saw lines of people milling around the promenade through the glass walls. Beyond them, the long block line of broadcast vehicles. The day was clear and bright. A gentle wind blew clouds across the sky.

CHAPTER FORTY-SEVEN

INSIDE

Anticipation filled the Arena, and I strolled back to my seat. I looked out over the Arena filling fast, suddenly hushed with reverence. Twenty-two thousand people there for Ali waited in mum silence. Thousands more milled outside on the steps of the Arena and strolled through the streets of Ali's hometown.

Politics at that time were hopeful but challenging. Trump had not yet been elected. I felt uplifted to be amongst people who shared the optimism and promise of liberation. Everyone in the room recognized Ali's greatness, compassion, and acceptance of all people, but most of all, Ali had somehow empowered each of them. Twenty-two thousand hearts emboldened.

Muhammad and Lonnie had planned the funeral for years. The secrecy, shared with a dozen friends, family, and service providers, remained unbroken. When Muhammad passed, the reverential process began. A security detail from Louisville flew to Arizona to oversee his privacy at the end of his life and thereafter. There would be no circus, no dishonor. According to Muslim tradition, his body was washed and cleansed with water, and lotus leaves carried from Saudi Arabia for the purpose. Across the country, people he had touched made their way to Louisville.

Back in my seat, alone in the crowded Arena, I was unprepared for the emotional onslaught that hit me. When the Arena lights dimmed, the stage lit, and Lonnie arrived with Muhammad alongside, silent tears streamed. I felt a sudden overwhelming sense of loss. Sitting there with memories of my time with Ali, I confronted the profound gift he shared with me and the entire world. It has taken me time to even begin to understand.

In that room were artists and activists, Presidents and athletes, and saintly leaders of a dozen faiths. Their tributes to Ali, spoken from their hearts so strengthened by the gifts he gave them, plowed right through me.

The story of Ali at an Olympic boxing match. The fight ends in a TKO, and Ali wants to visit the boxer in his dressing room, not the victorious fighter but the man who gave everything but lost this battle. Ali found the young man sitting on a stool, alone, his head in his hands, his disappointment profound.

"Hey brother, I saw what you did out there. You're good. Don't give up. You've got skills." He consoled, then the embrace.

Ali, riding home from church one Sunday morning with his daughter, sees an elderly man walking. His daughter stops the car. They offer the man a ride home. Upon leaving, Ali's daughter gives the man her phone number to call if he ever again needs a ride to Sunday services. Driving away, Ali asks his daughter if she would really go pick the man up if he called.

"Yes, daddy, I would." She responded.

With tears in his eyes, Ali says, "Darling, that is me in you. You are on the path to heaven."

Natasha Mundkur, a University of Louisville student who had never met Ali, captured the essence of the man. She spoke of Ali, who reached up "through the pages of a textbook and touched the heart of an eight-year-old girl whose reflection of herself mirrored those who could not see past the color of her skin.

But instead of drawing on that pain from their distorted reality, she found strength, just as this man did when he stood tall in the face of pelting rain and shouted, 'I am the disturbance in the sea of your complacency, and I will never stop shaking your waves.'

And his voice echoed through hers, through mine, and she picked up the rocks thrown at her and threw them back with a voice so powerful that it turned all the pain she had faced in her life into strength and tenacity.

Impossible is an opinion. Impossible is nothing...Impossible is never enough to knock us down because We are Ali...he is from Louisville, Kentucky, and he lives in each and every one of us. And, his story is far from over."

Celebrities and politicians spoke, and the tears flowed during their comments too. But the glimpses of what Ali meant to people struggling to sort out life, fulfill the simplest dreams, and even to love themselves shook my world.

There is a greatness in Ali that I am certain I will not see again and cannot describe here. It is found in his kindness, his respect for every person, the inspiration he gave to those people closest to him, and the masses he never met. These are the gifts of a great person; add to them the apparently limitless depth of his convictions, and we begin to fathom the man who is Muhammad Ali.

I wiped my eyes on every dry bit of fabric at hand that afternoon. The couple beside me whispered, seemingly troubled, but I was at a loss to explain. I struggled to say simply,

"I knew Ali."

CHAPTER FORTY-EIGHT

I AM ALI

Ali was born into a harsh world, the West End of Louisville, a poor, segregated neighborhood with all the forces of poverty and systemic racism piled against him. Ali heard the slurs; he saw the "colored only" side doors and seats at the back of the bus. He suffered humiliation and watched his parents suffer them too.

But somewhere, there was a spark. It may have been the officer who invited him to the boxing gym to channel his anger when his bike was stolen or his parents who sacrificed to buy him an even nicer bike, a motorized scooter. But something gave Ali hope that bore a mission.

I began to understand the historical magnitude of his ascent at the funeral in the words of Dr. Kevin Cosby. He instructed:

"...to appreciate what Dr. King meant when he said, 'The Negro needed a sense of some- bodyness.'" We need to "understand the 350 years of no-bodyness that was infused into the psyche of people of color. Every sacred document in our history, every hallowed institution, conspired to convince the African in America, that when God made the African, God was guilty of creative malfeasance.

All of our sacrosanct documents from the constitution said to the Negro that you are nobody. The constitution said that we are three-fifths a person. Decisions by the Supreme Court, like the Dred-Scott decision, said to the Negro, the African, you have no rights that whites are bound to respect."

The Supreme Court supported the Dred-Scott Act, often considered the worst decision ever rendered by the Court; it declared African Americans were not and could never be citizens of the United States.

"Even the Stars Spangled Banner, of which we sing only the first verse, says in the third,

No refuge could save the hireling and slave.
From the sorrow of night or the death of the grave...."

Prejudice by decree and institution fostered a sense of no-bodyness. Then came Jackie Robinson, Joe Louis, Jesse Owens, Rosa Parks, and Muhammad Ali.

Even before the Voting Rights Act was finally passed in 1965, Ali dared to stand up. "Muhammad took the ethos of some-bodyness to unheard of heights:

"I am black, and I am pretty!'" he proclaimed.

When Ali first said it, "black" and "pretty" was an oxymoron, Dr. Cosby told us. The first black millionaire in America made products to help blacks escape their "Africanity." Bleaching products and hair straighteners. Blackness was nothing to embrace.

Dr. Cosby continued, "Muhammad Ali was the product of a difficult time. And he dared to love black people at a time when black people had a problem loving themselves. He dared to affirm the beauty of blackness. He dared to affirm the power and capacity of African Americans. He dared to love America's most unloved race. And he loved us all."

When Ali shouted, "I am black, and I am pretty." He shouted it loud so that both sides, the oppressed and the oppressors, confronted the message. He found the strength to tear off the chains of oppression and to see himself as a complete human being.

Ali's compassion exposed bigots and their lost humanity. Their hate makes their world smaller; it cuts them off from the beauty of diversity. They are uncomfortable with themselves, ill-equipped to see grace in people, even in those they choose not to hate.

Ali's greatness rose through his ability to love people, all people.

Ali forced the world to look at him. He forced the world to confront his whole being. For centuries, bigots were blind to black people. Then there was Ali, undeniable.

Ali might have stopped right there. He could have been an activist for the black community, antagonistic to whites, hating bigots. But Ali had grace. I am humbled that for all the hurt he felt, he had the grace to forgive and to live the forgiveness.

Ali's fights, indeed, his life, are a metaphor for the journey of black America. Following centuries of oppression or twelve brutal rounds in the ring, Ali was still pretty, barely marred by the battle.

PART TWELVE:

CHAPTER FORTY-NINE

ARCHER ALEXANDER

I saiah eased back on the arm of the giant press, and the heavy drum began to turn. With each revolution, another pamphlet fell into the hopper, ready to be cut and folded. Most of the printings served the students in the Benton School; this flyer announced a Wednesday evening meeting of the Free Abolitionists in the school auditorium.

Professor Eliot hired Isaiah, now a freeman, first to keep the press clean and then to assist the printer. Now Isaiah eagerly stayed to print small jobs in the little shop after hours.

Tensions grew in Saint Louis. Every day, fights broke out; some days, there were full-scale riots. Even though eighteen hundred free blacks outnumbered the slaves in the city, Missouri was still a staunchly pro-slave state. Saint Louis was a major market for selling slaves "down the river" to the dreaded plantations of the South.

Professor Eliot did all he had promised Master Newhouse to free Isaiah, as he had done for dozens of former slaves over the years. He filed the letter of manumission and brought Isaiah into the Benton School community. Isaiah lived on a tiny farm on the edge of the city proper with a former slave, Archer Alexander, and his family.

Isaiah rose each day before dawn, filled with the hope of a free man. He helped with farming, tutored the children, served his afternoons in the print shop, and then worked into the night, refining his ability to operate the press. Isaiah worked with energy; emancipation was coming, and soon, even the

South would be free.

It was well past midnight when Isaiah finished the flyers. He carefully bundled several small stacks and packed them into his satchel. As he made his way back to the Alexander farm, he dropped the bundles at the homes of abolitionists committed to distributing them for Professor Eliot.

Itinerant speakers were scheduled to address the men of Saint Louis to promote the cause of abolition; they would debate immediate, universal emancipation versus gradual emancipation decreed by local ordinances.

Isaiah strode confidently through the streets; still, he carefully avoided passersby. Even as a freeman, he could be abducted. Men, women, and even entire families disappeared into the grasp of the traders and disreputable steamboat captains happy for the profits.

With the Spring moon full and the night sky clear, Isaiah hurried along, enjoying the sweet air and doing as he pleased. He often stayed out under the stars until the wee hours when sleep came easy, and his heart was whole, grateful for his freedom.

He arrived back on the farm late into the night, startled to meet Archer sitting on a bench just inside the gate. A short white fence circled beds of flowers that surrounded the yard.

He sat with Archer. "It's a beautiful night," He began.

"Oh, that it is Isaiah; I am here grateful to the Lord and Professor Eliot for the privilege. In the mornin', I'll be plowing that field so we can get to planting beans and tomatoes and corn, everything we need to feed all my children, all of us together again."

"You were apart?" Isaiah asked.

"We was sold all over the South we was," Archer began talking in low tones, "I hate to even remember all my children gone, my wife too."

"I'm sorry to ask," Isaiah lamented. "It was thoughtless to upset this sweet night."

"Oh, I think about it every day. I thank the Lord for bringing me here and the miracle of bringing my family too. It was Professor Eliot that hired a man to find my children after he brought my wife back to me. He said he could not sleep in peace until my family was back under this roof."

"Isaiah, you are younger than me, and maybe you can understand what I want to tell you. I've never told no one about the confliction in my heart. Professor Eliot, I am ever grateful to Professor Eliot; he got me here, and he brought my whole family back to me. I need to say it, Isaiah, I need to tell you. No one gave me freedom; I took it.

Ever since I was a small boy, I dreamt of something like freedom. I did not know what it was then, but I wanted my momma and daddy with me. I wanted schoolin' and no one beating no one. I hid inside myself. I hurt.

When I grew, I tried to escape, and they brought me back. They strung me up in that barn; my toes just brushed the floor, and they whipped me. The second time I tried to escape, they whipped me, left me hanging like that for hours, and then whipped me again. I didn't die because I wasn't free, and I wasn't dying till I was.

Then I did escape, and I got here to Saint Louis and met up with Professor Eliot. He helped me, and I liked him. I worked hard for him, cleaned up this house, and built this fence. I worked the fields for him all day, and he paid me well. In the evenings, I planted these flower beds. I'm so pleased to be free.

One day three men came here to look for Professor Eliot, that is what they told me, but they really came to steal me away.

They told me they'd turn me in for cutting on the trestle bridge, but I didn't know nothin' about it. They beat me senseless with their clubs; my head was cracked and bloody. But I could not confess to somethin' I didn't know nothin' about.

Isaiah clenched his fists, cradled between his knees. He looked at Archer in stunned silence. He thought to speak, but Archer went on.

They rounded me up with a dozen other men to sell us to them rice plantations. They took us to the river and kept us in a room over a tavern where the steamboat captain was waiting for dawn to sail. They put us in that room with liquor and locked the door. We could hear them carrying on downstairs a terrible amount of drinking. I didn't take drink; I was calculatin' an opportunity."

Archer shook his head in reflection. He opened a paper stuffed in his breast pocket and handed it to Isaiah; he had written down the story:

"I puts my head fru de winder to see what kind of a chance I had at escaping. The moon it was shinin' bright as day, and, ef you'd believe me, thar was the biggest kind of a dawg a-walkin' backerd and forrerd, and he jess looked up at me, a-kind o'winkin,' as ef he said, 'No, you don't!'

I had thote them slave-ketchers had been mighty keerless, leavin' us up thar without a watch, but now I onerstood it all. I sot down on the box, jess flustrated. I hadn't no more hope, not a mite. Sure enough, the Lord had done forsook me.

I leaned my head down on the winder-sill and cried like a chile. How long it was I don't know, but I 'speck I cried myself asleep, for when I looked up again I felt fresher and more cheery-like.

The moon had gone down behind the trees, and the shadders was black, but over to the east, I seed the fust little show of daylight. I put my head out agin, and thar was the dawg settin' down and watchin' of me. He knowed his business, sure. There didn't seem no way out of it, nohow.

But a way did open itself most unexpectedly, in accord with the nature ef dog and ef man; for suddernly, I heard off in the woods, three or four hundred yards away, the barking ef a coon.

The dog heard it too, and that was too much even for his faithfulness. To tree that coon was his first and most earnest vocation, and off he started as fast as his legs would carry him.

"Now's my chance," I said to myself: "the Lord points the way." I took a strong hold of the rope, dropped myself down gently to the ground. The box was heavy, but so was I; and it "wobbled," and when I let go it gave a "ker-thump" on the floor.

I knew that this must wake up the slave catchers, and I slipped quickly round the corner of the house in the shadow of it and waited.

Sure enough, the door opened, and one of the men came out. He looked up at the window and saw the rope hanging down. Then he heard the dog over in the woods and called out to his mates,

"The niggers have got away, and the dog is after them!"

They all rushed out, not very clear-headed after their night's carouse, and, without stopping to look, "made tracks for the timber."

When I saw this, I couldn't help larfin, though skeered to death, to see them men fooled so bad by their own dawg.

But I wasted no time, and, keeping the house between me and them, I ran like a skeered dawg until I was well out of sight before they could have discovered their mistake.

At about a half mile's distance, I came to some slashes, where it was all wet and mashy, and I put right through the swamp so as to kill the scent.

I was at that time close to the St. Louis road, but it was getting light so that I could see the tavern I had left, and I was afraid to keep on. I found a place where the bushes were thick and lay down among them so as to be completely concealed. Ef you'd believe it, I dropt right off asleep like a chile in its cradle. I was jess tired out and a'mose dead."

The hiding place was well chosen, for when I waked, about ten o'clock, I peeped through the bushes and saw the slave-ketchers and their gang on their way from the tavern to the ferryboat.

They had failed or had not attempted to trace me. Still, I was afraid to start out on the open road, for some of the men might be around, watching for me, and, although I was drefful hungry, I kept right thar until dark came.

As soon as it was clear dark, I got a-goin' and walked steady all night along the road till I come to whar the houses begin outside of St. Louis.

"You see Isaiah," Archer continued, "I broke them chains. I freed myself. Now Professor Eliot made it all legal and such, but I freed myself."

Isaiah leaned against the low bench, lulled in the scents of the garden, and thought of his journey. He grew tired as he thought back to the pen with the low door and the months in the ship. Then he realized that he, too, freed himself as he weathered beatings, educated himself, and journeyed a thousand miles to freedom. Emancipation was coming for all, but there must be more he could do.

CHAPTER FIFTY

THE MEETING

Wednesday afternoon Isaiah set the podium and arranged chairs in the auditorium for a meeting of the Abolitionists. He put a single chair behind a curtain to the side of the stage where he could sit unseen and listen to the orators.

Outside, students of the Benton School roasted chickens and baked cornbread in iron pots over open fires. Men from across the city gathered for a meal and to hear the orators. Isaiah got his cornbread and roasted chicken dinner, then slipped behind the curtain, waiting for the meeting to convene.

The first to speak was Professor Eliot himself.

"Gentlemen, I welcome you to the Benton School; we are here in service to St. Louis and the great state of Missouri. Our work is urgent. We must come to an agreement to save the Union. I tell you, the only way to abolition is gradual. Since the election of President Lincoln, seven states have left the Union. If we go forward with universal emancipation, more states will follow, and we will lose the support of the crucial border states. Listen to reason! Lincoln himself supports gradual emancipation."

Professor Eliot pleaded with Saint Louis city fathers to back away from the strict abolitionist movement. The hundred men packed in the small auditorium broke into a heated political argument about the path forward for Missouri, one of four border states critical to the Union.

That Spring, Eliot himself had bought a dozen slaves and freed them, demonstrating that slow, methodical abolition was the only way to avoid massive economic disruption. Even in the far north, white workers worried that the freed slaves fleeing the South would come and take their jobs.

Isaiah sat curtained off, the debate tossed in his mind. In the weeks since his arrival in Saint Louis, he learned the politics of states he had never heard named in the isolation of the Newhouse plantation. But his dream of emancipation, once so imminent, now appeared years away. Abolitionists disagreed on even the framework of a plan.

Peering across the room, Isaiah saw a tall, well-proportioned man with noble grey hair long to his collar and a trim chiseled beard step to the podium. The room fell silent. Frederick Douglass, himself an escaped slave, dared to speak openly in Saint Louis, still a gateway for slave traders.

Douglass gripped the podium and slowly looked over the room packed with slaveholders, abolitionists, freedmen, and escaped slaves. He held their gaze for a long moment, then he began.

"What on earth is the matter with the American Government and people? Do they really covet the world's ridicule as well as their own social and political ruin? What are they thinking about, or don't they condescend to think at all? So, indeed, it would seem from their blindness in dealing with the tremendous issue now upon them.

Was there ever anything like it before? They are sorely pressed on every hand by a vast army of slaveholding rebels, flushed with success and infuriated by the darkest inspirations of deadly hate, bound to rule or ruin. Washington, the seat of Government, after ten thousand assurances to the contrary, is now positively in danger of falling before the rebel army."

Douglass spoke for the immediate emancipation of all slaves as a moral right and to allow freedmen to fight to save the Union. He spoke of lives under the whip, of mothers and fathers, sisters and brothers torn apart, sold off to different plantations, all beneath the flag of the United States of America.

He spoke of a child cowering in the door of a lowly cabin listening to the mournful cries of his mother pleading for mercy between cracks of the whip. He bellowed in tones that shook the room. Isaiah rose from his chair.

'There are no mercies under the lash! My mother prayed for the soul of her perpetrator. Her misery would end when she met her God; the perpetrator would burn for all the days of eternity. But what of the sacred promise of the Constitution of the United States of America?' he asked.

"The American Government and the American Constitution are spoken of in a manner which would naturally lead the hearer to believe that one is identical with the other; when the truth is, they are as distinct in character as is a ship and a compass. The one may point right, and the other steer wrong. A chart is one thing; the course of the vessel is another. The Constitution may be right, but the Government is wrong."

His voice rose with the truth of what he said. Douglass mined the aspirations of men for good. The Union was the light. It was the promise of the Constitution. Slavery was a curse. The great orator soared:

"The story of our inferiority is an old dodge, as I have said; for wherever men oppress their fellows, wherever they enslave them, they will endeavor to find the needed

apology for such enslavement and oppression in the character of the people oppressed and enslaved."

"No man can put a chain about the ankle of his fellow man without at last finding the other end fastened about his own neck."

There was no time for gradual emancipation; the whole was foul. The stench was cast over all of America.

Douglass concluded,

"...Now let the freemen of the North, who have the power in their own hands, and who can make the American Government just what they think fit, resolve to blot out forever the foul and haggard crime, which is the blight and mildew, the curse and the disgrace of the whole United States."

Regardless of their stated beliefs, every man rose from their seat to cheer. For several minutes they stood. Isaiah watched Frederick Douglass, humbled by the power of his own words, walk from the podium, drained and exhausted.

CHAPTER FIFTY-ONE

D.C.

Though the pace of life in the 1860s may seem slow and romantic by our standards, the events surrounding the Civil War and Emancipation came with feverish urgency. Fierce arguments broke out on the streets and in brewhouses. Few citizens held neutral positions. It took great skill to navigate politics while moving from community to community. Isaiah made up his mind before Douglass finished his speech; he would give up the comfort of Saint Louis to serve Douglas as he might.

No one argued when Isaiah told them of his spontaneous plan to leave Saint Louis to travel with Frederick Douglass. But, Douglass protested; he could continue to attend to his own affairs. Isaiah insisted he accompany Frederick so the great orator could devote all his energy to the cause.

Douglass was to leave early the following day, Isaiah packed his few belongings, and before the sun rose, he waited at the carriage for Douglass to appear.

For months Douglass traveled a grueling schedule of daily speeches in towns small and large. Far more people heard him speak in the 1800s than any orator of the time. He campaigned mainly in the border states, but as the war progressed, he took his message north, where the sacrifice of battle was great. The Union strained under the demands of the war for supplies, men, and money. The economy was on the verge of collapse as the government printed more and more money, and inflation soared. Every northern soldier who enlisted to fight left his farm or his livelihood to do so. In the South, slaves continued to work when Confederates enlisted.

In August 1862, Douglass delivered his speech "How to End the War" to a packed chamber in Baltimore. He called for the immediate emancipation of slaves to allow them to fight for their freedom.

"We are ready and would go, counting ourselves happy in being permitted to serve and suffer for the cause of freedom and free institutions...Every consideration of justice, humanity, and sound policy confirms the wisdom of calling upon black men just now to take up arms on behalf of their country." He concluded.

Isaiah met Douglass as he left the stage; a crowd of protestors circled around them. "Why preach to us," a man shouted, "we have no power."

"You speak so clearly but do no good." Another shouted. "We can do nothing to repair the ills you declare; go tell Lincoln!"

"Our businesses are failing; our sons are slaughtered, and the war never changes. You want your freedom, go fight!" shouted another.

"This war is to save the Union; if you want freedom, go fight for yourself, we are tired of speeches." They protested.

Isaiah pushed between the crowd and Douglass. He steered Douglass to a door near the rear of the building. Their wagon was there, ready for the next journey.

In front of the hall on Main Street, tempers flared. Abolitionists preached for the end of slavery, but most people just wanted the war to end. Anxiety was at a boiling point.

Before the crowds noticed their departure, Douglass climbed up to his seat, and Isaiah walked the skittish horses down the dark street away from the shouts, fires, and occasional gunshots. At a safe distance, he climbed up to sit next to Douglass. The two men rode in silence. Douglass withdrew, deep in thought.

"Isaiah, I need to do more. The Union is failing. The South sends more soldiers while the slaves stay home and keep working. We don't have enough men to work and fight too. This war has to end before the saboteurs wreck our supply lines. An easy war is a long war, a thing we cannot afford. We have to fight now and fight hard."

"But what more can you do," Isaiah asked, "you speak every night. I hear the weariness in your voice. What can you do?"

"Speaking every night has not made the change we need. I must meet with Lincoln. We are going to the capital. I will knock on his door." Douglass announced.

Isaiah stopped the carriage. He climbed from the open seat and walked to the crossbuck doors fitted into the rear of the wagon. Over the past months, he built a small cabin on the bed to protect their possessions from rain and theft. There was room there for Douglass to sleep when his weariness was too great.

Isaiah returned with cornbread and water. "I will drive through the night," he declared. "we can be in Washington by morning."

The men rode in silence twelve miles to Halethorpe, where Isaiah fed and rested the horses while Douglass climbed into the bunk arranged in the rear of the wagon. Isaiah poured a strong cup of the morning's coffee from a cold pot stored in the bed, climbed the buckboard, and began the long ride to D.C.

The twelve-hour journey ended in the late morning at the steps of the White House. Isaiah tied off the wagon while

Douglass took his place in the line ascending the stairs to Lincoln's office. A long row of white men filled the staircase, each with a grievance or point of advice. All were anxious to share their views with the President.

Douglass planned to wait all day, even for two days, if that was what it took to meet President Lincoln. He gave his card to the clerk and took his seat on the stairs. In just ten minutes, as Isaiah joined him, a Marshall called "Douglass! Come forth."

A man in the line chided, "Damn it, I knew they would let HIM through."

Isaiah looked to Douglass, and he nodded, confirming he wished Isaiah to accompany him. The two men presented themselves at Lincoln's door. Lincoln sat low in an overstuffed chair, his feet stretched out amongst stacks of papers. The President's face was lined with fatigue and worry. His countenance brightened when Douglass began his introduction.

Lincoln cut him off, saying, "Mr. Douglass, I know who you are. I have read about you. Sit down. I am glad to see you."

Douglass studied Lincoln; was he merely a politician or a man of sincerity? It was immediately clear, Douglass saw no superiority in Lincoln's disposition, nor did Lincoln condescend. Lincoln greeted the men as equals.

Lincoln told Douglass he had read and considered his speeches each time they were presented.

"I see you think me vacillating on positions critical to emancipation." Lincoln began. "With careful study, I do not think the charge will bear out. My steps may be slow, but the direction singular."

"I do not doubt your fortitude on this matter," Douglass replied, "it is the pace of change that troubles me. Freedom cannot come quickly enough for the men and women and children chained by slavery."

"Yet I cannot move too quickly, or we will lose the border states." Lincoln countered.

"The Union hangs on a tether. The people have to march with me, or I will march alone. We offered the Confederacy fair payment to purchase the freedom of all the slaves, the cost would have been no more than ninety days of the war, but they denied us. Their commitment to this strange institution is strong."

"Sir, I may have a remedy if I may offer advice. You lead this powerful nation; I am but an escaped slave. Isaiah too was a slave. Yet we are ready to fight for freedom along with all of our enslaved brothers. If you free all slaves right now, they will join the fight against their oppressors. Sir, we can turn the war!"

"I see the wisdom of what you say, and I have thought deeply. Should we take such bold action, will the border states rebel? Will they throw their support to the confederacy?" Lincoln pondered.

Isaiah sat in awe of these great men. He mulled Lincoln's hesitancy. The border states were a powder keg, and time was short.

Isaiah blurted, "Emancipate only the seceded Confederate states! Throw them into turmoil!"

Lincoln looked to Isaiah. Isaiah felt his cheeks burn with embarrassment; he continued sheepishly, "I have no right...."

Lincoln raised his hand, signaling Isaiah to pause. "That may be a brilliant strategy. We have freed the slaves in D.C. with little consequence and in Maryland and Virginia. We need men to fight with conviction. Honorable men, fighting for their freedom, will always win."

"Sir, I am humbled by your forthwith sincerity." Douglass began, "I could well speak with you the entire day and deep into the night, but there is a line of men waiting with similar thoughts. I will go and continue my work to recruit black soldiers to the cause. Black troops have already proven their bravery and commitment. You can do more with a pen in fifteen minutes than I can do in my lifetime. I am satisfied you will proceed as fast as conditions warrant."

Lincoln stood, "Thank you, gentlemen. Mr. Douglass, never come to Washington without calling upon me."

Lincoln sat back in his chair, his arms gently folded; he appeared to immediately drift off in deep thought. Isaiah and Douglass rose to make their way past the men still lining the stairway.

CHAPTER FIFTY-TWO

CELEBRATION

Full equality under the law finally came on the ninth day of July 1868 with the passage of the Fourteenth Amendment to the constitution of the United States. Douglass and Isaiah shared a tearful embrace; their hearts soared. The decades of oppression were over. Chains were broken across the South, and thousands of escaped slaves finally walked free and equal in the North and across all Southern states.

Douglass planned a full month-long celebration speaking every night, a glorious, grueling recognition of liberation. Yet, Isaiah, exhausted, was to leave in the morning, traveling back to North Carolina to reunite with the former slaves of the Newhouse Plantation and walk as a freeman under the Angel Oaks where the whip cracked those many years ago.

Isaiah boarded a train in Baltimore, heading south in the early morning sunshine. He would make his way to North Carolina through Richmond, Virginia. The locomotive puffed dark smoke that billowed white as the train rolled out of the station. The old engine chugged on as the train sped through the countryside north of Washington, D.C.

Isaiah thought about how different it felt to travel as a freeman amongst freemen. He did not fear that he would be abducted. He did not study other blacks to consider if they might be escaped slaves on the run. He leaned into the seat and let his head lay back. He felt the welts across his back and heard Mira's cries, but for the first time in his life, he felt the power of a free man in a free country. The years he had left were his.

He had not thought to return to Africa to find his village and the farm in the gentle valley for many years, but now he dreamt of his mother and father, who certainly had long since passed, and of Mira, herself enslaved, probably in America. Would he know her face?

In D.C., Isaiah descended the train at the Washington Depot. He wore new leather shoes, a gift from Douglass. The smooth tops were laced tight around his ankles, but the toe pinched mightily. He adjusted his gait and hurried along the wooden platform strewn with boxes and the trunks of travelers leaving the agony of the South for the promise of New England. Isaiah would continue his journey south that evening, but he had to visit the new Emancipation Memorial just unveiled in Lincoln Square. The Depot was less than a mile from the Square, so Isaiah hustled along, hurting feet or not.

Douglass saw the memorial when it arrived crated from Italy. A tremendous recognition of Lincoln and the power of the slaves to break the chains of oppression, but Douglass quietly lamented the thin tale it told.

SIR: Admirable as is the monument by Mr. Ball in Lincoln park, it does not, as it seems to me, tell the whole truth, and perhaps no one monument could be made to tell the whole truth of any subject which it might be designed to illustrate. The mere act of breaking the negro's chains was the act of Abraham Lincoln, and is beautifully expressed in this monument. But the act by which the negro was made a citizen of the United States and invested with the elective franchise was pre-eminently the act of President U. S. Grant, and this is nowhere seen in the Lincoln monument. The negro here, though rising, is still on his knees and nude. What I want to see before I die is a monument representing the negro, not couchant on his knees like a four-footed animal, but erect on his feet like a man. There is room in Lincoln park for another monument, and I throw out this suggestion to the end that it may be taken up and acted upon.

FREDERICK DOUGLASS.

At the central station in D.C., Isaiah boarded a train for Richmond. It was late; the train would run through the night. Still a poor man, Isaiah settled into the coach car; a sleeper was out of his reach. He ate cornbread and drank water from a skin slung beneath his jacket. The rhythm of the old locomotive lulled him to sleep. He awoke when the train stopped abruptly.

They had reached the border of the Commonwealth of Virginia. Isaiah looked up to see the conductor, along with a thick burly man, push through the door of the coach. They stopped at the first black couple seated to Isaiah's left. In a moment, the couple rose and walked toward the rear of the car. The two men stepped to Isaiah.

"The railroad here operates within the laws of the Commonwealth of Virginia. We cannot proceed until we lawfully comply with the state's law. This car is now 'whites only.' We have equal accommodations for you. Please move to the colored's car. This way." The conductor instructed, pointing to the rear of the coach.

Isaiah stared ahead, not sure how to react. The burly man tapped Isaiah's leg. Isaiah considered the thick, varnished cane. He thought back to the stick that split his cheek when his horrible journey began.

"C'mon now, move along. The train ain't rolling till we comply with the laws of the Commonwealth. Out of your seat or off the train!"

Isaiah stood, picked up his satchel, and walked forward to the exit. He would not walk to the back of the train. He opened the door at the head of the coach. He looked to the conductor and the man now holding the cane midpoint of the shaft, ready to strike.

"May God bless you," Isaiah said, and he climbed down the steps onto the berm.

The moon shone brightly in the western sky. Stars lit the night all around. Isaiah listened to the gravel scrape beneath his boots as he walked up the tracks alongside the idling train.

A man leaned out of a window in the coach car, scolding, "That's private property you're walking. You're trespassing. I suggest you get clear of the railroad, boy!"

Isaiah saw a lantern and three men approaching from the front of the train. He ran from the tracks for the protection of the forest. The men did not follow. They climbed back aboard the train when its whistle sounded, and the train chugged slowly away.

The train's lights soon disappeared down the narrow slice cut through the thick forest. Isaiah returned to the tracks and followed. He could still hear the locomotive in the still night, but there were no lights, no sign of a town or even a homestead. He walked several miles along the track and then came to a crossroad that led to a wooden bridge over a rushing stream. A signpost near the head of the bridge read, "Loudoun County." Beneath the official county sign, a cryptic notice:

I AM
COMMITTEE

1st. No man shall squat negroes on his place unless they are all under his employ male and female.

2d. Negro women shall be employed by white persons

3d. All children shall be hired out for something.

4th. Negroes found in cabins to themselves shall suffer the penalty.

5th. Negroes shall not be allowed to hire negroes.

6th. Idle men, women or children, shall suffer the penalty.

7th. All white men found with negroes in secret places shall be dealt with and those that hire negroes must pay promptly and act with good faith to the negro. I will make the negro do his part, and the white must too.

8th. For the first offence is one hundred lashes—the second is looking up a sap lin.

9th. This I do for the benefit of all young or old, high and tall, black and white. Any one that may not like these rules can try their luck, and see whether or not I will be found doing my duty.

10th. Negroes found stealing from any one or taking from their employers to other negroes, death is the first penalty.

11th. Running about late of nights shall be strictly dealt with.

12th. White man and negro, I am everywhere. I have friends in every place, do your duty and I will have but little to do.

Isaiah felt a sudden cold breeze; he shivered. He thought to just lay down right there and let the life drain out of him. He was exhausted.

From the road, a path trailed down to the river. Isaiah heard the gurgle of water filtering through rocks at the foot of the bridge. Wearily, he trudged down to a tree trunk laid along the low bank just above the stream.

He sat, then leaned back to lay full length on the log. The water gurgled; the stars circled in the sky. Isaiah did not mean to sleep but closed his eyes to think. He had to find Douglass; their work must continue.

The moon was at the horizon when Isaiah awoke. He smelled the faint smoke of a campfire somewhere in the night. He rose, and with the notice to his back, he hurried up the road away from the bridge.

The crunch of the gravel road faded into the silent sound of his shoes stepping into the sand as the road tightened to just two tracks. The lane cut narrowly through the dark wooded hills. Isaiah saw the distant flicker of a log fire; a village must be nearby.

Uncertain and fearful, Isaiah kept to the shadows covering one side of the road. As he approached, he saw the fire billow a dense white cloud of smoke, then flames burst high, singeing the leaves of an overhanging oak, illuminating a mound of pine branches piled near the flames. The fire raged. Then he saw the ghostly visages of white-draped men, hands in the air, and a drum began beating low and slow.

Isaiah left the road to disappear into the trees across from the clearing. Isaiah studied the scene. A mighty old oak reached out toward the fire and back into the blackness of the woods. Then, through the murk of the billowing smoke, just above the hands of the exulting ghosts, Isaiah saw the upturned heads of six black men dangling by their necks. Isaiah groaned aloud. His stomach knotted as he spun away, running in a crouch until he gagged, vomiting as he struggled to stand.

Isaiah crashed through the brush, terrified, angry, reeling in the disappointment of failed decades. If he alerted the murderous ghosts, if they pursued him, Isaiah never knew. He ran. He did not look back. The horror of the scene burnt deeply into his consciousness. He could not look again. He ran.

Again tears dripped over his scarred cheek. Cresting a hill, Isaiah stepped, but there was no ground. He flew from the bank, flailing headlong into a stream. His satchel floated in his grip. The cool water engulfed him. Isaiah struggled, then laid back, adrift, facing the stars. He surrendered to the flow. He felt despair and elation, humiliation and pride, and most of all, he felt his sense of self lean hard against an immovable force. With gentle resistance, he began his drift across time.

While the decades piled atop one another, the constant humiliations of segregation wore on Isaiah. In time, Douglass was gone. Isaiah lost his mighty voice; his passion seethed invisible to his oppressors. Isaiah lived on bearing the burden for unspeakable decades. Then there was Ali.

CHAPTER FIFTY-THREE

"SERVICE"

The rain poured down as I drove home from my mother's condo in Clearwater Beach, up I-65 along the eastern outskirts of Louisville, on my way to Michigan. It was five hours to get home and six hours till dawn. I was glad for a full tank of gas and a jumbo coffee. Then, just seeing the sign for Louisville sent me back, I reminisced about my friend and the journey he set me upon. Louisville is synonymous with Ali. The Louisville Lip. A great heart. A legendary fighter.

Curious, I typed "Ali gravesite" into my GPS just to see if it registered. Before I finished typing, the directions came up. Ten miles ahead and just minutes off the expressway, I could sit in his presence once again. Late night or not, there was really no decision to make. The exit appeared, I merged onto the ramp and turned west onto Grinstead Drive.

Grinstead weaved over rolling hills, dark and wooded, then passed scattered houses entering Louisville. I drove through an old commercial neighborhood wishing the quirky-looking taco place was open all night. The wipers whipped back and forth at full speed against the downpour, even on the slow, quiet avenues. The GPS guided me along narrow streets crowded with parked cars. A couple of minutes further on, I was alongside Cave Hill Cemetery.

A short, wrought iron fence sat atop a fieldstone wall bordering the Victorian Era grounds. Grinstead followed the gentle hills under towering oaks as old as the ancient stone wall.

At a stop sign, I turned onto Baxter Avenue, drove slowly, then stopped in front of the main entrance to Cave Hill. A broad white sign announced, "Closed," A heavy chain locked the gates shut beneath it. I would not visit Ali tonight.

The heavy downpour slowed enough that I could peer through the fence to gauge the vastness of the densely packed rows of gravestones. Long arcs of low stones bent off into the night. I thought to circle around to see if I could find the maintenance barn that I had glimpsed in a photograph of Ali's plot.

I drove a city block or so, studying the cemetery, then the road veered away from the long wall and into a neighborhood of craft-built homes on tidy residential streets. The windows were dark; only my low-beam headlights disturbed the quiet.

I got disoriented on the winding roads and took a chance to get back to the cemetery by turning left onto Dudley Court. Water flowed along the curb. Parked cars pinched the narrow street to a single lane. In one long city block, Dudley Court ended smack against Cave Hill.

I parked, if just to stop driving for a minute, then stepped out of the car to straighten my legs and breathe fresh air. Rain splattered against leaves in the overhanging trees, then slapped in fat drops against the dark pavement. At the end of the cul-de-sac, I considered the fence surrounding Cave Hill.

It was taller than my reach, so it would be a trick to climb over, and a misdemeanor trespass seemed a bit extreme. Then I saw an ornate little service gate between stone pillars tucked behind overgrown junipers. I walked to it. A chain wrapped through a leg of the iron fence and then back through the black wrought iron of the ancient gate. The chain made a couple of loops through the fence, but the lock closed around just one link---I pulled the chain through, and the gate pushed open.

My heart raced. The dripping rain splashed over me and ran down my neck. I hurried back to the car to retrieve the Eddie Bauer rain gear my dear wife had bagged up in the trunk. I pulled on the jacket and ballcap, tugged the hood over my head, and whispered a thank-you for her vigilance.

I slipped through the gate, carefully pushed it shut, and re-laced the chain through the bars. Inside, the grounds were eerie, it was a cemetery, after all, but I had a mission. I wanted to see the granite stone that will announce Ali for eternity. I wanted to sit on one of the benches that flanked the walkway up to the gravesite, and I knew Ali would be happy if he knew I stopped by, actually me or anyone else on the earth---Ali loved people.

A stony dirt path led uphill from the gate. In just one hundred yards, I could see the big maintenance barn up ahead. It had stood out in the upper corner of a photograph I found online. Typical of Ali, he chose his plot in a common corner of Cave Hill, not in the section with lofty obelisks and granite crypts. His plot was downhill and slightly to the right of the metal barn.

The rain fell harder as I walked alongside a row of overhead doors and then across the parking area to a walkway just wide enough for a single vehicle. A dark green stripe ran up the middle of the path. I followed along for no reason but that it was there.

Paths and narrow roadways crisscrossed the dense landscape. A few hundred feet on, I worried I might not find the site in the dark and rain. Then suddenly, right alongside the path, flowerbeds reminiscent of the farm in Berrien Springs; then I saw the flanking benches, and up the hill, Ali.

The rain all but stopped while a foggy mist filled the air. The wind halted momentarily, then billowed from the south, feeling warmer and wetter. The gravesite is nestled in the hill under a magnolia tree just above a small pond. Two stately black granite columns flanked Ali's memorial stone; it read,

"Service to others is the rent you pay for your room in heaven."

I knew the quote described Ali's life, but the word "service" troubles me. "Service" connotes sacrifice and duty. It does not entirely fit Ali. His kindness never seemed a burden, his compassion was genuine, he found unbridled joy in pleasing people, and he inspired the people around him.

I sat on the granite bench to the right of the walkway, huddled in my coat, contemplating the stone. The rain soaked my knees just below the outstretched Gore-Tex. And once again, emotions hit me. I quietly churned inside, feeling a mix of awe, humility, inspiration, and overwhelming loss.

In my reverie, I did not notice the hooded man suddenly next to me on the bench. I did not see him approach or sense when he sat down. My eyes may have been closed and my thoughts deep, but there he was.

"He changed everything for me." The man said, his hands crossed in his lap. He sounded somehow far away. His voice was strong and clear, but there was a distance I cannot describe.

"For more decades than you can imagine, my world slipped off into a distressing state of being. I was nobody even when I succeeded. I was nobody, or so I thought. I bleached my skin. I straightened my hair. I learned to speak like a white man. But the melanin in my skin was heavy; it dragged everything down."

His voice commanded every fiber of my attention. What he said, the strange remoteness in the sound of his voice, and still, it was like I knew this guy. Maybe I should have been concerned that a stranger slipped next to me on a bench in a rainy cemetery in the middle of the night wearing a hood that completely obscured his face, yet I was pleased that dawn was a way off so, in the darkness, I could hear his story.

"It's a shame they shot Abraham," he suddenly blurted, "no one anticipated how strong it was or how deep and how long the hate would last. First, his Emancipation Proclamation, then the Fourteenth Amendment, set us free. Then just seven years after that amendment broke the chains of slavery for good, they took the land back and tied us to the plantation with economics, not chains."

"That was so long ago," I said, but I heard my words and immediately regretted the comment. "I know it was horrific...."

"No, no, no, no, no, no..." his voice trailed gently off into silence. He hesitated, then said, "I sounded like I was complaining. That's not right. There are facts. Let me tell you the truth since we are here sitting in the shadow of Ali. You know?... I am Ali. You must be too sitting on this bench in the wee hours in the rain. He did something to you, too?" he hinted.

"I was so proud we fought to be freed." He said. "Finally, there was nowhere I could not go, and no whip was waiting to tear my skin. But then dancing Jim Crow all black faced and talkin' like de black man hisself a juk. Aww, jum down turn youself 'round, jumpin Jim Crow."

That's what he said, mocking the black man, and it caught on and became everything they needed to tamp us down, and when it wasn't, they burned us out in Tulsa and mocked us more and more.

He paused in silence, then, in low tones, he hummed the tune, "Turkey in the Straw".... Barely audible, he whispered the song under his breath, and the melody lingered.

I drifted into memories of childhood birthday parties and raspberry popsicles from the Good Humor man. Then he sang unfamiliar words:

"Nigger love a watermelon
ha, ha, ha, ha! Nigger love a
watermelon, ha, ha, ha, ha!
For here, they're made with a half a
pound of co'l There's nothing like a
watermelon for a hungry coon."

"Oh Lord," he paused, "those lyrics changed some with the times, but the tune's always been there reminding us. Imagine the ice cream man playing it continuous, driving through the neighborhoods. That reminding and the lies, and the hanging, and the humiliation, it all beats me in the head day after day after day.

Every hour of my life, I calculate my situation. Is that bus coming free for me and the color of my skin, or is the committee on board waiting to toss me off and whip me?

Maybe the committee is outside the door of my home, waiting to hang me from a craggy branch. Maybe I'm walking on a street, and I take a moment too long to look down when a white woman passes, and then I am running down that street where I should be walking, and more and more of those supremacists are joining in and gaining on me. They carry a whip that will take one-hundred slices out of my back if I survive, so the next time I look down quicker, quicker, so they don't imagine me embracing her ivory skin."

"But I can see you never felt the whip. Don't worry; I can't fully describe it to you. But I can tell you it tears you just like it tears me. It tears my wife just like it tears your daughter. And when I hear my momma scream "Mercy" between the lashes, it is your momma in your ears weeping with you because you can't do nothing either."

They never had to pass a Federal law against lynching you. Oh, but they did pass one against lynching me. It's just a fact. It passed on the nineteenth day of December 2018. There were two hundred previous times it did not pass, and it stayed federally legal to watch a black man hung from a branch in these United States of America.

Forty-seven hundred and forty-two men and women hung in trees before it was federally illegal to participate in the hanging.

Ole' Rubin Stacy in Miami Dade, Florida, he got terrible hungry, so he knocked on a door to ask for food. But he so frightened the white woman who answered, I mean, he was a black man, so that woman screamed, and Rubin was arrested for attempted rape. Then six policemen let a mob get to him, and that mob took Rubin, and they hung him from a tree alongside the house of the woman who made the complaint, but he was just hungry for food.

Oh, and they gave us the right to vote too! In nineteen hundred and sixty-eight, the federal government passed a law to stop states from making laws that kept black people and poor people from voting. So now they twist districts and play tricks to "tamp down the black vote." It's the same thread pulled right through from those emancipation days, and it's the same supremacists doing their work too.

I was wondering from a long time ago, am I somebody? Am I nobody? Everything good in America is white. This melanin in my skin is dark, not black, but sometimes brown or even a creamy mocha.

And I fell in love with a mocha skin girl who put her arms around me and kissed me, and I was somebody! I was the man who loved her, and I took her for an ice cream sundae.

We walked, her arm in mine; the sun was shining so warm. We just walked right into that ice cream shop and sat down at the speckled green counter for a chocolate sundae with two spoons. And that skinny little guy slapped her right off that stool.

His momma sat two stools down, and his feelings were hurt because his momma was sittin so close to a mocha skin girl. Slapped her right off the stool, and when I hollered, I disturbed the peace, and that skinny fella collected up a gang that grew more when they drug me out the door and across the street.

They drug me by my shoes till they fell off, then by my britches till they pulled off, and I was half-naked scrapin on that ground, and my girl cried. I heard her cry. And I thought of how I would look at her again, and she would look at me after me scrapin half-naked on the street.

Day after day after day, every hour, I negotiate for the melanin in my skin. It's heavy. I am so weighted down, worrying if I can grocery shop here or if I'll get stopped there for a police safety check two hundred times without getting beat or shot. I know I can get through one-hundred stops because I already did that. And the supremacists and the voter suppression, I see that continuous. The chains of slavery were broken, but terror replaced the horror. There was strange fruit in those trees. I get so tired of the fight, the same fight decade after decade.

Then, here he comes! In that dark hour when we even doubted ourselves, he showed,

"I am the Greatest! I am black, and I am pretty!"

Some of that pretty likeness is carved into the Emancipation Memorial in Washington D.C. because Muhammad Ali's great-grandfather, Mr. Archer Alexander, met up in St. Louis with Professor Greenleaf Eliot, who collected the money to go to Florence, Italy, to find the sculptors to cast that Emancipation Monument.

Professor Eliot gave the sculptors a photograph of Archer Alexander as guidance for the casting, and that's why Ali's likeness is on that Memorial in Washington D.C... 'ole Archer Alexander passed on some of those same looks to his great-great-grandson, Muhammad Ali. He was so pretty in his face and in his soul.

I heard Ali, and I watched him give old Howard Cosell those big words right back in his face. He was pretty and a poet. And he forgave, and he loved everyone. He was a golden gloves champion shut out of those Louisville restaurants, but when he came home from the Olympics famous, they opened their doors.

Ali was big; he did not need to insult them; he just wanted dinner. And when they stole his World Heavyweight Championship crown and sentenced him to five years in prison, he stood with the Constitution of the United States of America, fighting right on to the Supreme Court to win his title back. And he won it back. They stole three prime years of his fighting, but he did not insult them.

"I fought for what I thought was right, and they fought for what they thought was right. How can I be angry with them for only trying to do what they thought was right?" he asked.

"Oh, Ali was somebody! I found his spark in me. I am not three-fifths of a man like the Constitution once said; I am a full man. I am Ali!"

The rain had slowed. When I hadn't noticed. I pulled the rain gear from over my ball cap and looked to the hooded man. My mouth opened to speak, but I paused. There was an aura, like the morning on the driveway when I first saw Ali. Not a glow, but an atmosphere, powerful.

As the visage rose to leave, I leaped to my feet, ready with an outstretched hand, but the figure had spun away. I saw only the deep shadow of his hooded face and a glimmer.

In the ebbing darkness, there was light. I caught that mischievous twinkle.

That's how I remember it...in the mist...next to the bench...at dawn...in the presence of Ali.

PRAISE FOR AUTHOR

Thomas: "It was a great story about a part of the life of Ali nobody has ever talked about. He has been one of my heroes for many years, and this story confirmed many of the things I thought about him."

Hotcat "Loved these personal vignettes about the GOAT who could have hidden behind his icon-hood but had the work of being human to finish. I also enjoyed the telling of the author's journey and the imagined travels through slavery. It's a page-turner!"

Becky "Any person in the world that appreciates the great life of Muhammad Ali will certainly enjoy reading this well-documented book of your days with your friend, Ali. Thank you so very much."

John "...the exquisite prose (like John Updike, with a gift for telling details) nailed parts of the locations as I know them...
you constructed that precise historical narrative with direct quotes worthy of Bob Woodward. ..I was surprised and delighted."

Jan "This book is a joy to read."

Made in United States
Orlando, FL
04 July 2024

48610018R00183